Not Exactly Murder

Margot Sinclair

BENYA PUBLISHING

Library of Congress Control Number: 2025941608

First published in 2025 by Benya Publishing

ISBN: 978-1-968455-00-2 (paperback)
ISBN: 978-1-968455-01-9 (ePDF)
ISBN: 978-1-968455-02-6 (ePUB)

Publication data:
Margot Sinclair
Not Exactly Murder
Volume 1 in the "Not Exactly" Series

Design and layout by Scribe Inc.

Benya Publishing
P.O. Box 799
Sullivan's Island, SC 29482

www.benyapublishing.com

Preface

Who remembers the '90s? The Clintons were in the White House. The SUV was the new thing. Martha Stewart was a household name. Cell phones were clunky things a few people carried in cars.

More important to our story Charleston, South Carolina, was still Charleston. Big patches of the city were shabby and ungentrified. The old families lived in the old houses and maintained the old rituals in their kingdom by the sea.

And there was and is an underbelly of the city of organized and disorganized crime that the visitors never see.

1

"Put the damn gun down," Rannie short-for-Randolph Ralston told her client sternly.

Gaston Garnett, Poet-in-Residence at the College of Charleston held her and the sheriff's deputy at gunpoint in the little interrogation room where Rannie had come to interview her client. He gave her a big grin. "I'm a suspect in an alleged murder. Now I'm a suspect in an alleged gun taking. Isn't that what they say? Everything's always 'alleged'?"

Rannie had come out here to the Charleston County jail to share confidences with her client, was ending up a hostage. Gaston's wife had been found shot dead. He and his wife were both raging alcoholics who battled in public. He was the natural suspect although the evidence against him was extremely thin. The cops had arrested him that morning. He called Rannie. She rode up to the jail on Leeds Avenue. And this bozo from the sheriff's department had brought his gun into the room against all regulations. And was now disarmed.

Rannie kept her signature poker face, but her heart rate was up real high. She was only twenty-seven, but five years of law practice in a seaport town had shown her what guns could do. She tried to reason with him. "This murder thing is nothing but speculation. Which you're busy adding to with actual documentary evidence."

Gaston was a bull of a man and a monster of egotism. Piles of white hair. His drunkard's eyes were still bright beneath bushy eyebrows. "I got needs and priorities of my own. Right now I'm figuring we'll bust out of here. Me holding my sex-bomb attorney hostage. Take off in a car on a wild, high-speed escape from the law. Go on a spree of violent felonies. You'll fall into the Stockholm syndrome. We'll make red-hot motel love in a seedy town. Then get surrounded by cops and die in a shit-storm of gunfire."

Rannie knew Gaston was a liar straight from the heart. Each day he reinvented himself anew. He could con you in the most persuasive detail. Convince you he had won a Silver Star in Vietnam, been a gridiron hero, had a medical degree in dermatology. Enough repetition and playback and he believed it himself. At least for a while. Then he'd come up with another one.

Rannie played along. "You see it as kind of a road picture," she said. "*Breathless* meets *Thelma & Louise*. Loopy lawyer gal and thinking man's desperado poet."

"*Southern* poet," he emphasized.

"Sure. Got to have the regional angle."

"Yeah. It would work better if you had grabbed the gun and tossed it to me. Because . . . you were nuts about me. Even though you had only seen me once. But you heard me at a poetry reading when you were seventeen and never got over it. All the way through college and law school you mooned over my news clippings."

"It'd make a good screenplay," said Rannie. "Try it out on one of your creative writing classes."

It did seem like a movie in a way. Gaston going for the gun with dazzling speed for a man so big. Whip. Blip. And there they were prisoners.

The stench of pinto beans wafted through the wire mesh window of the door. Lunch for the prisoners was a distant banging noise of trays and tin dishes, a babble of shouted profanities—"fuck you, muh'fokkah"—those kinds of noble sentiments.

Gaston was a celebrated poet which did nothing but get him a job teaching—the butt-end of the English department—sneered at because he lacked the Ph.D. He was way past fifty with a lot of heavy-drinking mileage on him. His face looked like a long association with disaster. Which it had been. At least until he married the romance novelist. But now she was dead.

"*Quelle rodomontade*," Gaston said in an affected voice.

Rannie didn't know if he was talking about his screenplay or the real life drama.

Lonnie Daryll Colson, the disarmed deputy in a tan uniform let out a big belch. His gut hung over his gun-belt heaving like a volcano about to erupt. Lonnie Daryll looked real shaky.

Rannie grimaced in disgust. "What's wrong with you?"

He sounded sheepish. "In the struggle and ruckus . . . I swallowed my chew."

He had said it almost with a whimper. Rannie closed her eyes and thought "numbskull." Big sweat stains under his pits. Embarrassing to even be in the same room with him. Now she'd be on the six o'clock news. Gun to her temple. Some negotiation specialist trying to match wits with her lunatic client who would simply revel in the attention. Rodomontade, my ass.

Lonnie Daryll sat down heavily in the second plastic chair. Hung his head between his legs like he was about to hurl up the contents of his stomach. "That gun, it's like a resource I hate to lose." He choked back a big heave, both hands over his mouth. Took them away cautiously. "Prisoners allus trying to disarm you . . . it's like one of my pet peeves."

Gaston seemed concerned. "Hey, I can empathize. There's a world of pissant nuisances out there. Students wanting to eat their lunches in my classroom. No manners at all. And these are seniors in college. And you know what I hate? I hate it when waiters say 'enjoy'. Can't they complete a simple sentence? Say 'enjoy your lunch?'"

"It's a bitch awright," said Lonnie Daryll. He let out a long drool, the early warning sign of a major up-chuck. Men always did that when they had gone five drinks over the line. And this bozo had actually swallowed his Redman. Nothing short of a wild boar could digest that.

Gaston lowered the gun to point it at the floor. "I'm undergoing a change of heart," he ventured. "With all things considered. Wondering if we can rehabilitate this whole scene."

Rannie told Gaston to put the gun down. Robocop here—she jerked a thumb at Lonnie Daryll—didn't want to lose his job. He'd keep his mouth shut about the disarming.

Lonnie Daryll brightened at that. Slapped his thighs

showing his agreement. "That's a signif'cant enough offer. Kind of exhibitin' our good will. You just set the gun on the chair." He pointed to the other plastic chair. "Simple enough execution."

Gaston winced.

"Sorry 'bout that. Bad choice of words. I'm kind of hoping we can see an extension of an olive branch here. Maybe a Christian theme type thing."

Gaston scratched the side of his face with the gun barrel, giving the offer a guarded appraisal. "I'm wondering whether what I've seen so far gives me confidence this deal can work."

"I see no need to formulate a report," Lonnie Daryll urged hopefully. "I think I'm empowered to act in that arena."

Gaston cocked his head suspiciously. "No hidden agendas?"

"*Tabula rasa* time," Rannie stuck in, nudging him along. "Multiparty agreement on it. Cross my heart and hope to die."

"We're down to the buzzer," Lonnie Daryll pressed. "Time for last minute heroics. You do a sweet alley-oop pass off'a that there gun. We'll all go to the locker room."

"I don't hear any opposition," Rannie encouraged.

Gaston twirled the gun on his finger, dangling it by the trigger guard, butt facing towards Lonnie Daryll. "Here now. I'm officially handing it over. Laying it down on the chair. Is that your site of choice? The way I see it, we've just got a temporary taking of property here. Nothing serious."

"I think that's fair and balanced," said Lonnie Daryll, rubbing his sweaty palms on the seat of his whipcord breeches as he stood up. "I'll give that some high praise." He snatched up his weapon and shoved it in the holster. Kept his hand on it in case Gaston had a change of heart.

"You're the runaway winner," Rannie told her client. "Fifty-fifty split. Everybody walks away and forgets this happened. Well not exactly walk away in your case. You go back to your cell."

Lonnie Daryll still looked a little wobbly. Without warning, he wheeled and threw up in the corner.

"Good God," said Rannie, stepping back in disgust. Had he gotten it on her?

"I told you I swallowed my quid." He urped some more.

Rannie got out as soon as they'd let her. She didn't care if Lonnie used Gaston's head for a commode brush. Malodorous pair of lamebrains. They both belonged in there with the rest of them. Drug mules and addicts, shit-hooks and lowlifes.

Out in the in-take area, she sat down, thinking she would have a little moment of cheap grace. A bored clerk watched a soap opera on a TV set up on the wall.

Rannie was trembling and sweating. It was February and cold as a bitch outside. Tourists who know the infernal heat, bugs and humidity of a Charleston summer don't realize how cold it can get.

The phone rang and the clerk sleepily told Rannie it was for her. Was she there?

Rannie thought, God-bless-it, I have to be plagued by my office. Has my brother got himself mired in malpractice again? "Am I here?" she said wearily. "I can neither confirm nor deny."

"It's your mother."

"I'm not here."

■ ■ ■

"I will not overreact," Mary Canty Ralston declared fiercely to her youngest daughter. "I will keep my normal sunny countenance." Her voice was as aggressive as it was loud. She wore a terra-cotta dress from 9 West and shoes from Ranzoni, the best shops in Charleston.

Moira Allegra Dewees Ralston tried to maintain an air of innocent bewilderment. Her round china blue eyes were watchful like a bird with a snake. She had expected her mother to react badly to her dropping out of college. But with Mary Canty there would always be a special edge of nastiness.

They sat opposite each other in the second floor sitting room of the great Regency style mansion at Number 1 Legendre Street with its view of the ancient oaks of Whitepoint Gardens and the glittering harbor beyond. A clear light of midday came through the windows into the high-ceilinged room with its double mahogany doors. The glowing hand rubbed floors were of true heart pine from a time when trees were so huge that boards two feet wide were cut from the centers. The fireplace was bordered by Sepia Delft tiles depicting Biblical scenes.

The 1838 house where Moira had grown up was a magnificent artifact from a lost age of extravagance. And Moira like her mother believed it and the other mansions of Legendre and Legare and Lamboll streets were symbols of a cultural superiority at which all Americans were properly awed.

Crowds of tourists always stopped to gape at the pure visual romance, moving on uneasily when they heard Mary Canty's unearthly screeching from within. Buffered by its ballast brick garden wall and elaborate parterres, the house was set too far back for them to peep through windows and see the Adams mantles, cabinets in Italian marquetry, the walnut harpsichord, all the splendid things that had been in the Ralston and Randolph families for centuries.

"I woke up to life's brevity," said Moira.

Mary Canty erupted. "Brevity? You're eighteen years old. You're as brainless as . . . as a cattail or a pussy willow or something."

Moira flushed scarlet. "I have decided I am a very serious person." She paused uneasily. "Beneath the surface."

Mary Canty smiled an acid smile. "How nice of you to reassure me on that point. As you cut your mother's heart out. And don't soften the blow. Don't slowly introduce your nutty notions by writing me a letter. By giving me the slightest warning."

Moira shivered and breathed through her mouth. She felt she was suffocating.

"You were an atrocious student at Ashley Hall," said Mary Canty. "I had to get down on my knees and beg—I mean *beg* Sweet Briar to let you in."

"I am looking for creative validation," Moira said through a small pout. The firmness in her voice was so unexpected she startled herself.

The statement didn't register with Mary Canty. "Don't give me that little determined sulk of yours. You look as stubborn and mulish as your father used to. Never could take correction on the smallest point that man. And you—how can you be so unaware of the dismay you are creating? All your life you've made me an object of ridicule."

Moira shrugged and twisted her hands in her lap helplessly. Through the window she could see the flame red winter berries of the pyracantha draping over the neighbor's wall. Fire thorn, she thought. They burned with the fire of her yearning soul.

"Your first semester grades were a disaster. Four 'D's and an 'F'. But what should I have expected after Ashley Hall? The only girl at the Latin Club slave auction no one would bid on. The girl who spent St. Cecilia's Ball in the bathroom with the dry heaves. A coming out party for a deb who wouldn't come out!" She paused for breath.

Mary Canty always made Moira feel so close to the edge. Days of dark displeasure. An undercurrent of suppressed fury. Sudden explosions of monumental rage. Now Moira had announced a major life change and her mother was making her feel like a truant from grade school.

Mary Canty got up and paced the room. "I am a person of simple chic. I am generous, I am gracious." She slapped the heel of her hand to her forehead. "I raise a daughter with an unslakable thirst for tom-foolishness."

Moira's despair shifted to anger. Her life had been a series of furtive knocks at the door of opportunity. Yet she always knew poetry was her destiny. How could it be otherwise? She had been raised in the house of her ancestors. With portraits and age-spotted mirrors, the mellow glow of old wood and timeless elegance. Chippendale scuffed by the boots of Southern cavaliers and chewed by generations of Labrador retrievers. She had returned to the prospect of her beloved Charleston to take her place in life and, by God, she would do it. She rose slowly to her feet.

"Go ahead. Corrugate me. Or castigate me. Whatever the word is. Cutting me up is your standard blood sport. You and Rannie both. All your . . . low-down insult."

Mary Canty gave her a sinister look. Her voice held a note of pure satisfaction. "Such a nice little display of sass and guts. And such big words for a girl who makes a 'D' in Freshman English."

Moira ducked her head. "I'm not a structured learner," she mumbled. "I am a poet."

"A poet? Because you have a knack for . . . for phrase-making? Those little moon-June ditties you used to write?"

Moira had expected this scene to be brutal. But college was so much worse. That awful business of having to get to classes on the opposite side of campus. The Phys Ed requirement of swimming the length of the pool when she had almost drowned. All the girls making fun of her. They made her feel like a circus clown slipping on a banana peel. She'd have to pick herself up and force a grin, laugh with the crowd as they laughed at her. She cried so much her roommate had moved out.

Moira looked down at her shoes. "I have been told my work is publishable."

"By whom?"

"Gaston Garnett."

"Who on earth is that?"

Moira sniffed. "Quite probably America's greatest living poet. Certainly the South's."

"What happened to Robert Frost?"

"He's dead, mother."

2

"Yeh-boy," drawled Collier Ralston into the telephone. "Bait a trap with pussy and you'll catch me ev'ry time." He laughed at his own folksy earthiness.

Rannie stood in the law office doorway staring at her older brother. With his feet up on his desk, he looked as he always did—like a scourge of trifling laziness.

Collier glanced up, caught her standing there with that implicit challenge loaded into her stare. He hunched into his chair and muttered a hurried good-bye into the phone. Then asked briskly if she got the lawsuit filed in time.

She said she did. He said great, they were a well oiled machine. She said she got it filed two minutes before the clerk's office closed. Two minutes before the statute of limitations ran. Two minutes before they would have been in line to be sued by the client for malpractice because Collier had sat on the case so long he'd forgotten about it.

He gave a weak, stuttering kind of laugh. "You're a real charmer, Rannie. Wherever you go, you carry an atmosphere of damp, chilly menace."

"The house needs painting. You know what the bandits are charging now? Thirty thousand dollars. *Thirty thousand.*"

Collier waved it away as a minor nuisance. "All this money business, it's like a monomania with you."

"Thirty grand. I think it's a strong, unambiguous message."

Collier said could she ease up? He was under big stress from the legislative work load.

Rannie snorted. "Rhetorical grandstanding or whatever you do up there."

"If you're referring to the Confederate flag, I think I'm the voice of moderation."

South Carolina was the last Southern state to fly the rebel battle flag from the dome of the state house. Blue cross of St. Andrew on a red field.

When Collier was being the voice of sweet reason he'd point out that the flag was not an in-your-face symbol of resistance to racial integration. It had actually preceeded that. In 1960 the US government had proclaimed a Civil War Centennial and suggested the states that had slugged it out do various stunts to memorialize the event. That was when the flag had gone up.

Collier was a battlefield reenactor. Dress up in Confederate uniform and play war. It had seemed okay when he was a teenager. But he was grown now. When he was all decked out he looked like he was in the full flush of juvenile behavior.

Collier tried to smile disarmingly, the smile he used when one of his girlfriends caught him with another one. "So here you are. Standing around like . . . what? A presiding irony?"

Rannie said she had been working all day without let-up.

Her hands were grimy with work. Collier glanced about negligently. Said well since she had gotten that suit filed his desk was clear.

Rannie said acidly, "I'm sure you could find some work to do around here if you'd organize a search."

He looked at the door helplessly, wanting to scuttle out to freedom. It was hard to picture him as a state senator but he sure enough was one. Thirty years old, and according to him, being talked about as Congressional material.

Rannie had never understood state politics. You couldn't particularly link a national party label—Republican or Democrat—to their platforms. It just seemed to be a pack of good ol' boys cutting sweetheart deals. Land deals. Highway deals. Shameless one-time tax breaks for the rich and powerful.

That was the promise that Collier always dangled in front of her. They'd be in on the looting and pillaging. He'd be the rainmaker. But mostly he was into the bevies of little college girl interns. Blonde political groupies whose names ended in 'I'—Traci and Tammi and Staci—who would show up for the all-night drinking and poker parties in the Wade Hampton Hotel in Columbia. Roaring drunk legislators and lobbyists stalking the halls, bed sheets wound around them like togas.

Their mother Mary Canty never tired of telling you what a beauty she had been in her youth, and you could still see the traces of it behind the smoker's wrinkles on her lips and the sunbursts at the edge of her eyes. Collier got the looks. He was male-model handsome. Then Moira although she was so insipid it was hard to think of her as pretty. Rannie? Well, Rannie knew she was a special case.

It took an unusual man to appreciate her amazon queen looks.

Four Ralstons. All of them still moiling around under the same roof because the house was such a white elephant; it just drank money. It was built in 1838 when there was slave labor and an endless sea of trees across South Carolina. Now the contractors saw the address and doubled their prices.

And Rannie was the only one earning any money. And the more she earned the less the others seemed inclined to pull their weight. So she was trapped in a kind of labyrinth from which there was no escape.

Mary Canty was crafty beyond measure. Give the woman an unlimited budget and she'd manage to exceed it. Once she'd gotten hold of a charge card of Rannie's and run up $15,000 of debt in two hours. Then simply refused to discuss the matter. Which was an easy pose because every day from noon until three she was drinking at the Carolina yacht club and from three until pass-out time she was drinking at home. And she was a late riser.

"Well, don't let me hem you in with protocol," said Rannie. "Go drive up to Columbia and dick around. Answer the call of the wild."

Collier raised an eyebrow. "Dick around," he said abruptly. "There always was a common streak in you."

Rannie narrowed her eyes, giving him a warning glance. He had been physically cowed by her ever since she had conked him with a spice mill when she was nine and he was twelve. It had taken thirty stitches to close the wound. That had certainly caused a stink. The endless round of tests to see if he was brain damaged.

Collier took her suggestion and left. But kind of quietly obstinate like she wasn't ordering him out. All the sibling rivalry of a lifetime glared out of his eyes.

Rannie knew she was a bastard. Or bastardess. Whatever you called it. Born on the wrong side of the blanket. The news had hit early via a loud confrontation between her parents that meant nothing to her when she heard it as a five year-old child but grew in importance as she got older. "So I indulged in a bit of naughty fun," Mary Canty had told her husband. "What do you expect, you dickless wonder!"

It had never bothered Rannie. The father was unknown. Her "daddy" was the one who raised her, and she was always confident in being his favorite. Collier was a slippery eel from the get-go. Moira was such a simpering mess. Her crying jags should be studied by medical science. When she wept it was noisy and wet and without the least restraint. The astonishing, endless wail drove others off and provided a protective blanket.

Mary Canty? Rannie didn't even have an Electra-style competition with her. Mary Canty was nothing but verbal abuse and bombast. In a town rich with legendary drunks, she was in a class all her own. She took her blood pressure medicine with vodka and vermouth.

Rannie's daddy spent his married life finding reasons not to be home. And Rannie was always with him. Watching him try cases in other counties. Freezing in duck hunting blinds. Walking behind him across broomsage fields, the dogs rigid on a point, waiting for the covey of quail to explode in front of them.

The sign on the door said "Ralston & Ralston." Her daddy

had put it up when Collier joined the firm in the old People's Building on Broad Street. When Rannie came in, he had never gotten around to adding a third Ralston or maybe "The Ralston Firm." And that was because "Big Collier" had died of a heart attack when "Young Collier" told him about the high school-age page girl he had knocked up and the flabbergasting sum of money she wanted to restore her virginity.

As the sky turned purple with streaks of pink, Rannie got ice out of the small fridge and the desk bottle of Jim Beam from the drawer for an end of the day drink just like her daddy had done. When she was a little girl and would come faithfully each day to walk him home he always had a smell of Beam on his breath. She drank it the way he did in a squat Old Fashioned glass with just a bit of ice to cut it.

Traffic was thinning out down below. Broad Street was the old business street of law offices and realtors and small insurance agencies. Flat roof Federal period buildings with all kinds of different facades. Italianate. Romanesque revival. After six in the evening it could take on a strange timeless quiet. Except for the car models, it could have been 1940.

South-of-Broad lay the hidden alleys and courtyards, the antebellum mansions with scrolled columns holding up triple piazzas. Spanish moss draping the oaks. Palmettos and banana plants. Although desecrated more and more by tourists, Charleston truly remained a city with the power of hypnosis.

A big flock of grackles swooped overhead. Rannie was alert to birds, even the trash ones. She and her daddy used to go on the Audubon Society bird counts. Roam the woods all day. Take joy in spotting a ruby crowned kinglet.

She could see right into the lit window across the street. And lo and behold, as she lived and breathed, there was Rhett MacReady—the son of her daddy's former law partner. He had gone to Virginia to college. Then been some kind of army commando. A Ranger or something. The newspaper had carried a photo of him in a black beret. Now he was back home.

Her eyes began to dance. She started to throw open the window, yell across the street and wave. But controlled the impulse.

Rhett MacReady who had painted her debutante portrait.

Behind an office closet door the scandalous portrait lay buried among old case files. Four feet by three in a beaux arts frame. The 18-year-old Rannie Ralston languorously nude. Showing her already voluptuous breasts. And my she had a healthy glow.

Buck naked, her daddy had said in horror.

I've got to go lie down, said Mary Canty.

Rannnie smiled broadly remembering the whole heady experience. The whole wonderful, romantic thing.

So now Rhett was back. She hadn't heard about him going to law school.

■ ■ ■

"I will never represent you again!" Rannie snarled into the phone.

In the next room Moira stiffened. Her sister needed a muzzle on her. It was like she was gripped by demonic possession. Rannie bellowing into the phone and then ending it with a resounding: "Fuck you and the horse you rode in on!"

Moira closed her eyes and breathed deeply, trying to picture a blossoming azalea bush. Each evening, the Ralston cocktail hour was like lying on a bed of nails.

The room glowed with the light of a wood fire casting flickering shadows over objects that had been in the family for multiple generations. Moira sat in the chair where the periwigged Fanshawe Ralston had smoked his long-stemmed clay pipe. He had ridden with Francis Marion and nearly been hung by the British. Her feet rested on the carpet Colonel Runneymeade Ralston had been wrapped in upon his untimely death.

Glass covered book shelves with leather bound volumes of Sir Walter Scott. Exhibition cases with relics of the Southern past. Horse pistols, swords, daggers. A derringer that John Wilkes Booth was said to have left behind when he came through Charleston with his acting troupe in 1859. Stuffed Carolina parakeet and carrier pigeon, both now extinct species. A Yemassee Indian skull with a tomahawk sunk in it.

Rannie strode into the room, face red with anger. She moved like a man when you thought about it. Snatching up her drink and rattling the ice in the glass. Just like Daddy used to do.

Mary Canty's voice was its usual evening slur. "Why must you bring your ghastly work into the house? Was that call from someone actually in jail?"

Rannie gritted her teeth. "That douche-bag. If ever I hated a client, it's him."

"I don't know where you got that trash mouth," said Mary Canty. "It's like terminal La Tourettes or something."

"I'm sure Rannie doesn't mean it," Moira chimed in. "She just likes to hear herself say vulgar things."

All her life, Moira had taken every opportunity to side with her mother against Rannie. It was the only mother-daughter solidarity she had ever had. But tonight she realized it was a tactical error.

Rannie gave her a cruel smile. "Well don't let the sad reality of my life interfere with your joy in dropping out of college. What will occupy you now? Spend each day sitting there like a diamond on velvet?"

Moira shivered under her sister's glare. "It's just a turn in the road of life."

"Or one more pratfall in an endless burlesque."

"I think I should have gone to Hollins." Moira was feeling her way cautiously. "They don't have a math requirement there."

"You were always hopeless at math," Mary Canty agreed.

"And they have their famous Writing Programme," Moira said almost desperately. "They've developed many famous writers. Annie Dillard. Lee Smith."

"Dillard and Smith write novels," Rannie snorted. "People actually buy novels."

Moira raised her chin defiantly. "Sylvia Plath made money. I'm pretty sure she did. You see her books everywhere."

Rannie rolled her eyes. "Sure. She stuck her head in the oven because she couldn't take the sudden onrush of good fortune. Thank you, Sister Moira for this wonderful night of revelation. I'm so lucky to be here with my family. I'd hate to be alone at a time like this."

Moira's eyes filled with tears. "I'm sure you know you're missing something in life by being so mean. It's just you don't know what it is."

"I paid for the spring tuition," Rannie accused.

"She was failing anyway," said Mary Canty dismissively. "Every subject." She stood up. Reached out her hand. "Let me freshen your drink, Rannie."

Moira sat up attentively. "You paid? What about . . . ?" She looked at Mary Canty. She had never seen her move so briskly. Clashing the bottles on the drinks cart. Slashing through a lime with a little serrated knife.

"You want more ice, Rannie?"

Moira was weakly insistent. "What about . . . ?"

Mary Canty interrupted sharply. "Moira, go upstairs and get my sweater. I'm freezing to death. This wretched house. I don't know why you won't upgrade the heating, Rannie. It doesn't cost all that much and . . ."

Rannie fixed Moira with a hard, suspicious gaze. "What about what?"

Moira tittered. She hated it when her sister made her do that silly nervous laugh. "My trust fund." Moira looked from Rannie to her mother and back again. "The one Daddy left me for my education."

Rannie narrowed her eyes at Mary Canty. "I paid her tuition . . . and she has a trust fund? Why did I not know about this?"

"Well, she's dropped out now. That will save you a

bundle. You should be grateful for once instead of always complaining."

"Twenty-five thousand dollars," whispered Rannie in shocked wonder. "I wrote two checks that totaled twenty-five thousand dollars."

"It's not something I care to discuss," said Mary Canty, making a chopping motion. "Moira can't possibly understand . . ." She trailed off with an air of resignation like they couldn't talk adult topics around a defective child.

Moira squirmed uncomfortably. She expected her sister to explode in one of her famous outbursts. Instead Rannie spoke in a level tone. A musing voice of weary calm.

"You know I have to do Collier's scut work for him while he plays grab-ass with interns. I get held at gun point by a client. A cop's gun. .38 calibre. Could punch a hole in my head big enough to shove a rolled umbrella through. Then said client has the gall to phone me here tonight."

"Don't carry on so," ordered Mary Canty. "You're such a self-dramatiser." She gave Rannie a new drink and lowered herself slowly into her chair. Said her back hurt from sleeping wrong.

Moira felt a growing queasiness. This business of guns and gaping holes. As a child, Rannie was always barging into the house with dead animals. It was one thing for men to hunt. That was their role in life. But Rannie would come back and lay out ducks and doves and God-knows-what-all on the kitchen floor. Just like a cat with dead mice. She simply revelled in the slaughter.

Moira tried hard to picture a nice floral image, but all that came to mind was Chinese snowball. And she hated those big white pom-poms.

Rannie bridled at her mother's insult and bulled on with a filthy story about the county jail and a policeman swallowing tobacco and throwing up. It was all so sordid and vile that Moira tried hard to not listen. Then Rannie dropped the grenade into the room.

"Gaston is such an asshole."

Moira could feel the first thrill of panic. It slithered up her spine and took hold of her throat. "Who?" she squeaked.

"Gaston Garnett. There's a poet in fine fig for you. Murdered his wife although I imagine he'll get off. The cops have got a major problem with the time line. Gaston was loud drunk in a bar at the time of death. Coroners don't know what they're doing. Most of them are just Baptist ministers who take a ghoulish interest in death."

"Have I heard this name before?" Mary Canty leaned forward in her chair. She sounded irritated. "Someone mentioned him."

"He lives on Middlesex Street." Rannie vaguely pointed uptown to one of the historic districts called Ansonborough. "Nice house. All his wife's money. She was an author. Now she's a dead author."

"Authors are all over Charleston now," Mary Canty bemoaned. "All trying to write about the city like they were 'been-heres'." Mary Canty showed no interest in the identity of the deceased. She belonged to the old school that bought books but never read them.

But she did relish a good murder. She leaned forward. "How was she killed?"

"One shot to the heart." Rannie put her finger in her mouth and made a loud pop. "Passed through her body and slammed her up against the wall. Fell to the floor. She thrashed a while before she croaked. They could tell from the blood smears. Must have died in absolute agony."

Mary Canty seemed intrigued. "So our poetic Mister Gaston has now come into her fortune?"

"What the devil's wrong with you?" Rannie snapped at her sister.

It was the last words Moira heard as the world began to spin and she fell over onto the Runneymeade Ralston carpet.

3

Over Collier's loud objections, Rannie had kept the law office in the exact shabby state it had been when their daddy died. Ratty old chairs with busted springs. Framed copy of the Declaration of Independence. Shelves of Southeastern Reporters even though she had that all on LEXIS-NEXIS now.

Down below was Broad Street, a corridor of ego-tripping lawyers, the 18th century Exchange Building an eminence at one end, the Four Corners of the Law at the other. With the roofs of the old walled city spread out below, a glorious treasure-trove of preserved architecture and subtle snob gradations. In a world smothered by asphalt and strip malls, the ratty old antique place where she had grown up had risen in status to a staggering piece of beauty.

At 8 a.m. Rannie sat at her desk looking across Broad street, filling up on caffeine, wondering what Rhett was doing, what kind of a practice he was going to start.

She leafed through the Post & Courier, found herself staring at the bankruptcy announcements, the classifieds where men said they would no longer be responsible for their wives' debts. She might be in there soon disavowing her mother.

Life was not good in the house of ill-will at Number 1.

Legendre. The frantic pace of bill paying was getting to her. Thirty thou to paint the place. Keep the rot contained in some minimal way.

Her sister saw the house clouded in a romantic haze of the past. Candelabra glowing and the parquet ballroom sighing with the sounds of a waltz. As linen-suited planters mounted the broad stairs with hoop-skirted ladies on their arms. And ebony house servants in striped vests and long aprons toted crates of wine from the cellar and pulled corks.

Rannie saw it as a dying white elephant of falling plaster, short-circuited wiring, leaky pipes and outrageous property taxes. Anything of real value had been hawked to Yankee antique pillagers during the Great Depression. Leaving a clutter of artifacts from her berserk ancestry.

The Fanshawe Ralston chair. It was just a broken-down chair where he used to pass out nightly, tanked on Dragoon punch. During the Revolution, he had betrayed his horse troop to the British in exchange for his own sorry neck. They were all hanged, leaving him alive and unaccused in his treachery.

The Colonel Runneymeade Ralston carpet was nothing but a factory woven rug. His corpse was wrapped in it before being transferred to a coffin. He had blown his brains out after being caught embezzling from the Planter's Bank in 1888. You could still see the blood stains, but otherwise, so what?

Moira had a trust fund, and Rannie had been suckered into paying the tuition bill to Sweet Briar. We must get Moira out into the world, Mary Canty had urged. Her swindler of a mother was utterly unrepentant.

Her mother was an "I told that man" kind of Southern

woman. As in "I told that man if he thought he was going deer hunting he just had another think coming." Or "I told that man if he wanted in my britches he was going to damn well marry me. And before that happened he better get finished with college and start earning a living." Her daddy had been a saint to put up with it.

At breakfast, Moira had been up surprisingly early. Writing her little ditties in a notebook with a fountain pen from the 1930s. Trying to make a rhyme with Lenten roses. "I love the purity of the morning light," she mused. "And the sea as a shimmering backdrop to my life."

Rannie told her to enjoy her day of grandiose selfishness.

"You're like a frozen custard that never got thawed out," Moira had answered snippily.

Rannie spoke in an elongated purr. "You are so-oo Charleston. A type mercifully rare in the rest of the world."

"And you are just dog hair on a cashmere sweater," sniffed Moira. She examined the notebook in front of her carefully. "Not that I am one to harbor hostility like a sister I know."

Rannie wished a good dose of E. Coli on her and went to work. Left her there with her herbal tea and that pinched little expression on her face.

Moira having the vapors last night. Crashing down to the floor like the End of Time. God knows what had set her off. Moira didn't need a reason to behave like a mental defective. All that mess of gaudy blond hair like a human daffodil. It was like it had leached out her brain.

Frozen custard in a pig's eye. Rannie was a potential volcano of passion. It was just that romance in her life was a past due date. She didn't know any eligible men to even muse upon lustfully.

Rannie wanted romance and total surrender and eternal love. Not that she had ever seen much evidence that it existed. When Mary Canty was in a cold mood, she used to address her husband like someone she had barely met. And when she was ripped, she treated him like a chimney sweep who had tracked on the carpet.

But now there was Rhett MacReady.

Rannie rummaged in the closet with all the dead files and tax returns and trash that should be chucked out. Dug out her portrait in the scrolled frame. Beat the dust off it until the varnish glowed again. And there it was. Rannie Ralston debutante. In radiant health. Eyes alight with mischief. And without a stitch on.

I am Pure T. Woman, she said half-aloud. I'm not some slender, lofty sylph, my face a smooth blankness of perfect pores. I don't float into a room with narcissist written all over me. I have big breasts built on aggressive lines. Powerful hearty thighs. Fresh shining skin.

It was traditional in Charleston to commission a debutante portrait. What had happened was Rannie had been entrusted to pick the artist. The assumption was she'd go to the usual society artists, widows and spinsters who eked a meagre living from art.

Rannie had selected Rhett MacReady which had raised some eyebrows, but Mary Canty figured what the heck, he was a mere college boy. He'd be really cheap. And if not, she'd refuse to pay him at all. It was one of her favorite stunts.

Well, one thing had led to another that summer in the sultry warmth of Charleston, and Rannie had ended up posing nude *and* losing her virginity. She had talked dirty with a lot of girls in her time, heard a lot of confessions about "getting carried away." But in all that explicit palaver, she had never once heard of an orgasm the first time. Certainly not a screaming explosive one like she had.

The portrait had caused sheer pandemonium. "Cavorting buck naked," Mary Canty had shrieked. She had been expecting at most a plunging neckline. Rhett had gone back to the University of Virginia, and Rannie to UNC which ended the commotion. Needless to say, Mary Canty never wrote out a check.

And speaking of the devil, there he was again visible through the window across the street. Over there in lonely glory. With a back that was a pack of muscles.

The docket sounding was at nine. Half hour to kill. She'd just go see him. No warning. Just drop in. Very matter of fact. See how he reacted. He'd probably play the slow-talking country boy. That was one of his stunts when a surprise came jumping out at him. Very cool.

She crossed the street wending her way through traffic. A woman with a mission. Cast iron Corinthian columns around the door. Went up the stairs to the third floor with a head full of memories.

Night swimming with him naked off Fort Moultrie. Lying floating on their backs with the stars all overhead. And that fleet of porpoises had come up and rolled around them. Nudging them with their noses.

R. MacReady Attn.-at-Law lettered on the frosted door glass. She tried the handle but it was locked. She knocked, and Rhett opened it. Taller than she recalled. Absolutely looking down on her. The sharp realism of his jaw line and that cleft in his chin. The body that had moved on her with complete conviction. While she did the "don't stop, don't stop" soliloquy.

She gave him her best provocative look.

"Well here's a wave of nostalgia," he said, not showing the least surprise at seeing her. "Look at that power suit. Talk about a brand new incarnation. My memory is cut-off jeans and a t-shirt with a sword fish on it."

She followed him into the big room. Light coming from the tall windows that faced hers across the street. Saying, "Working for a living has become an anomaly in my family. I'm the only productive Ralston. Collier's a Senatorial do-nothing. Moira's still the same bright little buttercup. So I get to defend dudes who shoot speed into their arms."

"Is it complicated?"

"You take their money, plead them guilty. Just like our daddies used to do."

"How does the bar accept you?"

"As you'd expect. You throw a few elbows and they treat you like a hobgoblin."

Then it struck her. This wasn't a law office. It was an art studio. Canvases everywhere. Easel. Rags. Palettes. Paint splatters on the floor. A sofa, armchair and bed over in one corner where he seemed to be living. Big book case filled with folios and art books.

Rhett did a little flash of brush work on the canvas, chucked the brush in a can of turpentine.

There was no heat in the room, and Rhett wore old paint daubed khaki pants and a gray roll-neck sweater that was frayed at the cuffs. He was painting, what? A hairy wild boar slobbering and squealing as it fought a pack of baying hounds.

"You're an artist?"

"I'd think you'd recall. Do you still have the infamous portrait?" He smiled, his eyes sure enough taking her inventory.

Rannie was wandering around the room, running her fingers over a stuffed red fox, its fur the color of her hair. She chucked a squeezed-out tube of paint lightly in the air. Caught it. "The portrait? Oh, it's around somewhere. Probably buried up in the attic."

"It ought to at least have an honored place in the bathroom."

"You never went to law school?" she inquired casually.

Rhett shrugged.

"But the name on the door?"

"My daddy's old office. You remember he moved here after the break-up. Part of my minor inheritance. I get to squander an office."

"He moved here after the ruckus over the painting."

"I don't think we need to take the heat for that. Our daddies were both stealing from each other every chance they got. They lied about everything. Got up each day primed to lie early and often. The truth was not in them."

Rannie said, "I don't spend a lot of time traumatized by guilt." God she'd like to jump all over him with new enthusiasm. She'd show him the difference between a girl of eighteen and a woman of twenty-seven.

"Well, sometimes," he said, "I look around me at the world and burst out laughing. Cope by braying my head off."

"You always looked like your daddy when you laughed. The matinee idol looks. Gary Cooper blended with Alan Ladd."

That brought a really nice smile. "Well you got Big Collier's look about you."

She touched her face. "Are you serious?"

"Yeah. I spent a lot of time studying you as you might recall." The smile again, the eyes going right into hers.

"But why not law school? We used to say we'd be partners."

He shrugged. "I'm thinking of being the wild pig artist of America."

Rannie studied the painting. "Why pigs?"

"Bill fish are taken. Ducks are an overcrowded field. Feral hogs are an available gig."

"It's a good pig."

"It's okay."

"No, you've pretty much nailed it."

"Thanks."

"The lost Lowcountry. Plantations and swamps. Crumbling Charleston with crepe myrtles and live oaks. Decorative iron work and little alleys. Jasmine spilling over the walls. I think of our lives back then as a kind of primitive Eden. You could have a sublime faith in the old place."

"Yeah," Rhett agreed. "I come back here looking for coherence and find things are changing. We used to stay up all night drinking at Cap'n Harry's Blue Marlin. Go out with the dawn pink above the rooftops, get a black coffee at the Iron Kettle. Now total transformation. Cap'n Harry's old thieves' den is outrageous priced condos. You can buy cappuccino. Mochaccino."

"A city of grace and charm being turned into a tourist industry at an alarming rate. Charleston has become like a corporate logo."

"Snap diagnosis," Rhett agreed. "But right on."

"I'm a simple and direct personality."

His eyes held a hint of mischief. "Some would call it obstinate."

"Complex situations come up, I try to stay in command. But I'm capable of strong affections."

"I remember that pretty well."

Rannie felt her heart pounding. God, yes, she would jump his bones without preamble.

No, it was time to play the rules. She said duty calls and went to the door. Maybe she'd see him around. Across the street neighbors and all that.

"Rannie?" he said.

Rannie hesitated, holding the door. She was breathing heavily.

"I always thought you were . . . I don't know . . . those piercing cat-green eyes . . . like a sphinx."

She spoke in a kind of elongated purr. "Well, maybe our worlds can find a way to communicate again."

He gave her a slow smile. "I read there are forty-five miles of nerves in the human body."

A dazed Rannie Ralston went out onto the sidewalk. Almost got hit by a car while crossing the street. She was thinking she needed to go on a crash diet. Lose at least ten pounds.

■ ■ ■

"Mo'fucka gone be a dead mo'fucking mo'fucka!" grunted the ugly booger next to Gaston Garnett. Dreadlocked hair. Biceps the size of smoked hams. Hideous purple scars of prison tattoos.

Moira Ralston looked thoroughly alarmed and pressed her knees more tightly together. Hugged her elbows so as to not touch anything. She kept shooting horrified little glances at the people around her. Trash women visiting their nightmare lovers.

Gaston Garnett racked his brain trying to remember where he had met this absurd girl. It was so hard to see her face through the yellowed plastic barrier of the visitor's room. Her voice was muffled. The plastic was a problem. Like trying to talk to the ticket troll in a bus station. And she kept a hand in front of her face in a vain effort to block the stench of the county jail. Soft little fingers with a birthstone ring. Was that a sapphire? What would it bring at Moneyman Pawn?

He screwed up his eyes. "And you are Rannie Ralston's sister? This is possible?"

Moira looked pained. She finally took her hand away. "Rannie doesn't look a-tall like us. She's something . . . well, very different altogether. That awful horse-radish hair. They say I have the ancestral Ralston mouth. You can see it in all the old family portraits. Copley captured it so well. Although Peale got it all wrong."

Gaston studied her little pink cupid's bow of a mouth curling slightly at the edges in her self-satisfaction. "Copley? Do you own this prodigious painting? I should so like to see an object of such vast worth."

"No, it's in the Gibbes museum." She seemed fearful of disappointing him. "The family sold it during the Depression. For way too little I'm sure."

"No mind." He reassured her with his avuncular smile. The one he used on fluttering little nervous nellies when he had put his hand some place that made them shriek.

"I've come to help you," Moira said with sudden resolution.

Now he was interested. He must tighten his grip on her li'l ol' brain. She was his bodacious lifesaver with the Ralston check book in hand. Bail him out to a scented bath and eighty proof bourbon balanced on his chest while he lolled in steamy suds. Then drying the old bod with lush monogrammed towels while savoring a second hit of hooch and contemplating the dinner menu.

"Fuggin' ass-wipe!" It came out "ice-wahp." A white man drawl. That evil 'Cooter' somebody down the row of prisoners lined up at the barrier. Big beefy face and porcine eyes. Slash from a broken beer bottle through his eyebrow and into the cheek. That boy was bad to the bone.

Moira gagged slightly like she might be sick. "How do you stand this . . . ?"

"This grimy hell of miscreants? I have body and mind control, the ability to adjust to a landscape of raging brutes. It is, after all, a world of self-interest and broken promises."

Now personalize it. Make her his ally against the world. "For both you and me."

"I knew you were strong," Moira gushed. "From that day at Sweet Briar when I heard you read 'Bad Drunk in Natchez'. It was such an earthy poem. And all those shocking four-letter words. But still I could tell the manly force just thrusting . . ." An alarmed look seized her face. "Well, displaying itself."

This Nervous Nelly opposite him. As a present day-product she was preposterous. Bred for ideals of the 1950s. The light was long ago turned out on the party for her kind.

He gave her the smile of sentimentality. Ineffable Byron, Keats and Shelley sentimentality. "My only suffering comes because I can't exercise my craft. This . . . this squalid milieu overshadows my ability. Clapped in the hoosegow by unfounded rumors. I feel disillusioned. Exploited by Fate."

"What about me?" said Moira. "I'm going round the bend just sitting here in this . . . in this boondoggle or whatever it is."

She almost seemed to be floating upward. Like she was levitating. Putting her mind outside her physical body.

Gaston said, "These hideous colors. I think it intensifies your character. You are love made force. You are a walk in the scented night."

"I want to write about the gardens of Charleston," Moira said fervently.

Gaston blinked. "Gardens?"

"Secret landscapes behind brick walls. Places of intimacy. Gardens are the spirit of their creators. You can feel it just by passing through. Poignant passages I call it. That's a *double entendre*. You know. From the French?"

Gaston thought, am I illiterate? I write treble and quadruple entendres, you little peabrain. I am the world's sunlit chamber. Its taste of caviar on toast. Locked in here with festoons of jabbering negroes and white trash from the sewers of North Charleston. While this vapid twit . . .

"Meander. Isn't that a wonderful word? And parterre. How it rolls off the tongue. Layered space."

Yeah right. The old Emersonian reverence for nature. Still, it might be interesting to cast the wicked eye upon her hidden valley. Her water meadow. Shady grove my little love. Yes, indeed. Make her squeal and dance to his hornpipe. He remembered humping that little bouncy sophomore at Sweet Briar in a cloak room. Giving her a jaunty hayride on the mounds of camel hair and tweed. Was that when he had met Moira?

"Parterre de luxe," purred Gaston. "Parterre of my lover's qwym."

Moira's blue eyes snapped open with the sudden effect of up-righting a baby doll. "Your lover's . . . what?"

He gave her his smile of generosity. "In my capable hands, your true gifts will take shape. With the right mentoring, you'll soon be an established talent."

"I don't need the mainstream media," said Moira. "I can live for my craft. Like you. Small magazines would be enough. A sweet vindication for all the abuse I take."

Gaston was contemplating the infinity of the Ralston bank account. "I speak reluctantly. But I need serious legal representation. I can't make do with one of those bearded public defenders. They're so frail their chests appear concave."

"I'll find a way to make my sister cooperate," Moira solemnly promised. "I have a great optimism on that point."

"I will accept her back as my attorney without prejudice," he said charitably. "Mine is the true wholesome spirit."

"I knew you were a decent person. Rannie misuses everyone. Then rages at them when they dare complain."

"And I've got to be sprung from this place of doom. I must make bail."

"I don't have any money," explained Moira plaintively. "I do have a small trust fund I believe. I'm just hopeless about money. I wasn't raised to be involved in the sordid details of life. And Mother seems to live off Rannie. Lord knows my evil sister rubs our noses in it often enough so it must be true."

Gaston's brow furrowed thoughtfully. "Does your mother own her house?"

4

"We are sequestered here," said Moira. "Not just in a great house. But nestled within the small world below Broad Street. A self-sufficient community." She flashed her practiced smile.

"With possibilities as limitless as our dreams," said Gaston, returning the smile broadly. His white hair was shampooed and fluffy, his jowls glowing from a close shave.

Rain streaked the windows like little teardrops of sorrow longing to get into No. 1 Legendre and warm themselves at the crackling fire.

At that moment Moira felt she had entered the perfect conspiracy against the world. Gaston's charm was so intense. His vitality masked something definitely unresolved inside him. But that was in the nature of a poet. And it was in the nature of his muse to bring out the best in him. With her gift for intimacy Moira could easily ensure he met audience expectation.

Gaston had devoted three hours to a bubble bath in the old iron tub with claw feet, steaming the stench of jail out of his pores. Then clothed himself in one of her daddy's suits, a gray Harris tweed which fit him almost perfectly. Well, it was a little tight around the middle. British tailoring.

From Canada actually. And lace-up brogues. He said he felt he was entering a time capsule.

"With its old-fashioned pace," Moira went on, "Charleston is a monument. It encapsulates all that is best of the human condition. Like . . . like a pressing of autumn leaves found in an old leather-bound book." She looked to Gaston for praise of her imagery.

He had turned his attention to the drinks cart. "Ah Tanqueray gin. That smell of citrus. And a taste that fairly shimmers on the tongue."

Moira bravely soldiered on. "Some call our ways antique. But life flows without conscious effort."

Gaston rattled the bottles. "And can this be Plymouth gin? Oh frabus joy! Haven't had a Plymouth since the 70's. Gad what memories to sully the taste. Leisure suits and disco. That pious Mistah Jaw-jah Peanut in the White House." He unscrewed the cap. "Yes, the remembered spicy smell of lemongrass."

Moira chewed her lower lip. She had a great deal of experience with excessive alcohol consumption. Her mother had taken a stab at AAs. Drove to a meeting with a silver flask of rum, kahlua and crème de menthe which she offered round.

"It is said that Charlestonians are like the Chinese. We eat rice and worship our ancestors. If we have a reputation for being difficult and overbearing it is because we are a city under siege. Modernity lies camped outside our gates."

"Indian tonic. Yes, quinine is definitely called for. Nature's finest medicine."

Moira closed her eyes and breathed deeply. He had

been in jail. She said, "I really can't stand the common camellia. It's got blossoms as big as grapefruits. The sasanqua is smaller and has a grace about it. And its leaves aren't so coarse."

Gaston tipped his glass back, spilling a good bit down his chin and shirt front. "Ah, let the good grappa flow down my parchèd throat. Banish the faces of walking dead men staring at me from behind steel bars."

Moira's eyes popped open. "Those lines . . . they're from *Linear Notes* something something."

Gaston gave a small bow. He was very pleased with his celebrityhood. *Linear Notes in the Topography of Pansexual Troilism.* "Do you know the poem title?"

"'Undoing the Sated Past'?"

"Pre-zackly. A noble failure like so many of my endeavors. I was living on the Tuscan coast at the time on an NEA Genius Grant. Savoring the chianti and the deep burnishing sun."

"Oh no," Moira contradicted. "It's not a failure. It's an elevator . . . elevating. I remember so vividly." She closed her eyes and recited:

"When Shelley did
in Spezia drown
The surf was up
and the poet down."

"What? What?" Mary Canty came across the threshold holding a long cigarette and a short drink. She stumbled slightly at the edge of the carpet. Recovered.

Gaston leapt up and spread his arms wide. "I adore

and relish your home and hearth. It reverberates with solemn silence like a great cathedral."

Mary Canty snorted. "Silence? My oldest daughter will be here soon. Her noise switch is permanently on." She tried to sit down gracefully but ended up sprawling in a chair. Then realized she wanted a refill. Stared at the drinks cart.

Gaston knew the emotion and quickly took her glass.

She told him the suit looked good on him. Far better than on her late husband who wore it like a guano bag. Always hanging loose on him.

Gaston reared back in mock surprise. "Your . . . *late* husband? Has my eyesight begun to fail me? You can't be any older than thirty-five."

She didn't contradict the absurdly low age. "Yes," she allowed, "I am widowed." She paused thoughtfully. "Much as you are, I believe."

Gaston held up a hand. "Speak to me not in tones of low-down desolation."

"My husband was a perfect fool," barked Mary Canty. "I haven't missed him once." She knocked back the drink he handed to her.

Gaston's eyes narrowed. His lips spread in a sly smile. "My wife was violent, unstable, quite probably a secret drug addict."

"Big Collier gave me three ungrateful children and a load of grief. I married him because that's what women did back then."

"Claitey was a theatrical aspect of my life. I wed because I was young and insatiably curious about the female zone of life. A madcap adventure that led to a hall of mirrors in a Fun House of schizophrenia."

Moira couldn't believe the turn of conversation. True, she was glad to know Gaston had been unhappy in love. But her mother could reduce any memory to a cesspool.

In an outburst of enthusiasm, Moira prodded Gaston to do please recite a verse for Mother. He said he felt an enormous hesitation. She said oh pretty please do 'Magnesium Flash of Salty Vernacular.' And stared at him in earnest concentration.

Gaston's voice rose in pleasure. "My folkways period. I was at Sewanee at the time. An agrarian populist in Osh-Kosh B'Gosh overalls. Raising hymns of the people into the fresh mountain air of Tennessee. Intoxicated by that atmosphere dense with sap and longing. They said I was extravagantly gifted. All I knew then was that I would be leader of a great enterprise. And so I raised a mighty noise.

> Life's a weaving and a fabric
> A gravitas filled with mirth
> And in our saintèd lusts
> We transcend laws
> Mere mortals be subject to."

"My you are good," Mary Canty enthused. She took a deep drag on her cigarette. "Touching. Astute. Whatever the word is."

Gaston nodded deferentially. "It is my humble stock in trade. Stringing words together in halting rhythms."

"Your work is so Southern," Moira gushed admiringly.

"It's our need to keep the past with us. To strip bare the tensil fraud of the present."

"The doctor says I have high blood pressure," said Mary Canty. "But I think he's lying. Doctors say that to everyone who likes a cocktail in the evening."

"Liquor is the unguent of the brain," said Gaston.

Mary Canty laughed and laid a hand on his knee. Gaston cut his eyes to her hand.

"My cholesterol hovers at 240," said Gaston.

"I think that's rather, well, enchanting," said Mary Canty. "A man such as yourself who is controversial and . . . provocative." She rested her chin on the back of her hand and gave him a significant look.

"Your mix of luminosity and physicality," he murmured. "It could lead to a dangerous dalliance."

Moira thought, what is this little charade?

She said, "I really think I am at heart a 19th century Romantic. Wistful, sentimental, sometimes sad with a sweet melancholy. I dwell apart from ordinary people. I think they are simply wrong about most things."

The front door opened and slammed shut. Rannie thrashed around in the hall shaking her umbrella, hanging her raincoat on the deer antler hat rack. A big clang as she rammed the umbrella into the brass stand. Footsteps trudging up the stairs. "What a god-awful bitch of a day," she proclaimed. "I think I've been rendered clinically dead. Damned clients treat me like a service-industry professional. May as well be a bartender. A hairdresser."

The jitters ran all through Moira. Rannie stood framed

in the doorway seething. Barely containing her self-destructive force.

"Is this an A-list party, or can anyone join?" Rannie paused. Saw Gaston. Her jaw fell open.

"Ah, the talented spitfire Miss Rannie," said Gaston expansively. He stood up in welcome, saluted her with his glass. "May I call thee mouth-piece? Or barrister o'mine? You are a true triathlete of piss, vinegar and brimstone."

Rannie moved sideways across the room to the drinks cart. Sniffing the air like an animal that senses a trap. She poured Jim Beam into a glass with three cubes of ice. Swirled it. Talked aloud to the room at large.

"Most days I think I have peripheral-vision. I know when the Hoot Owl Gang is sneaking up on the campfire. But now I'm what? Dry-gulched? Bush-whacked?"

"Hi-yo, Silver," Gaston chortled, flopping back down and extending his legs. "Do join us. We're having prodigious fun. Whole lotta shakin' goin' on."

Rannie eyed him, swallowed a third of her drink. "I've got a mother who goes over budget with every purchase. But don't take my word for it. I'll show you the MasterCard bills. Let the numbers speak for themselves." She looked at Moira. "And dear sister. What did you do all day? Sit around on a tuffet?"

Mary Canty spoke to Gaston. "You'll love it here. It's like the Fourth of July fireworks without the *joie de vivre.*"

Rannie looked at Gaston. "Psycho killers receive obsessive love letters in prison. Get married on death row. Holding hands through the bars with some little waif who longs to descend into Hades. But you've invaded my home.

Do you figure you'll get some action here? Moira with the clamped thighs."

Moira ducked her head and blushed a bright scarlet.

"Rannie of the unzipped lip," said Mary Canty. "Raising you was like tending a cactus garden." She waggled her glass at Gaston, and he jumped to get her another refill. And to sweeten his own.

Moira took a deep breath. She could feel her armpits go moist with the tension of it all. "This is an absolute fit of cruelty, Rannie." Her eyes teared up. She was trying to picture nandinas and spireas. Purple phlox.

"Rannie lends a strong dose of fire," said Gaston with lordly calm. "I know it well. My father lashed me with a studded belt and made me thank him for every blow. He was a tent preacher who was known to handle snakes and talk in tongues."

Rannie eased herself down in a chair. Ran her tongue around her teeth. Drank some more. "Okay. I'm curious. How did you make bail?"

"I just signed some little forms for him," Moira interjected. "Something about the house."

Rannie's eyes were absolutely bulging. "You pledged the house? You forged mother's name?"

Moira's voice cracked tearfully. "You make the simplest act of decency sound criminal. You're just a mean old . . . shenanigan or something."

"For God's sake, don't start some tiresome debate," drawled Mary Canty. "I would have done it in her place."

Rannie glowered at Gaston. "And you're what now?

Handgun Man becomes the cuddly mascot of the Ralston family? We get the Unabomber plus poetry?"

"I think you're right for once," said Mary Canty warmly. "I think Gaston is just a great big old huggy-bear."

Both Rannie and Moira stared at her with their mouths open. Mary Canty's face was positively glowing. It was luminous. And she was batting her eyes at Gaston Garnett.

■ ■ ■

"Who on earth is Gaston Garnett?" Collier exclaimed. He was just in from the state capital in Columbia. Acting busy and in a rush so he could avoid any work. Couldn't even go to a simple work comp hearing for his sister.

Rannie held up a vanity-published collection of poems entitled *Cigar Mezzanine*. She opened a page at random and read aloud from "Succès de Scandale":

"Voyeuristic longings
On the wilder shores of sex
autoerotic lynching
Beg, borrow, fabricate
Orgasme de succès."

Collier was aghast. "That's poetry?"

"An early effort. That was from his aesthetic period. The first half of the '60s. Swinging London. Mod fashions. He wore a velvet suit and a scarf for a necktie. Haircut like that Rolling Stone who drowned in the swimming pool. That's what he told me at any rate. He finally settled on

Southern themes. *Catfish Dee-light. Bad Drunk in Natchez.* That got him a reputation as a regionalist, and he goes on the 'honey college' circuit. Agnes Scott. Converse. Randolph Macon. Hollins. Reads to little girls and paws them afterwards."

"I didn't know there were poets anymore."

"He's a true *artiste.* Last night he told mother she was tangy as a pickled peach."

"Pickled is right. She'd drink corn cob wine if there was nothing else available."

"And she told him he was just as sweet as pumpkin chip preserves."

"Dear Godfather."

"He seems to have uncovered a romantic streak in her we didn't know existed. Way down under the alluvial deposits of bile."

"He can't live in our house!" Collier almost shouted.

"He's doing a pretty fair imitation of it," Rannie answered dryly. "Treating it like some disability entitlement for him. When I left this morning, he was drinking Luzianne coffee with bleary eye and shaky hand after a night's boozing with Mother. He does like his toddy, our Gaston."

If the whole scenario wasn't such a horror, she'd have enjoyed Collier's discomfort. She leafed through a sheath of pink phone messages from disaster clients. Armed robber. Car-jacker. Rapist. She didn't want to return any of them.

Collier said it was horrible. It might even be unethical. Maintaining an accused murderer in your house.

"I can't say much to allay your fears. The really endearing part of the drama is I'm sure he did it."

"He did it? As in he snuffed his wife?"

"Murder most foul. The only original spin on the old theme is how he covered his tracks so well."

"And Moira brought him into our home?"

"It certainly stands her wholesome image on its head."

"You've got to get him out. That's all there is to it."

"I guess being free from commercial constraints gives you an off-beat perspective." She explained in detail how Moira had pledged the house on Gaston's bond. If Gaston disappeared, didn't make any particular hearing, the court would snatch it out from under them without delay.

She shook her head in despair. "So the two debacle-driven dingbats in my life have me over a barrel."

Collier stuck one hand in the side pocket of his suit jacket. It was a Jack Kennedy gesture he had studied. Collier really saw himself as Congressional material. "Most storms are of our own making," he huffed.

She cocked an eyebrow. "Does this mean that I'm at fault somehow?"

Collier chose not to press the issue. "A homily Big Daddy used," he mumbled. He could always hide behind his daddy's memory and rely on Rannie to back off.

"Speaking of self-made storms," she said, "I see you're scheduled to fly to New York." She opened the office check book to show the stub for Delta Airlines. Turned the book so he could read it in case he thought he could lie his way out. "Another girlfriend? Exhilarating young thing? Kind of far out on the frontier isn't it? Chasing Yankees."

"She's from Irmo, South Carolina. She just works in New York. And I'm in love. This is the real one. I'm going to ask her to marry me." His right hand seemed to be shaking a bit so he shoved that one in a pocket too.

"Well, this is certainly an emergent personality. The grown-up Collier makes wise lifestyle choices. Does this one do pageants?"

His smile was lopsided. "She's a set designer for an advertising firm in New York. She finds old mansions to rent for fashion shoots. Gets the props. Once she had to find a boa constrictor."

"Can she find work like that in Charleston? Because the last I checked, our finances were a black hole without bottom. You might need a two-earner household."

Collier was visibly shocked. "I'll be bringing in some big accounts by the time we set up house-keeping."

"What about Sheri-lynn?"

"She'll be up in Columbia," he said defensively.

"You don't think she'll notice you're married?"

Collier shuddered. He really didn't have the knack of juggling multiple girlfriends. His overlapping serial romances kept him in an ongoing state of peril from vengeful women scorned. He had gotten sugar poured in his gas tank, had his shirts slashed, even been sued under the grossly outdated breach-of-promise theory.

Collier pulled himself up. "Sheri-Lynn will have to understand that we're finished. She's a mature person. She'll win Miss Richland County this year. Have a good shot at Miss South Carolina. She'll be busy." But there was no conviction in his tone. Even less in his slumped posture as he trudged out.

Rannie sat back, glad to be rid of him. The winter sun through the window felt good on her body. Like maybe there was a promise of a warm snap out there somewhere.

She looked across the street where Rhett, alone, in profile, was busily painting away with a quiet and purposeful air. A glimpse of him always gave her a big jump in the heart rate.

She had always imagined he'd become a leading trial lawyer in Charleston. They'd share office space at first. Two ambitious kids fresh out of school. Learning from their mistakes. Become partners. Get married. A spirited couple like Spencer Tracy and Katherine Hepburn in *Adam's Rib*.

Now he had turned into some kind of jerkwater artist. Living in an empty office with no heat. Go around to wildlife art shows and try to sell a painting here and there out of a van. She ought to just stride across the street with a soul-saver's zeal and snatch him up, make him apply to law school. He wasn't too old if he got going right now.

He disappeared from view, breaking the focus of her thoughts. She looked at her desk piled high with work. Start out each day in a blaze of energy. Drive on in unrelieved grind like a hod carrier toting bricks. Fall down exhausted at night. Sex in her life conceptual at best. The only interruptions in the routine, messy disasters created by her mother. Rannie Ralston the anti-heroine for the new century.

There he was back again, cleaning up his brushes.

The end of the day had begun to crawl over the rooftops. She'd just linger at the window staring at him, all judgment suspended.

What was all that business about forty-five miles of nerve endings? She hadn't heard a word from him and it had been two days. No casual, let's do lunch. No bumping into her on the street and saying how about a quick drink.

Drink, she thought. She'd have to stop drinking if she wanted to shed the ten pounds. Pour as many calories down you with that as you did in a full meal. But if she did stop, how could she tolerate the evening with her family?

She picked up an SC Bar magazine and slapped it down on the desk in exasperation, making loose papers fly onto the floor. By the merest chance she noticed a criminal tax appeal. Some textile magnate got his tax evasion conviction reversed by the state Supreme Court. The lawyer's name was R. MacReady. Who the heck was that?

5

"Breasts like inverted champagne glasses," slurred Mary Canty. "That was in a poem I once read. Or a novel. Novelette. One of those."

Gaston Garnett's right foot hurt like hell. Had he kicked something last night? It was hard to remember much after midnight.

He leaned towards Mary Canty trying to reduce the space between the two armchairs, make things a bit more intimate. Was that beaming rapture on her face? Of course it was. She was in the company of Gaston Bayard Garnett, man of letters. Hoot 'n hollar celebrity. Hubba-hubba crowd-pleaser. A welcome addition to any house party.

And lunch was just minutes away. Or rather dinner as it was called in the South. The big meal. Which appealed mightily to Gaston Garnett, a man of tremendous gusto like an operatic baritone. A barrel-chested man who loved high-on-the-hog brawny food. Bloody roast beef the size of a basketball. Grilled double-cut chile pepper pork chops. Breaded lamb chops four-inches thick.

And while he waited with mouth-watering anticipation, the hardest-working man in show business must entertain. Regale his hostess with ribald tales of a horndog life lived without restraint. "My upbringing was unusually Gothic even by Southern standards," said Gaston. "I sipped from the spiritual font of many a saloon. Nothing if not evangelical . . ."

Why were her eyes narrowed? Was that suspicion? No. She wanted her drink topped up. Expected a man to anticipate her desires without her having to ask.

A small enough chore. Boo-ga-loo Gaston at thy service. Scurry to do thy bidding. Scurry, shit. He was hobbling. Lurching along in pain. A crippled court jester willing to fetch and carry in this house with the savory dinner smell of roast chicken stuffed with sage and wild mushrooms. And all portions gargantuan. And all the liquors quality labels.

Yes, there we go. Reseat ourselves. Hitch up the trouser legs to preserve the nice crease. The faint odor of mothballs. Here sharing the moment of perfection. "My first published poem was titled 'Lavender Ice-cream.' I was a young English major at Chapel Hill. In an aesthetic period. Oscar Wilde. Walter Pater."

"I despise lavender," Mary Canty said caustically. "Makes me think of old maids and sachet bags." She brought her glass to her mouth awkwardly.

Gaston wagged his head in slavish agreement. Doo-wah-ditty. Not much fervent acknowledgement of my importance. No mind. Cajoling the womenfolk was ol' 'scratch-'em-where-it-itches' Garnett's calling. In many ways he preferred the mature ones. Awaken their dormant passions and they were extremely grateful. Wear saucy undies and whale away at it like they had just come out of a woman's prison.

And her Ladyship here could be an artesian well of moolah. High cotton. Big rich. Highfalutin' manse with so much square footage in disuse. An ancient street with its canopy of spreading oaks, the sidewalks buckled from the roots, the yards filled with camellia and magnolia. From his room, the view of the harbor gleamed in tones of blue where shafts of sunlight pierced the clouds.

Now cosseted by pillows and a sound drink in the right hand. The distinguished fragrance of charcoal-filtered Jack Daniels Old No. 7. Rocks. Was it a fine moment? Does a martyr dig stigmata?

He would have to romance her, of course. Gentle words of seduction after twilight. Finagle her out of those expensive clothes. Nuzzling down her belly. To sniff her privates for the smell of ripe cheese.

"Sweet drinks give you bad breath," declared Mary Canty.

"Too true," Gaston agreed heartily. Then quoted lines of "Brazos Bust-head":

"Don't eat the pickled eggs
In that jar behind the bar."

"My cowboy period," he explained with uninhibited pride. "A summer workshop in Austin, Texas. Roper boots and bolo tie. Whipcords and snap button black shirts with embroidered roses on the yoke. Barrooms with chicken wire to protect the band from flying bottles. Big trough-like urinals in the restrooms."

"I loathe Texans. They're not really Southern. Can't imagine why they were part of the Confederacy. Kentucky and Tennessee are Southern. Maryland used to be. Missouri and Arkansas, but they're all trash out there."

Gaston let out a deep breath of exasperation. Tolerance equals enhanced profitability. And she was rich as giblet stock. Damn, his foot hurt like he had stepped up to his knee in a fire ant hill.

"Husbands and wives always want to murder each other," said Mary Canty. "It never seems exactly like murder when it's within the family. I don't understand all the brou-ha-ha about your wife's death."

"The late beloved. Now defunct." He saluted her memory with his glass. The grieving widower his latest incarnation.

No need to appear overly sad. Mary Canty felt no pity for man nor beast. Just like his wife. Claitey short for Claibourne Pusey. Tabitha Boone on her books. Yes indeed. He had *wanted* her dead. Guilty as charged on that desire question. But with mitigating circumstances. He sometimes saw her through a blinding red mist. Her face an uncanny resemblance to her mother's. Swilling Johnny Walker Red. A mouth full of cashews. As she went through the whole list of his short-comings. Theirs was not a lyrical production. Claitey railing viciously. Him glancing at his watch as the night advanced. Wanting to slip away by the outside staircase to jukebox revelry.

Night life in college towns had its boisterous aspects. Beer in plastic cups. Cute-butt waitresses who patrol the room to pour shots in your mouth from a bottle. The young and the feckless. With the Big Bopper wearing his RayBans in the cool gloom. All garrulous good cheer. Straight-throat a tall Budweiser to win the chug-a-lug contest. Regaling the sweet young thangs with literature and life. Confiding his loneliness to those who hinted at therapeutic coupling with the verse master. A two hour session at some Dew Drop Inn.

"Manys the time I wanted to kill Big Collier," Mary Canty reminisced. "Maybelle Sprunt caught her husband fooling around. Opened the trunk of the car and found a sheet cake with happy birthday and the name of his girlfriend. Shot him in the hip with a .22 pistol. Then had to drive him to the emergency room. They saved his leg because she drove so fast and got him there in the nick of time. You would think he'd have been grateful, but he wasn't. Typical of a man."

"So much misinformation on my tragedy," said Gaston gloomily. "They will persecute me to the max. I submit to dear Rannie. Rely on her to make justice prevail."

"Rannie's the gold standard for total bitchery," Mary Canty agreed. "Girl would argue the hind leg off a Billy goat. I tell people my daughter has a soul. She likes birds. They answer, 'Hitler loved dogs.'"

Gaston drank deeply of Jack Daniels and memory. She didn't exit gracefully my Claitey. Seeking that diffused halo of light. She wanted meditation, yoga, the mysteries of the East. She needed inner peace. But got jam up, utterly twisted and disheveled by her inner demons. He had separated his fate from hers. That was all. No more. Because dead romance novelists tell no tales.

"'A spritzer?' I said. 'Never heard of such a thing.' The most damnable drinks. Long Island Ice Tea. Can you imagine? I said, 'Who brought me here? Call me a cab!'"

Gaston stared at her in astonishment. What was she talking about? Was she delirious?

Whatever it had been, Mary Canty changed the subject abruptly. "I couldn't help but notice last night that we share an appetite for Italian wines."

Gaston nodded cordially. Yes, Jesus. Get the hell out of Dodge where so much vicious gossip might spoil the budding romance. Sun-drenched Tuscany. That was where he belonged. An ochre-walled villa with bright tile work. Great jars of black olives. Paper-thin carpaccio with arugula, chives and a sound lashing of olive oil.

Mary Canty said, "Moira's always going on at me about enjoying a high-ball at midday. She's got an impressive talent for nagging and little else. Poetry. In a pig's eye."

Moira. That put Gaston in a Jack Daniels-fueled reverie. Young Moira was like a slice of meringue. Divide her creamy thighs and find the blushing pink inside. Eat very slowly until she hit all the high notes.

And her sister Rannie in her office on the power corridor of Broad Street. Testosterone City that girl with her mussed red hair and Valkyrie thighs. Such a brace of siblings. Delicate ding-a-ling and robust ball buster in the same house. Such radiant dishes to choose from. And tap in turn their G-spots.

And Gaston knew how to love them. Most men would zero in on a primary ingredient. Gaston was creative but restrained. Meandering fingers. His touch all evanescence and shimmer. And he touched them everywhere. Until he reached the alabaster below the tanned bikini line. Where he gently gripped the wool and let it thread his fingers.

But he must keep his relationships healthy. No quandaries just yet. Devote himself to the crone before entangling with the maidens. What was the wretched woman saying now?

Mary Canty leaned towards him. "You may think this is a loopy idea," she confided. Choosing her words deliberately. "We could get together with real savvy."

Paydirt, Gaston thought. She was positively beaming. And was that a touch of appeal in her eyes? Now he was getting some traction. Reach across to squeeze her shoulder. A little of the touchy-feely.

"You do play bridge don't you?" she asked.

■ ■ ■

"Pea vines," Moira murmured to herself.

Anyone who saw her sitting perfectly still in her third floor room would imagine she was in an hypnotic trance, but appearance was misleading. Her mind was traversing the creative landscape, halting for a rhyme here, a daisy image there, and the troublesome answer to the choice between comma and semi-colon. Alone with her tools—pristine pages and an antique fountain pen—she sought the path to perfection.

At this precise moment, she needed a rhyme with 'vines'.

Pines. Fines. Dines. Sines. Was that a word? There had been that horrible business in high school math about co-sines that had so taxed her comprehension.

Across the top of her page she had written in exquisite calligraphy the title of her poem.

"Figs in Season."

It was a beautiful title and perfectly evoked Charleston's

gardens, those floral fairylands of cool green dappled with patches of sunlight. Banks of multicolored blossoms all designed to stun the eyes. The sounds of songbirds and seabirds in one perfect spot.

Then the muse descended. With a reverent hand, Moira wrote:

"When pea vines seek the sylvan shades."

It was perfect really. Moira was writing with a belief in her own good taste. She was exquisitely matched to her home and the Holy City by the sea. Its French Huguenot accents flowed in the blood of her pedigree. She was truly the *châtelaine* of Number 1. Legendre Street. Not her silly mother.

The title of the book of "jottings" as she would call it would be *Tendrils and Filigrees*. Or perhaps *Tendrils & Filigrees*. To show a delicate refinement while never deviating from her strong sense of time and place. Perhaps she would subtitle it *Jottings of a Charleston Lady*.

Titles came to Moira without effort. "Hearts of Palm." "Slender Willows." "The Bathing Sea." They showed her superior capability at design. The problem was filling the pages with the lines of poetry. Careful craftsmanship was so exhausting.

Gaston had pronounced her talent far in advance of her young age. But composing even a single line was an agony. Her sister with all that bumptious manishness just didn't understand the suffering of the artist. With all her years in college, Rannie had never once had to describe the delicate tracery of a cobweb. In fact the stress made Moira so morose she had a gnawing doubt that she could take a lifetime of writing.

"Artifice ain't art," Gaston had proclaimed emphatically

when she asked his advice. "No clichéd adjectives no time," he had commanded stoutly when she pressed him further.

She called him Gaston now. No longer Mister Garnett. They knew each other that well. He was granting her truly unusual access. Still he was so reticent, even guarded around her. Knowing they should keep their relationship on a professional basis. Although Moira felt her delivering him from prison had placed them more in the Flora McDonald—Bonnie Prince Charlie category.

Flora had been like a spiritual guide, leading her true prince over the seas to Skye. There was a mighty symbolism there. Woman's role as muse to direct the distracted and tortured soul of man to salvation. Because Flora had been a simple peasant girl, Prince Charlie had not married her. And thus gone into a rapid decline of debauchery and uselessness.

A shadow passed over her face. Well Moira was certainly no peasant. But this heavy social drinking Gaston was doing to placate her wretched mother was careening out of control. Last night he had actually stamped his foot through the little stool with the crewel work Pekinese. Making some emphatic point or other.

Drink or no drink, there was really no excuse for what he had done. It had the appearance of violence. And given the dreadful mistake about his role in the murky death of his wife, bourbon to excess added a sinister aspect. She really needed to persuade him to follow her example in abstinence.

"Kentucky bourbon staves off lunacy," her daddy had always said. Which was a bewildering attitude. But he was a man of single-minded character. He never suffered the endless complications of the artist's soul.

Perhaps, Moira thought, she should forthrightly propose to Gaston that she appear with him when he began his circuits of the women's colleges once more. True, she lacked his theatricality. She was too uncompromising in her insistence on good manners. On keeping her composure. But it would provide a balance, a measure to the performance. A golden mean.

Filled with a sudden vigor, Moira rose to her feet, left her desk and descended the broad circular stairs. Past flat colonial portraits. Ancestors in ruffed collars and powdered wigs. Rehearsing her little speech.

"I'm sure it would be tempting the fates on a grand scale," she would begin boldly. "But I really think I should be a much more visible partner."

Would he laugh, call her impulsive, even zany? And decline. Or consider it with a sudden seriousness? Give it a judicious appraisal. Then say yes of course they'd get on famously. Perhaps impulsively embrace her while quick color rose in her cheeks?

Moira was breathing heavily. Of course the advantages would be obvious. They would carve out an enviable reputation in tandem. Stir admiration in every audience. His mature talent, honed to a brilliant edge. Her fresh young voice and beauty and steady guiding hand. A May-December union. Well, not that bad. May-October. May-September?

Almost burning with excitement, Moira hesitated before the swinging door to the kitchen. An odor of roast chicken wafted out. And the harsh laugh of . . . of Gaston

Garnett. He sounded like an actor playing a pirate or one of Shakespeare's history plays.

"Wah-har! C'mere to me O beauteous octaroon wench!" Then something inarticulate like a sucking noise. Like someone slurping soup.

Moira paused, debating whether to go forward. Her nerve almost failed her.

A smothered exclamation: "Law, if you ain't one bad boy mutha-fucka!"

With this, Moira pushed open the swinging door to pay her surprise visit to the kitchen. Her lips parted as she prepared her smile.

Gaston Garnett was humped over Tamzi, the maid's 20-year-old daughter, singing "Chattanooga Choo-Choo" and dancing like he was in a conga line. And his hands . . . were up her thighs and under her dress. Tamzi glanced furtively across the room but made no effort to push Gaston away.

Moira's response was complete stupefaction.

Instinctively, Gaston stood bolt upright. Greeted her with remarkable composure. "Ah, Moira. Just in time for dinner," he said. "Trying to lend a hand back here. Seemed the democratic thing to do."

She raked him with a glance that took in everything from hunted eyes to gravy splattered shoes.

"You're . . . you're disporting yourself with the hired help," Moira gasped.

6

"So he gets a college student to drive him home. Even though he's been driving shit-faced drunk every day since he's sixteen."

"Yeah?" said Rannie. "First designated driver of Gaston's boozing career?"

A strong gusty wind was rattling the windows on the cubbyhole of an office occupied by one of the assistant solicitors—solicitor being what South Carolina calls a District Attorney. Lazelle Gaillard, was a deep polished brown with strangely cat-like eyes, the first generation of black lawyers to stick around Charleston, not take off for D.C. and a federal job. Work a few years as a prosecutor to learn the trade and then strike out in private practice. She was wearing a gray-ribbed sweater with a black turtleneck underneath. Gray wool skirt. None of it Tommy Hilfiger. She couldn't afford it on the salary. She sat there eased back in the gunmetal chair squeezing a rubber ball in one hand.

"And then when they get to the house, he says 'I want you to come inside with me. Something's wrong.' Go in together and there's the body. Shot right through the heart. One clean shot." Lazelle made a loud 'PA-DOW', pointed at her chest to imitate the bullet's path.

Rannie gave a short barking laugh. "So the cops pointed him like bird-dogs on quail. I can see their point of view. Domestic violence. *Cherchez le* booze-soaked husband."

Lazelle changed hands with the ball. "You should try one of these. Lets out the stress. Keeps your arms in not great but at least good shape."

Rannie looked around the pea green office, ancient paint clotted around the windows where each new layer had been applied without scraping. Close enough for government work. The walls were a mess of taped up wanted posters, court dockets, movie star pictures torn from magazines. Trash birds pecking on the window sills. Starlings and pigeons.

"Was Gaston really a jazz sideman on the trombone?" Lazelle asked.

Rannie snorted. "In his dreams. He was Poet-in-Residence at Tulane for a while. Got denied tenure. The creative writing professors always do. But the Big Easy will fuel your fantasies. Nights in the Quarter with Dixie beer and fried oyster po'boys."

"So he wasn't an advisor to a Vietnamese Ranger battalion either? Didn't win the Silver Star?"

"I think he was in a USO troupe. If they called it that. He claims he wrote jokes for Bob Hope and got blown and laid by one of the Playboy Playmates. I forget which one, but he'll show you her fold-out without a whole lot of urging."

"I knew he was lying about being tight with Malcolm X. A lot of your white professor types like to get their liberal credentials right out on the table first off. Tell you how they marched in Selma and Birmingham. Faced Bull Connor's dogs. You know that's bullshit. But he almost caught me on the Muslim thing, it was so off the wall. Until he said they had met on a pilgrimage to Mecca. Started speaking at me in Arabic. Which could have been Pig Latin for all I knew."

"He told you all this?"

"Gaston'll get worked up excited at the drop of a hat. I mean the man don't struggle to fill a silence."

"He's a special needs child all right," said Rannie. "But you see the problems with the case, of course."

"You mean it's all circumstantial. If even that. Mostly suspicion. No weapon. No physical evidence. We ain't got diddley-squat."

"And then you got that Court of Appeals ruling tossing one of y'alls convictions because it was all circumstantial."

"I know," said Lazelle. "No blood on him Gaston. No scratches. No powder residue on his hands. Nothing."

"The Grand Jury indicted him."

"Well, you know what that's worth. They'd indict a bowl of collard greens if we asked them to. Buncha folks wanting to get back to their jobs."

Rannie studied the coroner's report. The time of death was when Gaston had witnesses saying he was in a bar on King Street. And Gaston could camp in bars for days on end. "That does seem to clear him."

"Yep. It's *adios*, prime suspect." She waved her hand at the wrist bye-bye.

"Rats."

"You want him to be guilty?"

"It pays better."

"He had guns, but no match for the bullet. There was a shotgun in the house. And a .22 caliber pistol."

"Maybe he'd hunt squirrels in the back yard. I heard all his yarns the couple of times he hired me to get him off drunk and disorderly raps. Bill him by the hour because he talked so much. His wife signed the checks. Never met the woman myself. How do you size him up?"

"He looks like a double side of mashed potatoes."

Rannie grimaced. That made her think of all the meals she had been skipping. And a plate of lemon squares sitting on the kitchen table. Hunger gnawed at her like a fatal malady. "He's a real Deep South fat boy all right."

"Get his gut much bigger he'll span a couple'a time zones. A big, loud, triple-chinned ya-hoo. But maybe as a poet he's something valuable. Never met T.S. Elliot or anybody. There's two sides to anything."

"He's a boy for hard-partying," Rannie agreed. "Go carousing with college kids half his age. Put away the shots and beer. Hope to end up naked with some coed who thinks all the profs look good at closing time."

Lazelle got thoughtful. "Well, talking to him, listening to him talk to the cops, there was something funny there."

"What?"

"He give me kind of a spooky feeling. The way he'd look around. Like he was full of fear."

"I think his brain got maimed for life sometime back a ways."

"Nice shoes," said Lazelle. "Come from Bob Ellis?"

"You'll be able to afford them when you get out on the

economy." Rannie lifted one foot, turned her ankle this way and that. Said, "So you're seriously thinking about cutting Gaston loose? Even if I don't push the issue?"

"I've got a jail full of dirtballs now I got to process. It looks like an overflow hole of Hades up at County. All of them candy babies. Crank. Horse. Crystal meth. Most of them doing a Saint Vitus dance in the cells. I finally get a decent murder, chance to prosecute something high-profile, my desperado turns to doo-doo. I can't mess around with this fool. Hand the case back to the cops."

Rannie thought a moment. "How about you hold off until I've gotten a fee out of him. May as well have a little unofficial fine levied on him for being a general jerk-off. Help me defray my costs."

"You want me to enter into a bad-faith scheme for you to rip off your client?"

Rannie did an easy smile between girls. "Let's just call it professional courtesy on the part of a gal who hopes to one day quit this butt-hole prosecutor's job and earn a handsome living as a criminal lawyer."

Lazelle pondered the ethics of the issue. "What's it like out there? Like pitching horseshoes? Looks easy but ain't?"

Rannie stood up, shrugged. "I dunno. Kind of like a big pie fight maybe."

Lazelle opened a desk drawer and dropped Gaston's folder in it. "What I think just happened is I kind of lurched here and the file got knocked off my desk and mislaid for a while."

Rannie paused in the doorway, having a sudden ache for a bacon-lettuce-tomato sandwich slavered with mayo.

Wondering if the agony was worth it. "You know Rhett MacReady? Is he a lawyer?"

"Seems to be."

"Not much of one," Rannie argued. "He paints pictures of pigs."

"And wins big appellate tax cases whupping up on the Attorney General. They're so mad about that up in Columbia they can't see straight."

Rannie cocked her head to one side. "Are we talking about the same guy?"

Lazelle smiled. "About six-three. Weigh in at two-ten. Kind of NFL free safety size. He's a nice, nice looking boy. For a white boy. Not that I'm prejudiced."

"He looked better when he was a teenager. Or maybe there were just fewer men around."

"You kind of running deep with emotion? It sure shows."

"What? What does my face look like?" Rannie was thunderstruck. She the master of the poker face.

"Like an unholy sunburn."

"It's hot in here. They've got the heat cranked way up."

Lazelle got kind of an impish grin on her face. "What'd he do? Take your cherry or something?"

"Nothing I want to talk about."

"Well mercy on you, sister."

Rannie paused again. "You don't happen to know the size of the judgment that got reversed?"

Lazelle raised an eyebrow. "Only twelve fuckin' million dollars."

■ ■ ■

"Why am I flat busted? Let me count the ways," said Gaston Garnett in a sing-song voice. He fished a Krispy Kreme doughnut out of the white paper sack and bit into it.

The red-haired witch Rannie Ralston sitting over there considering her strategy. She had just delivered her 'it's-time-to-pay-your-lawyer' speech. Now staring at him with hard predatory eyes. It made him want to put her on his lap and spank her soundly with a hairbrush. That would sure fire up the blood in both of them.

"You've got your job at the College."

Gaston made a deprecating laugh. Finished devouring the doughnut and licked the sugar glaze off his fingers. "My salary. Yeh-girl. The joke's on me there. They pay me like gypsy faculty. By the course. No benefits."

Sorry sum'bitches, Gaston thought. The entire English department. Calling themselves pragmatists to rationalize their cowardice. Catamites. Boot lickers. They reacted to all stimuli in terms of base self-interest and craven dishonesty. Lecture the drooling undergrads with your line of sight just above their heads to not see the contempt they ooze. Then sip your faculty lounge coffee and play intellectual gotcha games.

He was the wild-hoggin' man of the Deep South. Ox-lifting strong, yet country ballad feeling. Bubba-boy Gaston who makes some bad mistakes and is the dad-blame better for them. Whoring and brawling like *God's Little Acre* got into a blender with *Elmer Gantry*. That was the cook book ingredients of a liberal education. Not like those dried toads with their warmed over journal articles on Jane Austen. Gaston sat in faculty meetings listening morosely. Contemptuous of the drab lot of them.

"So you just slip and slide through life, a case of arrested development."

Gaston would not be baited. He had been too long down and dirty with true adolescents. Little brats arguing with you over the difference between an A– and a B+.

"G.B. Garnett," he said "is the 'what's happening' poet on the leading edge of Southern literature. He finds pith and pity in the broad shoulders life of the common man. As simple a thing as a local news headline can start him off on his magical maunderings. 'Speed hump issue splits community.' 'Company flushes out port-a-potty vandals.'" He crossed his thighs, dug out a second doughnut and started on it.

"I don't work for free," said Rannie.

"I can think of nothing practical," Gaston answered blithely. He knew she was stymied. As long as he kept on the sweet side of Moira and Mary Canty, they'd have our Lawyer Lady Rannie toiling away to keep him out of the slammer. If only Moira hadn't caught him with that dark skinned gal in the kitchen. That was a sure enough stickler. Well, Moira was easily intimidated. Frightened little mouse. Doubtful if any man had even put a finger up her.

"What about your wife's money?"

Gaston gestured helplessly. "I'm not in the will. It all goes to a daughter by a previous marriage. Hence I had no motive to kill her."

"You don't say that with a lot of conviction."

He gave her his basset hound look of sadness. "Do you suggest I didn't love dear Claibourne, my sorghum molasses sweet Claitey-waitey?"

What version of his marriage to give her? The deeply bereaved needing comfort? Get Rannie sitting close enough to caress. God the deliquescence between her thighs. A flaming red bush emblazoning her twat. Such a bush as Moses must have followed into Sinai. And those killer knockers. Some congenial dining there. What a chore it must be to haul them around all the time.

"What I think is you slapped her around. She threw stuff at you. And she made you crawl for pocket money. But I'm just guessing."

"If you're going to get so het up about the whole thing, perhaps this gosh-darned ol' peckerwood should just skedaddle. Disappear for awhile. Get in a rusty Ford pick-up and drive away. Ditch it on the banks of the Mississippi with a farewell note under the windshield wipers. Leave you guessing. Did the boy take the fatal dunk in the Big Muddy? Or merely slid down the mighty Father of Waters on a coal barge?"

Gaston felt good. He gave her a bit of vigor there. And the "light out for Injun country" look in his eyes. Knowing he had her by the short and curlies. Mummy dearest had put up their great big ol' count-your-money mansion for his bond. Rannie wouldn't want to see them on the street living in a cardboard box. He'd love to be at the bond hearing. See Mary Canty abuse the judge and get thirty days for contempt.

Rannie rolled her eyes. "You jackrabbit and I'll have a

bounty hunter on you like a duck on a June bug. They're real talented in that respect. He'll bring you back hand-cuffed to an O-ring in the backseat of his car."

She glowered at him. Considering her next move. He tensed a bit. Got to anticipate it. Like a quarterback reading the patterns.

Rannie propped her head with her hand, spoke in a fatigued voice. "You used to beat up your first wife didn't you? The one you married in UNC grad school where you didn't get your Master's degree. Come home drunk and she'd be there with a hippie girlfriend—it was a hippy era wasn't it? Bellbottoms and long ironed hair on the girls. You wore love beads and some kind of batik shirt from Indonesia. No liquor-by-the-drink in those days. The South was all beer. But someone would always pass you a jay and that would get you really wrecked. You'd stagger in weaving erratically. They'd be drinking mint tea, waving incense sticks and bellyaching about your deficiencies. It would set you off and you'd slap around anyone who came within the ambit of your fury. It was the friend who called the cops and helpfully enabled the end of your marriage."

Gaston let out a squawk. "How did you . . . ?"

Rannie held up a folder. "Divorce file from North Carolina. Your *first* divorce."

Gaston shuddered. Valerie had reveled in the ecstasies of martyrdom. The intractable bitch was 23-years-old, and swore I'd stripped her of the best years of her life. When all women are infinitely recyclable. Reclaim their innocence if not outright virginity. But she lived for pessimism and gloom. She even sheared off her long hair so she looked like Joan of Arc prepped for the stake. Put him in a state of absolute nihilism.

He gave Rannie his I-am-at-peace-with-the-world smile. "I admit all. *Nolo contendere.* Is that what you lawyers say?"

"And the second one?"

"Linda? Well, she was a bit of what'cha call a moralistic quibbler. I was just back from 'Nam. Drank a bit. Ran around a bit. You know how young bucks are after a war."

"And you're a guy of unparalleled inventiveness. You tied her to the hood of the car and drove it at 100 mph. Passing a line of seventeen cars on a secondary road got the cop's attention."

To think I had once imagined Linda would make a sensual wife. Where had the idea originated? Making love to her was like trying to stuff a garment bag.

"You tried to choke the cop. Our Vietnam warrior who kills by conditioned reflex. He had to club you to the ground."

"I tap danced in a USO troupe. Gaston the Music Man. Mountain clogger and Virginia Reeler. You know that. I've never come close to killing anyone. Some exuberance maybe."

"So the poem of strangling Vietcong with piano wire is just one more desperate invention?"

Rannie could cross-examine the hell out of a man. But Gaston was singular in his cool. He placed his hand over his heart. "You've read my work? 'Undertow of Death'? Lemme tell you, friends and neighbors, I am touched way down deep. It's from my Vietnam Veterans Against the War period. I had long hair and a beard. Wore an army field jacket. I was the featured poet at peace demonstrations. Tim Leary and Allen Ginsburg were personal friends. We dropped acid together." He began to recite:

"Amurrican boys
On a killing spree
Roscoe, Al,
Jeb and me
We all went down
To the massa-cree
Locked and loaded."

Rannie interrupted sharply. "You gorked your wife didn't you? Just did it in a paroxysm of rage."

He shook his head sadly. "Claitey was into Eastern mysticism. For five years we had been practicing yoga. Greet every day with melodic fugues. Some simmering discontent perhaps. But no outbursts of choler. I'm not violence prone."

"What about the night you busted up that bar down in the market? When you first hired me."

"I was cold-cocked by rough-necks. Hoodlums decorated with body piercings and tattoos on their necks. It was all self-defense."

"What I'm guessing is on the night in question you came in drunk and Claitey got mad. The usual history. You nailed her. And then I see you sprinting back to the bar. Sweating like a pig despite the cold. Hanging out with college kids who don't remember if you left them for a time or not. Dumped the gun in a dumpster so it's deep in a landfill now."

Rannie was glowering at him with slitted eyes. Going to show him who was top dog. Claitey Pusey was like that. She'd always know just when a public occasion demanded she bring out the humiliating tale of him and the electric shock dog collar. She led a life of recrimination.

Gaston smiled to himself. There was only one gambit left. The Romeo Play. "You have such unwavering inner strength," he said in his voice of shy sincerity. "I've always been in love with you."

He proffered the remaining doughnut in the sack like a smitten school kid on the playground trying to win over his first crush.

7

"The sun was in your eyes," Gaston argued uneasily. "You couldn't have seen anything."

"I'm not a fool," Moira answered primly. "I know what I saw."

Gaston sat down heavily in a chair and stared at her. Why had he done it? Those fleshy ornaments on a woman's chest he could never keep his hands off. To suckle there on a dreamy flight to bliss. But he had barely gotten into the peanuts-and-cocktails portion of the flight when this little Puritan had to make her dramatic entrance.

She had flounced away. Yes, there was a distinct flounce in her step. And he had been waiting in dread for this confrontation. Praying it wouldn't come. The white massa' caught down in the slave cabins by Goody Two Shoes.

Do the poet's burden speech. Get her so lost in fervent rhetoric that she'll be nodding in agreement with anything.

"Have you no sense of the poet's burden?" he began, leaning towards her intensely. "It's my calling to study humanity in all its exuberant lust and horny glory. To brave their drab and dim purlieus and view the lowest dregs hopped up on drugs, or sobbing drunk, beaten senseless by battering 300-pound wives in K-Mart polyester. Do you not realize how simple missionary gestures on my part can relieve their pain-wracked faces? It's destiny fulfilled for these simple souls to be touched in their hungry nakedness."

"I'm not sure that makes any sense at all," said Moira firmly. "But I'm very sure naked is something that ought not to be discussed around here. And certainly not *done* around the help."

Gaston looked around frantically. Where was that damned Mary Canty? He needed a rescue. A drink. A ham hock to gnaw on. A life size Dolly Parton doll with no voice box to cuddle at night.

Moira was looking at him strangely. And now she was shoving a poem at him. He winced. The gesture was so familiar it came to him almost nightly in recurring dreams of terror. Armies of gabbling women shoving their intense doggerel at him.

He read the poem in stark disbelief at its sheer awfulness.

FIGS IN SEASON

When pea vines seek the sylvan shades,
And noon day sun begins to fade,
Ho to the garden go I in fair delight
Armèd with basket and scissor
To snip with main and might.

He put it down, unable to read on. Closed his eyes and breathed deeply. I am in a trance, he told himself. I am rendered completely invisible.

"The volume is entitled *Tendrils & Filigrees*," said Moira.

Gaston didn't open his eyes. He smiled wanly. "That's nice."

"I need a mentor to promote my career."

What? Promote this little dunce? She must be off her rocker. Of all the importuning . . . He reared up seething, then settled back down. Hold hard, Gaston. Losing your temper is always an error. Sometimes a fatal one. Put on that avuncular smile.

"We'll need to get you an agent," he stalled. "And you can't approach more than one at a time. Not ethical, you know. All that letter writing back and forth can eat up months of time."

"Why don't you fix it with your agent? Just make a phone call."

"Well, um, possible conflict of interest," Gaston hedged. "Both of us living under the same roof. Unkind tongues would say you had undue influence over me. All those gossipy literary critics would bare their claws at that one."

"You don't have to live here," Moira said with startling force. "You could go back home."

Gaston looked stricken. What? he thought. Am I to abandon the comforts of No. 1 Legendre? This great mansion rearing in splendor. This pure, unalloyed place of refuge with darkies toiling in the kitchen. My God we're having pork loin braised in milk for that glorious big middle of the day Southern dinner. Maple glazed 'Carolina Ruby' sweet potatoes with bourbon whipped cream. Brown butter crook-necked squash with scalloped mushrooms. Biscuits with big slabs of butter melting over them. Hold one up and slurp it like an oyster on the shell.

He put his face in his hands and pretended to heave with emotion. "I couldn't possibly go back. The nightmare dreams I suffer in that House of Death's Door. Ghouls coming at me. Hunchbacks, and crones with shriveled breasts. Clubfoots and bloated children with empty bleeding eye sockets! It's unbearable! Can you recognize no part of my sadness in yourself?"

"You told me at Sweet Briar that I was publishable," Moira insisted. "I dropped out of college on your assurances of a stellar literary career." She nodded emphatically in agreement with herself.

Gaston put up his hands. "I might have exaggerated a trifle. Didn't want to snuff out the flame by too harsh a criticism. But this is really rough as a cob. Will need a lot of rewriting. We'll have to hire a book doctor—a poem doctor—to work the collection over. It will cost a great deal of money which I can't imagine your sister will be very glad to provide."

"What's wrong with you doing it?"

Work with sylvan shades? Dear Jesus he needed a drink. He squirmed in his chair. The humiliation. To think he had once wanted to hump this girl. The emotion seemed utterly remote now. What he wanted was to tie a knot in his donger.

Grimly, he wondered why he had ever married. Three times he had taken the fall. The enticing wenches see you as clay to be shaped by their scheming hands. You are put on earth to serve their needs. And you do it all why? Because you're young and horny and you listen to the siren song.

The career had all begun so well. The roving poet like

a troubadour singing of courtly love. Tell tenure to shove it. He was Odysseus on a voyage through an archipelago of nymphs. At each new college, the seas of eager female faces seemed to inject him with new meaning. A fresh invigorating chapter in a picaresque novel. To each willing sex slave of the evening he could whisper their meeting was entirely fortuitous. Arranged by a caring destiny.

He almost sobbed as he said half-aloud, "My life was all cruising with the top down on the interstate. Now I'm jammed up, blockaded in a bumper-to-bumper crawl."

Moira wasn't listening. She was saying, "I don't pay a great deal of attention to my sister's work. It is so utterly sordid. But I've learned a thing or two. For example, since I signed your bond, I can revoke it at my pleasure. I believe those in the bonding business refer to it in their vulgar parlance as 'streeting you' or 'pulling your jacket'."

What the hell was going on? Where was the massively skittish Moira, and who was this evil-minded virago who had replaced her? Gaston bared his teeth wolfishly. "Your mother will bail me out. It's just a matter of signing those forms."

"Not if she happened to learn what you were doing with Tamzi."

Gaston felt as if he had been sucked under water by a racing tide headed straight out of the harbor to the sea. Where his bones would sift five miles down to join the whale shit. He gasped for air. "You wouldn't consign me to Folsom Prison Blues! Have you no milk of kindness?"

"I think," said Moira, with a very satisfied look on her face, "you are going to promote my career. And I don't think we'll have any further a-do about it."

■ ■ ■

Rannie Ralston sat heavily in her office chair staring at a Tupperware container with a hardboiled egg and a stalk of celery. Her big lunch. Couldn't even eat salt with it because it would make her take on water.

On the roof across Broad Street, a red tailed hawk was devouring a pigeon. It almost made her envious. Hawks lived in the city year round, hunting the flat roofed buildings for rodents.

She had fidgeted something awful the evening before without a drink to dull her senses. Finally gone out jogging, made it about a half mile around Colonial Lake and collapsed against a tree feeling like she had appendicitis. Wishing for a mugger to put her out of her misery.

She had been a hard-core volleyball athlete in high school. But you lose stamina in a hurry even though you feel you're going flat out all day every day with a brute of a law practice.

Gaston Garnett was going to be a deadbeat in the most elemental sense of the word 'dead'. Flat broke when it came to legal fees. But always seemed to have pocket money. Woke up the whole house at midnight when he got a delivery of twelve chili-dogs. Devoured every one like Cronus eating his children.

She chewed her egg morosely, trying to get a bit of yolk to flavor each bite. She wanted to sit in an old time diner with a plate of Salisbury steak and gravy. Green beans. Rice. Fried okra. Corn bread. God she was starving.

They were stuffing themselves to the eyebrows at home.

Pork loin all dripping with juice. Sweet potatoes. Scuppernong pie. She tried to force her mind away.

Here's the old office, chockablock full of memories of her daddy and the old days of practicing law on Broad Street. For a time there, a mentally retarded colored man had hung around the office. Her daddy would pay for his lunch. Let him run errands, wear Daddy's shoes down to the King Charles Hotel to get them shined.

But even that led back to food. Her daddy used to take her down to the old Market and buy her a banana split. She'd sit there with him feeling like a little ten year-old princess. Eating a bite of each of the three flavors of ice cream in turn. Making them each last. All soaked in that soda-fountain chocolate. Saving the bright red candied cherry for last.

And speaking of re-tards, in came Collier in his usual party mood. Always expensively dressed. Just the right club tie, banker's gray suit and deep buffed black shoes. Calling back to someone to shake a leg and come on in. Showing his new squeeze the venue of his law life, a career for which he had neither talent nor enthusiasm.

"Is my name a symbol of infamy today?" he said tightly, nervous that she'd light into him. Wondering if she had enough good manners to declare an armistice. "And here's our office stalwart," he added too heartily. "My sis Rannie. Some folks say she's a heartless cannibal. But I know she's got some humor and soul under there somewhere."

And with that, Dale came in. The one Collier had said he intended to marry. But those intentions were not new. There had easily been fifteen before her. The cheapskate reality of his life always came along and ripped a hole in the stern of their Love Boat.

Holy Moses.

In the sheer beauty category Dale was a heart-stopper. Leggy and bosomy at the same time. No gush of charm. Just an easy apathy. And she gave off a vibrato. Every move she made was like prolonged foreplay. She was just plain damn erotically charged.

Dale extended a hand with a warm fluid movement. Rannie resisted the brief temptation to try to crunch it with her grip. She was almost as spellbound by Dale as her brother. The girl had hair so deep shiny brown as to be almost black.

They made small chit-chat and Rannie learned she was from Irmo, graduate of USC in mass communications, worked in New York in the fashion industry. Collier put in the story of the anaconda again, forgetting he had told it before.

"So, tell me something else surprising about Dale," Rannie said without cracking a smile.

Collier hesitated, breathing like a guppy. "I guess . . . I guess she's . . ."

"I'm not into guilty pleasures," said Dale smoothly. No elaboration. Just that one little zinger.

Rannie blinked, thought what? You're telling me you have a figure to die for? You're all bottled water and rabbit food? No beer and cheroots and double-fudge brownies.

"So, how's the Legislature?" Rannie asked her brother lightly. "You been introducing a touch of reason to the rebel flag debate?"

"You know I've been targeting insurance defense work," he sniffed, trying not to sound defensive. "Been going round all the industry lobbyists. It's not easy being the firm rain-maker."

Rannie stayed civil. Dale's eyes were roaming the room. Then she gave Collier the silent signal. The little semaphore that said 'I've done my social duty now let's split.'

"Well, be-bop-a-lula," said Collier with an idiot grin on his face.

"Sure. Rock on," Rannie said.

Dale flashed a final cinematic smile and went out with him, hips moving smoothly in a cohesive dramatic whole. The perfect visual complement to Rannie's too-handsome, feeble-excuse-for-a-lawyer brother. Heading down to Kiawah Island in the cold where the retired Yankees lived in three million dollar houses, played golf and counted their money. Walk on the beach. Collier throwing a shell into the crashing waves. Gulls piping. Come back and sit by the fire. Every breath she takes a bedroom serenade.

Yes, that lousy Collier kept hitting new highs. Taking her down to a rented villa on Kiawah Island. After months of the rental company dunning Collier, the bills would get slid into the office accounts. Rannie would spot them of course, get pissed, but she'd end up paying.

Rannie sat viewing the last smidgen of hard-boiled egg darkly, thinking of maybe stopping at losing five pounds. Take stock at that point. See if she needed to push on to ten. She hated celery and cottage cheese and a whole lot of other things in her lopsided life. A freeloading family. Every day setting new standards of extravagant dependency.

Dreadlocked Menace-2-Society losers for clients. Their affinity for guns and drive-by killings. Idea of culture is a kung-fu movie. They sulk through their guilty pleas. You tell them why have you got tattoos where a judge can see them. They stare at you uncomprehending. Yesterday one of them said to her, "Like, I am an icon of the night scene."

She reflected thoughtfully on whether she was in a defining phase of her career or on a short desperate slide to personal bankruptcy. She could have been a real estate lawyer for one of the big firms. Always get home at six o'clock and have your weekends guaranteed free. No frantic scrambling to get your clients and witnesses herded together and through the courthouse door.

She had chosen a freewheeling style. Nothing safe, mediocre, and boring for her. And she was good at it, dammit. Rannie Ralston could lay a visceral impact on a jury. There was always "buzz" about her on Broad Street. That Rannie's a chip off the old block. She's Big Collier's girl sure enough.

Well sure, her daddy was a profound influence on her. But she wasn't swamped in an Electra complex.

Looking across the street at Rhett's window ramped up her emotions even more. The surprise makeover of his lifestyle had been a real kick in the rear. But it felt good. Twelve million dollars. She was dying to know what his fee was. Did he do it on contingency? Take a third? Any remotely respectable number had him on easy street.

What would somebody pay for a pig painting? Five hundred? A thousand? Painting was just a nice hobby for him. One that made money rather than burning it up like yachting or gambling on golf. He probably had a very select law practice. Only taking on really big time tax appeals.

They had a background together, their adolescent hormonal melodrama. The precise emotion of teenager-in-love came back as she sat yearning to make contact but feeling surprisingly optimistic. A big tendency to believe in the invincible power of love.

Her smile vanished. But what? Here's another jarring note. There was a dark haired girl at the window. Now she moved away, walking around the room, picking up a brush or a tube of paint, setting it back down in a different place in a little subtle show of power. Rannie couldn't really see her and yet she could. Look at those pouty lips. Her breasts were prominent alright, yessiree. Not because they were so big, just thrust out by her shoulders being held back, hands behind her back. And she was giving him a heartfelt version of the old "hanging on his every word" routine.

Look at that body language. Just waltzing carnality. Jeez-us, Rhett. Some elementary psychology would tell you what she wants. Rannie shook her head in amazement.

The girl took hold of his face in both hands and planted a slow kiss on him. He made no effort to resist. His hands hovered a moment at her hips, then latched on. And there they were working their way around and sure enough gripping her glutes.

First Dale and now this!

"Well cry me an eff-ing river!" Rannie exploded. "I'm sitting here in a cross-fire of insults!"

She jammed the celery into her mouth and gnashed it like Godzilla eating Tokyo.

8
—————————————————————————————

"Where is the darlin' man?" said Mary Canty loudly. "Where is Ga-S'TON?" She waved her empty glass wanting a refill. Pronouncing his name like French.

At the drinks hour Moira treated herself to a small glass of extremely dry sherry. She felt really on top of her life for the first time she could remember. She almost could understand the urgency—the need to press on—that seemed to so infuse her sister.

It had taken her considerable effort, but she had at last wheedled Gaston's schedule out of him. Queens College in March. Converse in April. And impressed upon him the importance of her opening for him. Reading the first poem and then introducing him.

Gaston—she first-named him now—had declined to come down to supper. No doubt he was too excited by the road that lay ahead of them. The future was so bright with promise.

She had told him in no uncertain terms that he was to sharply diminish his intake of alcohol. And he would have to go on a diet. He was far too corpulent. Well he certainly got huffy at that. Shouting he could take no more reproaches from devouring Gorgon women. Claitey Pusey had been the master of the art, and mere amateurs like Moira were sandflies driving him mad with an annoying itch.

Moira had seized on that point and said that two failed marriages and a third one ending in murder might tell him he had a lot to learn about the female sex. All that drinking and overeating was just a frightened artist's desperate appeal, and a charitable-spirited woman such as herself was prepared to respond.

As for all that mulish sulking, well, she'd just have to be stronger than him. It wasn't hard really. Men really were the weaker sex. Yes, taking away that bottle of scotch he had hidden under his bed—her campaign of reform had begun in earnest.

Perhaps it was the glass of sherry, but Moira felt confident enough to confide in her mother that she would soon be reading poetry in company with the great Gaston Garnett.

Mary Canty didn't find it easy to digest this information. "You're going to read poetry. Aloud? To an audience?"

"Yes," said Moira sounding very pleased. But she wasn't allowed to enjoy her satisfaction.

Rannie came in slamming the front door. Her voice snarled from the hall. "That's it. I quit. I'm going to become a shuttle bus driver at an airport. Take people out to the Hertz rental cars."

"Don't have a hemorrhage, dear-heart," Mary Canty shouted.

"I have a lousy day, but it's finally over. I'm walking down Broad Street and look into an art gallery. You know how the whole street is galleries now, all the little groceries and cafés gone. And anyhow there's a painting of a wild boar in the window with a $30,000 price tag on it. Can you believe that? I bust my butt all day and somebody paints a picture and gets thirty thousand freakin' dollars!"

Moria tried to strike a brighter note. She said she couldn't understand why Rannie always had to be in a rotten mood. There were so many good things to look at in the world instead of just the awful ones, and the bare winter trees for example were just marvelous reaching beseechingly to the merciful gray sky, praying for the green sprigs of spring, that if you thought about nature and God it just made you a teensy bit subdued instead of all caught up in acrimony meanness.

Rannie poured her usual Jim Beam into a short glass. Sat down wearily. Put her head back and closed her eyes. "Okay, what do you recommend I think about? Jonquils and viburnums? Mmm, I feel better already."

Rannie's wrath always gave Moira a nervous stomach. All those probing questions made her feel like a prisoner in the dock. And all her ornate ideas came out nearly as baby talk. "You're just as sour as month-old milk," she told her sister.

Mary Canty balefully announced Moira was going to read poetry. Aloud. To a group of people who would sit still and listen. She sounded unconvinced.

"I can't conceive of such a thing," Rannie sighed.

"You always did have limited horizons," Moira sniffed.

Rannie forced a sickly smile. "I don't venture into the wasteland of the wholly irrational."

Mary Canty lit a cigarette. Blew long plumes of blue smoke out of both nostrils.

Moira crinkled her nose and waved the smoke away. "I have a fair amount of experience performing before groups."

Mary Canty gave a short laugh more like a dog's yip. "You as an angel in the Ashley Hall Christmas pageant. That was something I'm never likely to forget. The way you managed to fall sprawling into the middle of the manger."

"You certainly surpassed yourself," Rannie agreed.

"It will be at the Citadel," Moira asserted, as if that ended all debate. In a world of change for the worse, the Military College of the South kept the old and best ways alive. Everything there was validated by heritage and tradition.

"Bunch of jug-eared, callous rowdies," said Mary Canty, dismissing the idea.

"Daddy was a Citadel grad!" said a shocked Rannie.

"Don't remind me," said Mary Canty. She downed her drink resentfully. "All those awful class reunions. Listening to his fool friends reminisce about pranks in the barracks. The time they stole that horse mascot from Furman, broke its leg trying to get it into the van and then had to shoot the wretched beast. They would split their sides laughing at the most atrocious cruelty."

"Shoot it?" gasped Moira. Both hands flew to her mouth. In reality, she was terrified of horses, but they played a large role in her romantic dreams.

"Don't tell her," sighed Rannie. "She'll have to go throw up."

Mary Canty said, "That ridiculous sword he was so proud

of. Those uniforms. At least the moths got to them and I could throw them out."

Rannie stood up suddenly. "What about Daddy's sword? Where did you put it?"

Mary Canty spoke around the cigarette dangling from her lips. "God knows. Up in the attic somewhere with the rest of the rubbish."

Moira and Rannie were both speechless at the sacrilege. The sword had always hung in their daddy's study along with all his other memorabilia.

Only the phone ringing seemed to prevent Rannie launching herself at her mother's throat.

"What is it now?" Rannie barked into the phone.

Then her voice fell to an indistinct murmur and they couldn't hear the words. She came back and sat down, a little smile playing about her lips.

There was a silence broken by Mary Canty asking what the call was about.

"Oh, nothing."

"It's never nothing," Mary Canty persisted. "You sound like a pouting teenager. Wanting me to pull it out of you." Irritated, she shook the ice in her glass.

"I'm going duck hunting. Saturday morning."

Mary Canty took the news without overt enthusiasm. "How absolutely gruesome. It's freezing cold out there."

"That's when you hunt ducks."

"Is this a required part of your job?" demanded Mary Canty. "You're always in some predicament."

Rannie stared at her mother exasperated. "People go hunting for fun. Daddy was always hunting. Deer, duck, quail. Whatever was in season."

"Your father was in an endless flight from responsibility. The man could barely earn a living. The over-draft stories I could tell you. Who are you going with?"

"With Rhett MacReady. Remember him?"

"How could I forget?" Mary Canty said with evident distaste. "The portrait painting Casanova."

Moira thought, what is that look in Rannie's eyes? Is it a haunted look? No, she was humming a little tune as she tonged ice in her glass. It was from a Disney movie. *Sleeping Beauty*? Yes, that was it. "One Day My Prince Will Come." Rannie was . . . *cheerful.*

"What on earth is wrong with you?" Moira exclaimed.

■ ■ ■

Leaving the family scene, Rannie crawled up in the huge attic feeling right pleased with herself. Didn't curse when she got the cobwebs in her hair and the dust made her sneeze.

Rhett had just been readjusting to Charleston slowly. Any girl he met probably flung herself at him. But when it was a question of the girl for duck hunting, Rannie came instantly to mind.

The attic space was enormous like everything in the house. As a kid she had played up here a lot, made a little house delineated by a quilt on the floor. Moira was afraid to come up, so no one bothered her.

There was her old telescope she used to watch the loons that wintered in Charleston, sitting out on the harbor that seemed mild next to Canada. There was her bird scrapbook with feathers and sketches and sightings.

The sword was just dumped in a stave barrel with old umbrellas and canes. Straight blade. Gold cross hilt with the Citadel seal. The Ralstons went back generations in the long gray line of Citadel grads. An unbroken chain, at least until Collier got thrown out for smuggling a girl into the barracks in a duffel bag.

Collier was really nothing but a stiff dick tucked inside an otherwise empty suit. No delayed gratification for that boy. As a lawyer he was incompetence writ large, and as a politician even worse. He could strike an attitude, but that was pretty much it. If there was something dumb being hatched up at the state capital, he'd at least be on the periphery of it. He was a mudbath of scandals and ethical lapses.

She put the sword down and rummaged some more. Tailor's dummy. Broken down chairs. Old leather luggage and steamer trunks with bright stickers from the days of ocean liner travel. A Randolph had just missed traveling on the Lusitania when it got sunk.

Box of old framed photos. There was the Ashley Hall back court screaming and hugging each other after seventeen-year old Rannie hammered in the last winning ace for the state volley ball championship.

And by golly there was the photo of her and Rhett on the docks holding the big wahoo during that sun-bleached magic summer when she was eighteen. Rhett in a long billed cap, faded khaki shorts and no shirt. Skin a deep bronze. Washboard abs. Her breath came out in a long sigh.

Thirty thou he gets for a pig. That's what those rip-off house painters wanted. A team of ten working for weeks scraping and painting. How long did it take Rhett to knock out that pig? He had done her portrait in under two weeks, and that had included a lot of time when he wasn't painting because he was lying on top of her.

She had sneaked the portrait up into the attic, but Moira in a freakish visit up there caught a peek, got all awash in hysteria and tattled of course. The aftermath had been surprisingly painless. Her father had just left the house and gone off to try a capital case in Colleton County.

Rannie was an achiever all through school which had balanced out her misbehavior. And other than that, what? Various fights with boys. But that was nothing. Even when she slashed the tires on Cotesworth Kershaw's BMW her daddy had taken her side. He hadn't even scolded her over the painting.

"I guess you'll take after your mother's side of the family," he had said. That was it.

A great many negative things were said about Mary Canty, most of them true even if a bit exaggerated. Her mother had a garish reputation for extramarital flings when Rannie was younger. Once or twice there had been wicked whispers of it at Ashley Hall by some little snip who suddenly found herself slammed up against a locker.

Rannie hadn't had much opportunity to test her daddy's theory that whore's blood percolated in her veins. Bearable men had been scarce on the ground. Rhett was her one memorable romance.

She dug in a footlocker she'd used in college and found the great big Mako shark jaws that brought everything back with heightened recall. Their summer of love.

She had finished her freshman year in college and had her debut at St. Cecilia's in the spring. He had been one of the escorts. The studly U. Va. rising senior in a dinner jacket. Giving her the slow looks. Monopolizing her dances. When he smiled, his eyes went hypnotic.

All summer, Rhett had been into shark fishing. Would paddle out on a surfboard and dump a big grappling hook loaded with grisly meat. Surf back and wait for the line to jump taut. Then reel in some monster. They finally banned him from Folly Beach because he scared the tourists so badly.

When he asked her to go with him night fishing off Fort Moultrie, there had been nothing coy in her yes. They had dragged up the big Mako near midnight with the beach abandoned. Soaked with salt water, gritty with sand. A primitive blood lust of the moment raging. In the excitement, his eyes seemed to be shooting out electricity.

She had grabbed his face and started kissing him, tumbling down to roll in starlight and sand. A lot of really deep kissing and suddenly her bikini bottom was snatched off.

"I know it seems contrary to my nature," she had said, kicking her feet free. "But I'm new at this."

"You can wing it," he said.

And she had. And was left gasping and voiceless. With constellations floating overhead.

Feeling good about all things, Rannie came down from the attic with the jaws, the sword and the fishing photo. There was still a dynamic between her and Rhett that bridged the passage of the years. And if that little tart in his office got in the way, she'd choke her chicken neck.

Gaston had finally dived into the booze. He was shaking up a martini and telling Mary Canty that what with the juniper berries in the gin and the wormwood in the vermouth it was a medicinal concoction.

"Why are you dragging down that rubbish?" Mary Canty demanded of her daughter.

Moira enthused to Gaston, "That's Daddy's sword. He was on the regimental staff at the Citadel."

"And was he ever," moaned Mary Canty. "Brutal hazing of the freshmen. He'd wear a tennis shoe and a leather shoe so he could run down the gallery and it would sound like he was walking. That way he could catch freshmen doing something and 'rack them' as they called it in their silly slang."

Gaston heard the word 'rack' as though it jolted a lost train of thought and fixed on Rannie's breasts.

Moira had no earthly idea what he was looking at. Rannie thought there are folks who can change a room with their presence. Moira can lower the I.Q. to basement level.

Gaston raised his glass and recited:

"Oh give me a crack
At the cowgirl rack
And ride me into the sunset
That's from 'Deadwood Saloon Lament.'"

Rannie thought what a galoot. Always blathering on. No pregnant pauses, lapses or hesitations. She could see him hitch-hiking in the rain, imagining himself a badass fugitive. And talking aloud violently so any driver would be terrified to stop for him.

She shook her head bemused. None of them bothered her in the least now. They held no relation to her perfect path to the future.

And then and there she decided to buy a Land Rover Defender and to hell with the cost. Mud spattered all over it. Cool hunting gear in the back. And she'd buy a water dog. Lab or a Boykin spaniel. Give it all a good smell of the outdoors.

And she would find serenity in the arms of a tax law-yerin', hog paintin', hunk o' burnin' love.

9

"Whoa!" joked Gaston, throwing up his hands. "Who let the dogs out?"

Two figures of the grotesque stood framed in the doorway of Gaston's tiny college office. They didn't laugh at his wit.

Almost obscenely thin Smythe in his Tuesday and Thursday gray suit and mud-drab necktie. The stump-like bearded Smedley in garish madras Bermuda shorts and sandals with white socks. Bruce Springsteen t-shirt. An overcoat over the ensemble because it was so cold outside. They sat down uninvited. Fellow members of the English Department dropping by for a visit.

Gaston always thought of them as Mutt and Jeff. Or Weasel and Stoat.

Smedley with his copy of the *NY Times*. Gaston read obscure hick town weeklies. The *Elkins Valley Dispatch*. The *Etowah Clarion*. Filled with the voices of the land of possum and sweet 'taters. 'Funeral Limo in Fiery Crash.' 'Grits Queen Pay-off Scandal.' 'HS Coach Hopping Mad.'

"There have been student complaints," began Smedley studying his white socks. Wiggling his toes.

This jerked Gaston awake from the quiet somnolence of

his afternoon nap at his desk. He looked from one to the other suspiciously. Beanpole Smythe and Fireplug Smedley. They toadied to the department head, adopted whatever position was calculated to stroke her fur in the right direction.

Smythe cleared his throat. "They don't feel quite comfortable with a man who abuses women."

"Abuses?"

"Your . . . um . . . wife."

"I did nothing to her," said Gaston, inserting a semiquaver in his voice. "My wife was foully murdered by parties unknown!"

Smythe looked pained. "That's not the standard of proof these days. It's a matter of how students feel. And they feel you're the sort of man who would do such a thing."

Gaston demanded to know the names of his accusers. This was denied. Females had a right to privacy according to Smythe.

Gaston pressed his palms together with ferocious, isometric energy, grunting and grimacing. Then, letting go, his shoulders fell slack. "I'm in a personal crisis and this is your idea of collegiality?"

As he anticipated, they expressed grief and concern all in low tones, afraid of being overheard by the thought police. At no point did they suggest the students might be malicious liars, wildly fantasizing or even simply wrong.

Gaston wrestled with a growing conviction that the department head wanted him gone. "Won't you even give me a hint as to who they are?" he pleaded. "I can talk them round. I know it. I'm popular with the students."

They stared at him. It had been the wrong tack. Their student evaluations were the pits. But with the power they and others like them held in the faculty, they made certain that student evaluations never counted in the annual merit tally. Only publishing in scholarly journals.

"You'd only make things worse than they are," urged Smedley.

"Bring them in here," Gaston pressed. "Or I'll meet them on their turf so they don't feel intimidated by my alleged authority. You can both be witnesses. Surely they can be made to understand that I am blameless."

Smythe coughed behind his hand. "Unfortunately, your reputation precedes you."

"Yes," Smedley echoed. "The hijinks you've gotten up to around here—the brazen drunkenness at the Christmas party where you fell into the tree—the smashing of those outdoor sculptures at the art building—all your disconcerting outbursts in front of the class—well, the girls in question, um, the female students, feel that this is the—dare I say—god what a cliché—*icing on the cake.* They say they could see it coming. Feel it coming. They're very into intuition and sixth senses."

"Sho'nuff, honey-chile," Gaston protested in his Southern poet's drawl. "I've blundered into the con'sarned gray areas in my cotton pickin' time. I've availed myself of opportunities here, there and way down yonder in the paw-paw patch. But I'm not a genuine, get-down crim-i-nal."

Smythe said, "We've tried to shield you from the worst of it. But, truth be told, they don't like the way you . . . um . . . look at them in class. You've been charged—the worst of the charges—with staring."

"Staring?"

"Yes," said Smythe. "It's best to look somewhere above their heads. It's less open to misinterpretation."

"The actual charge," added Smedley, stroking his beard, "is excessive staring."

"*Excessive?*" Gaston erupted. "Do they have no vocabulary? What about lurid staring? Lascivious staring? Lubricious staring? Leering? Ogling? God, do you realize how low the SATs of these kids are?"

"You know we all share concerns there. The poor preparation of the incoming students, I mean."

Gaston laughed acidly. "My attorney will bring a Jane Doe suit against the little whining bitches. She'll ferret them out and get their names. Sue their pert young asses off."

Smythe winced at the word 'bitches'.

Smedley shifted uncomfortably. "In academe, self-preservation's the name of the game. No one willingly takes on a student today. You bring lawyers into this—you'll leave here with shit sticking to your shoes that can be smelled for miles."

Gaston sneered silently. Weasel and Stoat. The hatchet team of the department. What they lacked in courage they made up for in back-stabbing, lying and treachery.

He thought, I have wallowed on young honeys in drunken revelry. Shared spliffs as big as fence posts. Swum naked with them in forest streams. Been on the receiving end of bathroom blow jobs at costumed Halloween frolics. Where-oh-where did this new rigid morality come from? This lynch mob justice?

"I wouldn't press this," Smythe warned. "You're on a year-by-year contract. You have an expectation of non-renewal under any conditions. And you've got ample months here to find a new post. You're accustomed to moving on."

"Like a one-gallus tenant farmer with his belongings piled into a mule wagon!" Gaston roared. He pounded ferociously on his desk with his fist. Smythe and Smedley jumped up out of their chairs and retreated towards the door. The stumpy Smedley body-blocked his way out first.

Gaston came around his desk in pursuit. "Yes of course you must ride me out on a rail. The lone outlaw element of the department. Crush the free-spirited. Let there be no laughter and dancing to the Pipes of Pan in the groves of academe."

The skeletal Smythe backed into the hall, putting up his hands as if to ward off a blow. "The department head is prepared to give you a *positive* recommendation as long as you slide on out in May without a fuss."

The pair scuttled away like body lice. Exhausted from his fierce emotions, Gaston fell back into his chair. The claustrophobic walls of his tiny cubby-hole office seemed to be moving in even closer. His coronary arteries felt ninety percent blocked.

All his artifacts and souvenirs he'd have to pack in boxes once again. The moose head. The Elvis doll locked in an unseemly embrace with the Dolly Parton action figure. The photo of him dressed like a hayseed posing with a mule. Ceramic picaninny eating watermelon. 'I brake for boiled peanuts' bumper sticker.

Oh to wet the whistle. But he could no longer drink in his office since the neo-Prohibitionists had instituted the after-hours desk searches. Fuck the 4th Amendment when the sacred goal is keeping faculty sober role-models for the impressionable young.

The precious students with their borrowed federal tuition dollars. Getting trashed from Thursday through Sunday. The Morals Brigade couldn't make the slightest impact on them with their binge drinking lectures and healthy lifestyle presentations. So they lash the faculty into a corner like feral beasts.

Imaginary dialogues roved through his brain. He showed his flagrant contempt to the department head. Cut her to ribbons in debate. Cross-examined her mercilessly before the Faculty Council. Exposed her as being without wit, wisdom or scholarly proclivities.

He wanted them all to die a hideous and agonizing death. No one who knew the truth could call it murder. Abandoning all self-control he shoved his desk over on its side and heaved the chair about the room, repeatedly smashing it into the walls.

A fierce headache jackhammered in his skull. His throat was desperately parched. He felt "swole up like a pizened dog." Things could not possibly get any worse.

■ ■ ■

Moira sat at the long Chippendale dining room table savoring her lemon tea in an afternoon of intermittent rain. Just getting Gaston and Rannie out of the house that morning had jangled her nerves. To calm down, she had created an arrangement of colorful gourds and dried sun-flowers in a woven basket.

Rannie with her endless sense of teeth grinding rage and betrayal. Her ability to take the smallest thing up to a high level of generality. Rannie paid for tuition at Sweet Briar. But she has to dramatize it into a ticket to the poor house.

"Every day I see you like a jury verdict," Rannie had moaned. "I've been found guilty of nameless crimes."

"Well, you're just a cart before the horse," replied Moira, smiling indulgently. Rannie could not understand sponta-neous feeling. The sense of wonder of the child. The emo-tional requirements of the mystic.

With Rannie gone, the great house had drifted into a dramatic silence allowing Moira to get on with her writ-ing. Some families have a happy cohesion. The Ralstons did not. That Moira had heretofore disguised her depths around them was only natural. Petrified from an early age, she had been a bystander to life. Forever yearning. Lost wandering down roads to nowhere.

Now she had closed the loop in her life and come home to her origins. The house with all its history had given her an emotional vigor she had never known before. Moira was writing at an exceptional level. At precisely 4:30 p.m. she had finished "Figs in Season." She really ought to hang a sign on her bedroom door. "Do not disturb. Genius dwells herein."

True, the magnetic attraction between Gaston and her-self had played its sprightly role. The mysteries of human attraction defy analysis, but still it seemed so natural that they were in love. Despite their differences, they were unified in an obligation to art. And, as such, their union approached ideality.

After finishing her tea, Moira mounted the wide winding staircase and turned the knob on Gaston's room. To go through his things was not an invasion of privacy. It was a gesture of communion.

Gaston was profoundly lonely. The slow and solitary journey of the poet burdened by his brilliance. He needed her badly. By merely entering a room, she could convey a festive spirit. Buck up the crestfallen. Cheer the dolorous. She was melody mixed with harmony.

Going out the door to class this morning he had done a bit of a Virginia Reel and blown her a kiss. Proclaimed himself off to work his way up the food chain. He had such enormous restive energy, no doubt a reflection of his mental turmoil. His voice didn't seem to rasp so much. Denying him strong drink the night before had helped, and Moira had been a good Samaritan to do it.

Honestly, the man was just a disorderly little boy at heart. Clothes dumped on the chairs. Shoes kicked everywhere. Such a depressing melee. Moira picked up a tweed jacket and gave it a vigorous shake. Hung it in the closet.

Most would call his personality a difficult one, alternately brooding and volatile. Clouds precede lightning, after all. But Moira had her ways.

In one of their many meaningful interchanges, she had told Gaston a poet should learn through inspiration, not from sordid investigation of the world's dregs. He had nodded in embarrassed agreement. It was a subtle manipulation on her part, but effective. She was a quiet storm, full of purpose and unshakable ideals. He had recognized that when she delivered him out of the county jail. And her refusal to tolerate his drinking and his unspeakable behavior with the maid gave him comfort.

Together they would return poetry to its gilded glory. It would not be easy for him to deal with her suddenly increased popularity. Perhaps he'd be jealous of her abrupt climb to acclaim.

Moira plumped up the pillow on the bed and was utterly discombobulated by what she found underneath. A *Playboy* with a colored girl on the cover with a revealing décolletage. Which was a very unpleasant reminder of that incident with Tamzi, the maid's daughter. Among the articles listed was one entitled "Talking Oral Sex."

What on earth?

Moira had gotten glimpses of such magazines in stores before, but she had never actually looked in one. It was like entering the dark thicket of the male ego. Cigars and cars and alcohol. In the center was a fold-out section with a horrifying display of total nudity.

Moira flung the magazine in disgust onto the bed and as it landed, an envelope fluttered out. It had been opened, and she couldn't resist seeing what was inside.

What she found was a check from Farrar Straus & Giroux for $100,000. The notation on the accompanying letter said it was the final one-third advance against royalties for Gaston's novel *Carolina Flame-Out*.

One-third.

Moira could do math on that level. Gaston had received an advance of $300,000 from one of the most prestigious literary publishers in the world.

That simple bit of paper was a graphic picture of Gaston Garnett. This was the history of a man. Youthful promise. Long deliberate toil. Final triumph. This worldly success was his gift to her. His enduring gift of love.

Breathlessly, she phoned Rannie, impatient at being put on hold.

I am vindicated, her heart sang. They will eat their words. All their endless rounds of charge and counter-charge. Saying there was no money in art.

"And I will rub their noses in doo-doo," she said aloud in a sassy voice.

Moira allowed herself just a tad of celebratory vulgarity.

10

"The solicitor will paint you as a professor parody," Rannie warned Gaston. "Spend your time showing off for little girls who want a short, torrid affair with an older man. Plying the underage libido with alcohol. Playing philosopher king in a student apartment with your ZigZag cigarette papers and a plastic bag of reefer."

Rannie was starving, and it made her more irascible than ever. She had to fit into her old hunting pants when she went out with Rhett.

From her office window she could see the pilot boat bouncing on the chop out to a huge Maersk liner. Dark clouds hung low on the Atlantic horizon like a box closing over the city.

Gaston Garnett lolled in the client chair, eating boiled peanuts from a greasy sack, protesting his innocence and sense of violation. "I'm sure the Solicitor is seeking reelection, and I bear the brunt of his publicity seeking." He flipped shells in the wastebasket. Wiped his greasy fingers on his sock.

Rannie told him he would probably face the electric chair for his wife's murder. She had gotten the word from the solicitor's office that day.

"And Ms. Ralston dips into her kit bag of scare tactics. I had no motive. I adored my wife. She forced me to drink organic carrot juice, but that was her sole fault."

"Which is why the neighbors report y'all screamed and yelled and threw big objects at each other."

"Am I wrong, or are you a bit peeved?" observed Gaston.

"You're not wrong; you're right," Rannie agreed. "Went by an art gallery and saw a painting of a wild boar being chased by dogs through kind of a palmetto jungle slough. Mud and slobber flying. A lot of snarling fangs and wicked tusks. $30,000 price tag on it. I passed by today, and it was gone. Sold. Bam. It hadn't been there a week."

He propped his foot on the wastebasket. "Not an easy task pursuing the creative dream. Havoc and misery for most of us while a favored few prosper."

"But let's say you wanted a wild boar painting. Would you pay a significant premium over the standard scenes of marshes at sunset? The best of those is going for ten thousand."

Gaston seemed mildly offended by this injustice. "What kind of a signal does that send to artistic youth? Life is a crap shoot? One artist is strangled with his own entrails while Dame Fortune lavishly anoints another. A truly wise society would support the creative as the Dutch do. Buying their work and storing it for the coming of a more enlightened public age. That would resonate with me."

"All that resonates with you is ninety proof liquor and the sound of your own voice."

"*Mea culpa.* I am the Peck's Bad Boy of the poetry academy. I'm said to be gifted but self-destructive. I fumble the opportunities presented me by the muses and Fate. And then flee the mess. Gone like a cool breeze."

"Let's call it like it is. You've had a lifetime flirtation with freewheeling insanity. You rut with young girls right smack in the workplace on a Clintonian scale. You behave like a hooligan at poetry readings."

"Thank you for that bracing reminder of my failures. I am a shiftless, apelike creature who should be locked in a cage and fed with raw meat on a stick thrust through the bars."

"Let's get down to brass tacks, Gaston. It's time to pay your lawyer."

Gaston argued he was penniless. Clad in clothes from her father's closet. Begging Moira to make him a peanut butter sandwich for lunch and please leave the crusts as he needed the nourishment. He vowed he felt like an old dog who had never learned any tricks at all.

"You've got a state college job. A regular paycheck. Meanwhile you freeload at my house. Braised tenderloin with green peppercorn sauce. Turkey with a brown sugar rub. Crabmeat-and-oyster dressing."

"I'm in the process of being fired. And poetry, be it the most gifted or the veriest hackwork pays like the ring of small coins in the church poor box. I can't be expected to be your personal gravy train. And anyhow, your constant harping on fees has given unintentional focus to what can only be called your base, vulgar greed. There are those—and I don't want to be telling tales out of school— but there are those in the Yacht Club bar who describe you as an outright swindler."

Rannnie blew a strand of red hair out of her face. "As if I care. They all use the big firms for their legal work."

Gaston paused meditatively, then at leisure produced the sexual longings that were always on his fevered brain. "I'd love to see you in a tank top. Your enormous jugs bulging at the edges. I would tenderly lift them free in awe-inspiring display."

Rannie looked at him like something she had scraped off the bottom of her shoe. "I hear you've sold a novel. No doubt it's a thinly disguised autobiography."

Gaston rose exulting to the bait. "My life is an American epic. The Yoknapatawpa series. *Giant. Raintree County.* As a character, I am elementary and stable. It's the events that give my saga a degree of power and duration. Yes, duration. It will echo down the ages."

"I imagine it's more like a tour of a killer's internal landscape."

Gaston scoffed. "Yarn me a yarn. I am the mildest of God's creatures. A co-dependent with the dainty-feelinged world of men in touch with their feminine side."

Rannie tapped his thick file. "You live in a context of booze-fueled mood swings and terrifying violence."

Gaston challenged her to name one single, solitary incident.

"You operated a go-kart track in grad school."

"True."

"You had a girl friend at the time in addition to your wife."

"Yes, little April with her pert 32-C breasts."

"In a drunken rage you attempted to run over her with a kart. Pursued her around the track."

"She was into organic foods. I couldn't stomach another barley tofu casserole. It was just a rogue impulse. No harm really done to her."

Rannie almost sympathized. She thought of the fresh baked red velvet cake with the vanilla icing sitting on the kitchen table. "So how much did they pay you? The publisher, I mean."

Gaston tut-tutted. "Just a piffle."

"I gotta hand it to you. You're a black belt in the art of lying."

"I deny your charge. I am merely in training."

"How about 300,000 piffles?"

She saw the pause come into his eyes. He frantically slapped the pockets of his jacket, thrust his hands in one then the other.

Rannie smiled. "I've got the check, Gaston."

■ ■ ■

"The word *'mésalliance'* would not begin to do it justice," moaned Mary Canty. Her son Collier had presented his fiancée that afternoon, and the proposed match had gone down poorly. Or, as Moira said, like a lead balloon.

Moira had helpfully tried to tell Dale important truths about the Charleston culture. How there was no more true 'she-crab soup.' In the old days, the mature females—the 'sooks'—used to be thrown into the pot with their egg sacs. It gave it a rich flavor unknown to the modern world. Dale said, 'really?' Just completely disinterested, that girl.

Dale had refused a drink even though it was well into

the afternoon. Which had forced Mary Canty to keep going out to the kitchen to take hits straight out of the bottle. Which had caused her on one such trip to knock a tray bearing teapot, cups and small sandwiches on the floor.

"That black outfit," Moira whispered. "Like a funeral. I'm told they dress that way in New York. It's some sort of fad."

Mary Canty glowered over the rim of a tall scotch and soda. "Collier always was a dolt. Just like his father."

The pair sat under the regard of stiff portraits of deceased Randolphs and Ralstons painted by obscure ante-bellum artists, a grim reminder of proprieties and a proper social order.

Moira didn't approve of cutting people up, but the odd sensation of unity with her mother did provide a tonic of pleasure. And for once she was not the object of family abuse. "At first I thought it was some crude practical joke," she said sadly. "Marrying out of his social set. And not even a Charleston girl."

Heavy banging on the front door announced that Gaston Garnett had arrived home absolutely knee-walking drunk, unable to turn the knob, imagining that the door was barred against him.

"Such a commotion!" exclaimed Moira, letting him in. "You certainly haven't learned any manners since you left here this morning. And don't you go near the drinks cart. You smell like a brewery as it is."

"Sneak-thief!" he wailed. "Purloiner of the skimpy means that stood between me and utter destitution!"

Moira just brushed his pointing finger away. She knew he was going to go on about the check, and she just didn't want to listen to a word of it. Rannie always nagged her about contributing to household expenses, and the check was a way to stifle the accusation for a while. Gaston certainly didn't need it. He lived for free under their roof.

Besides, they had this whole business of cutting up Dale to get on with. Moira gave Gaston a thumbnail sketch of the lower-middle-class interloper who was about to make Collier's life such a misery.

"I'm completely humiliated," Mary Canty added. "The wedding announcement can avoid the papers altogether if we're careful."

Gaston flopped heavily in an armchair drawing it close to Mary Canty. He seemed to be getting his wits back, just a little slur to his words. "You weren't favorably impressed I take it."

"A tee-totaler. God, I could feel the piety just oozing out of her."

Gaston threw up his hands in mock alarm.

Moira sighed in despair. When Dale said she didn't drink, Mary Canty had stared at her in horror. As if all her plans for mother-daughter-in-law fun had been crushed before they even began.

"A scarlet woman on youth's perilous path to manhood," added Gaston, entering into the spirit of the occasion. He put one thigh over the other heavily and swung his foot.

Mary Canty drained her glass and held it out, rattling the ice, at Gaston. She liked to be waited upon and the maid refused due to her habit of throwing things when she found the service inadequate. To Mary Canty, the coloreds were more uppity than ever.

Gaston mixed her a fresh drink. It did not escape Moira's attention that he seized the occasion to fix one for himself as well. He flopped back down, in the process moving his chair closer yet to Mary Canty's. In his disheveled clothes, he looked suddenly old to Moira. As if he and her mother might be retirees in a home for aged drunkards sitting plastered on the front porch as the sun went down.

"We tried to be reasonably civil to her," Mary Canty allowed. "Everything she did seemed practiced like she had just brushed up with an etiquette book."

"She's just a concentrated dose of common," Moira added.

Gaston took out a notebook and made a note. He always liked a good turn of phrase. "Home? Family background?" he queried like a cub reporter for a newspaper social column.

Mary Canty waved her hand dismissively. "Some out-of-the-way place. Ima or something."

"Irmo?" asked Gaston.

"I suppose that was it."

"It's a suburb of Columbia," he supplied. "Donna Rice hailed from there. The fair honey who wrecked Gary Hart's campaign for the Presidency. They should erect a statue of her as Irmo's most famous daughter." He laughed at his own humor.

Mary Canty rolled her eyes as though Donna was a fitting poster-harlot for the outlandish burg. "They're going to be married in a Methodist church. I've always thought of Methodism as some sort of overwrought flim-flam and not a real religion at all."

Mary Canty was Episcopalian of course. The Randolphs had been St. Michael's and the Ralstons St. Philips, these two edifices being at the top of the Charleston social scale.

Since the death of her husband, Mary Canty never rose before noon, so church was out of the question. Still, she imagined she was a regular communicant just as she imagined she was a Republican Woman despite having not voted since casting a ballot for George Wallace in 1968.

"Preferable to a foot-washing Baptist," observed Gaston sagely. "Now there's some folks who really won't take a drink."

Mary Canty shuddered.

"One always wants the best for one's brother," Moira opined. "At the very worst I saw him going down the aisle at Grace Episcopal. It's on a terrible stretch of Wentworth Street—right across from those horrid College fraternities—but they do still have that darlin' blessing of the animals each year."

"Haw, that's rich!" laughed Gaston in a short bark.

Moira stared at him confused. He grinned back in that unnerving way that made her feel her slip was showing. It was another entry on her lengthy list of bad traits to break him of.

Mary Canty nuzzled her replenished drink. "I always expected Collier to marry for money. God knows he can't earn any. Find some homely rich girl from a good family. Sit down with the lawyers to work out a marital settlement."

"Everybody gets his whack, eh?" said Gaston. "Including the mater-in-law. Sound policy. But alas rare in this anemic age. World full of young twits chasing the chimaera of love."

"You're the only man I've ever met," Mary Canty said soothingly, "who wasn't a complete fool."

Gaston yawned. He held, he allowed, traditional views in matters such as these. Young Collier could not be allowed to become some trophy of the chase. Direct action was called for against this monstrous up-state impertinence on the part of a shifty suburban strumpet.

"Yes," Moira agreed. "Somebody needs to lambaste her lollygagging little red wagon."

Mary Canty asked if despite his numerous commitments Gaston might get his brain working on a solution. Gaston replied he had a minor accumulation of experience in the area of wrecking marital engagements. And he was willing to take a hand—purely, he insisted, for the benefit of Mary Canty whom he held in such esteem.

Moira sat up quite straight. Gaston had walked his fingers up her mother's hand and onto her forearm.

And followed up by giving Mary Canty a crafty smile. "Upon the return of a certain personal object of mine in the clutches of your red-haired offspring."

Mary Canty was completely mollified. She smiled at him as though she held his ability in the utmost regard. "There'll be no problem with that," she said comfortably. "I can be quite firm with Rannie when required."

"Yoicks! Gone away!" yelped Gaston in fox hunting parlance. "Point me at the conspiratorial maiden and let the horses run!" The image plainly gratified him, and he gave a throaty chuckle. Patted Mary Canty's hand. And then gently held it, stroking it with his thumb.

Moira identified it as a lascivious chuckle. And did not care for it in the least. The specter of a satyr had crept into the room. A dancing saraband of satyrs hand-in-hand with Gaston on his "Road to Parnassus" as he liked to call it.

11

"Do you know what it means to die for love?"

Startled, Rannie stepped back. The dark-haired girl had whipped open the door before Rannie could turn the twist bell pull. Despite the question, she didn't sound like a ghoul emerging from Ligeia's tomb. She was dreamy. And somehow resident here in Claitey Pussey's house on Middlesex Street.

"I've never come even close," said Rannie. She explained she had come to ask about Gaston Garnett. She was his lawyer. The truth was she wanted to explore the crime scene. See if she had any sudden insights.

"Oh, Gaston."

Was there something rhapsodic in the tone?

It was a human figure Rannie had to admit. Long straight hair parted in the middle *à la* waif from the 1960's. Pale white flesh like magnolia petals or the moon on a clear night. Her body gently curved and passive, cased in an ankle-length black velvet dress Guinevere might have worn in King Arthur's court. Faux pearl buttons on the sleeves. One of those unfathomable creatures who are always a subset on any college campus. Fasting and purging themselves. Ophelias scattering blossoms. Wandering catatonically like that creature in "The Fall of the House of Usher."

Rannie breathed in a faint tang of incense.

The girl put the back of her wrist to her brow in a stock dramatic gesture. "I spend my hours soul-searching and drenched in pain. My life is a wild rank patch of tangled briars."

"Do you manage to eat or do you have to return to earth for that? I mean is this a romantic or a clinical depression?"

"I rouse from my despondency to compose small lifelines."

She recited aloud from a poem which she had apparently written. Or maybe Gaston had.

"When all resistance melts
I smooth your scented hair
And sing of nervous nipples
And taste the snake of Paradise."

"Nervous nipples?" said Rannie.

"It's an image under development," the girl sniffed. "Poetry is a dynamic process."

"You wrote that? You don't say. What's the title?"

"The working title is 'The Odor of Wild Mint.' I mean to capture the intense drama of Gaston Garnett's life and loves."

As it turned out, the girl's name was Tabitha—Tabby for short—saddled with Claitey Pussey's pen name. She was Claitey's daughter by the second of four marriages.

Somebody named Boone. Which meant Rannie had blundered into the home of a grieving child whose mother had most likely been murdered by her stepfather.

But young Tabby didn't seem to be exactly fighting back the tears. "The sanctity of life is paramount," she mused, ". . . yet, on the brighter side, mother's dreadful death has liberated him."

"From what?"

Tabby gazed soulfully at the sky. "His writer's block is gone. He's become quite fluent. The critical world will be taking a hard look at him again. The speculation is already intense, almost overheated."

"He's sold a novel," Rannie ventured. "For a fair piece of change."

"Well, yes, that. Although I understand there's some problem with it."

"Meaning what?"

Tabby twirled about like a dancer. "I can't allow you inside. It's"—she made her voice lurid—"a *crime scene*. But I can show you where they gamboled like young fauns as spring blossomed into the melting warmth of summer."

Tabby beckoned and Rannie followed around the house. It was built in some style that Moira would know about. Two long porches that are called piazzas in Charleston. Twin brick chimneys at each end. Long green shutters closed over the windows as if forbidding the late afternoon light to enter.

Their heels tapped on a herringbone brick walk bordered by azalea and camellia, brown leaves in drifts at their roots. A chill wind stirred the bare tree limbs, rustled the banana plants dead in winter. A deep green cast iron bench beneath a dogwood tree. Mourning doves calling.

A moderate sized swimming pool was filled with water, the surface a mat of leaves and twigs. It chilled Rannie to the bone just to look at it. She asked why they didn't drain the pool in winter, and Tabby explained it had been therapy for her mother. Claitey had been in menopause.

"She'd go swimming in this freezing muck when she had hot flashes?"

"Gaston would hurl her into the water," Tabby enthused. "Like the one-eyed Polyphemus flinging boulders at Odysseus' ship, he called it. He claimed it gave him a surge of power. A feeling of omnipotence in an otherwise henpecked existence."

"Hmm," said Rannie.

"Mother did like to dominate," Tabby said waspishly. "Her role in the marriage fable." She paused. Then produced like a vague afterthought: "And then the gun wrote the fatal chapter. But which gun, I wonder? The one gun or the two gun or the three four five gun?"

Rannie ignored the Dr. Seuss nonsense and asked if Tabby had witnessed any of Gaston's tirades.

"Dear Gaston is mercurial." Small tremolo in her voice. "Perhaps capricious. But there's no harm in him."

"He sure ain't no altar boy."

Reverently. "He elicits particularly strong feelings."

Rannie couldn't hold back a small chuckle. "Especially among the coeds."

Now dreamily. "He *will* stoop to conquer."

Another Rannie laugh. "An unrepentant tool on that boy."

Tabby went quiet. Her face scowled. "This has become an uncomfortable experience," she hissed, and Rannie was amazed by the venom in her voice. "I urge you to be gone. Anon. *Toute suite*. And with due haste."

Rannie went back down the narrow brick walk between the boxwoods. Thunder rumbled like a distant threat.

"Jeez," she mused aloud. "Talk about your malevolent eyes."

And then it struck her. The resemblance was almost uncanny except for the hair color. Did Moira have a dark twin she didn't know about?

Then something really awful hit her like a wet fish. Tabby had been the girl kissing Rhett MacReady right smack in front of his office window.

■ ■ ■

"Well, women novelists will show their wares," pronounced Mary Canty Ralston. "Tabitha Boone. *Quelle nom de plume*." Which was as snide as Mary Canty could be in French.

Outside No. 1 Legendre, the trees dripped with water.

Moira looked at the picture on the back cover of the romance novel that Mary Canty thrust under her nose. *Flames of the Carolinas*. Saw the enormous décolletage and grasped her mother's meaning. She flushed in momentary embarrassment.

"It's just as well Tabitha's gone. I loathed her last book. Lost the touch, poor old thing. And a talented man like Gaston could only be held back by her."

Moira cringed. Her mother seemed openly jubilant that Gaston's wife was dead.

The family portraits hung there overseeing things as Mary Canty paced the floor wagging the book in one hand, gesturing with her glass in the other. She had knocked back a bottle of Chablis at dinner, gone through a large portion of Madeira in the afternoon and now was into the evening Scotch. She would typically pass out by eight or nine.

"'Colonial lusts and loves,'" Mary Canty read aloud dramatically. "'A novel of searing revelations.' Bosh. I can't get past the first chapter."

"Because you fall asleep so early," Moira said in a small voice.

"Exhausted," Mary Canty retorted. "No one knows the pain of selfish children. Bad enough you're swanning around up in your room reading your feeble verses aloud. But Rannie expects to have her little Perry Mason moments." She drained her glass and eyed the drinks cart like it might have moved.

Moira said, "Rannie is never above a bit of 'poormouth' rhetoric. Is that the word? Rhetoric or random or something."

"She always seems to be underperforming with her law practice. And she does have her little weight problem, bless her heart." Mary Canty laughed. "Do you know what your father said? I'll never forget it. It was her sixteenth birthday and Rannie had insisted on wearing some tacky dress. Hanging out here the way she does." Mary Canty gestured with cupped hands in front of her breasts. "Anyhow, he said, 'She looks like something that would jump out of a cake at a stag dinner.' Isn't that just precious?"

Moira's antennae went up. Rannie worshipped their father. Was it possible he had secretly disliked her?

Mary Canty said, "Ask the girl to contribute some token sum to the household accounts and she explodes. Even dear Gaston has started to complain about her miserliness. We were rigidly disciplined in my day. Honor thy father and thy mother was taken seriously."

"She's like a toddler crying for attention," Moira ventured.

"I think," Mary Canty stated, "if Rannie is going to make her nightly whine for sympathy, she has a corresponding obligation to show positive results from our emotional support."

At that moment, Rannie erupted through the door in a white-hot fury about everything and everybody in American jurisprudence, especially some client she kept calling a "scumbag." She made a bee-line to the drinks cart and began clunking ice into a squat glass, continuing to give them an in-depth account of her "day of perdition."

Mary Canty snapped at her. "Rannie, you've got something that belongs to Gaston, and he needs it returned immediately."

"Sure. When hell freezes over." She sucked in the aroma of Jim Beam like a life-giving elixir.

Mary Canty said don't dare goad her or try to turn her pleasant household into a denunciation scene. And what was this "thing" anyway? Gaston was quite distraught over it. Rannie explained it was a check, closed her eyes as she savored the first deep drink of the bourbon.

"How big a check?" asked Mary Canty, always alert to the main chance.

"Substantial."

Mary Canty gave her a beady eye. "I'm thinking of having a face-lift for Collier's wedding. It will help me fight off the despair."

"Sure," said Rannie deadpan. "Spend away. If you want us all paraded through the street by creditors. Herded destitute into the bankruptcy court. Go to it."

"It's a mother's prerogative to seek some minor joy in her only son's marriage," Mary Canty said haughtily. "You make every little thing into a dramatic power struggle. Force me to operate autonomously from my own daughters. I'll have to break up Collier's engagement all by myself."

Rannie looked Moira straight in the eye in a way that always made Moira cringe. "I met someone out there just like you today."

Moira blinked at her. "How is that?"

"Demented."

Moira clenched her fists. Her brain could run a newsreel of meanness inflicted by her sister. The time Rannie cut up the Scarlett O'Hara Barbie which Moira had sewn all by herself. The dead squirrel under her pillow. Just dreadful.

But now she had visions of being glamorous and self-assured. She would read at the Citadel to a rousing ovation. The exact nature of her readings would be kept under a cloak of secrecy even from Gaston. This would become a big factor in creating trust between them. As a team, they would be competitive in a global poetry market.

"I intend to read my poetry at the Citadel," she murmured. And then added more loudly: "To a rousing ovation."

"Of course you aren't," said Mary Canty abruptly.

Moira stared at her mother with a very real dismay.

"You'd make me a laughingstock."

Moira promptly burst into tears.

12

The little Broad Street cafe was jammed with a lunchtime crowd of lawyers chowing down on sandwiches and burgers and super sweet ice tea the way Southerners drink it. Rannie was having a salad fit only for rabbits. Disgusting.

Rannie said, "So this bozo is charged with three counts of armed robbery, three counts of conspiracy to commit armed robbery."

"Yeah," said Lazelle. "Aurelius somebody. I've seen the file."

"And one count of failure to stop for a blue light."

"That's cops for you. They always like to load them up with the small stuff. Think we can plea-bargain better. Say, 'Okay we'll drop the blue light if you plead to the rest.'"

Rannie pointed a finger. "But the kicker is he's arrested following a high-speed chase on Interstate 26. And he tells me his defense is he wasn't present at the crime. He was just giving some friends a lift, and when the cops came after them he panicked."

They both laughed. Lazelle said, "He'll have to do a little better than that."

Rannie finished her salad and ordered a black coffee. She was so hungry that in the middle of a guilty plea she had just blurted out "cornbread and succotash." Went on as though she hadn't said it while the judge and her client stared.

Gaston Garnett came in looking like a double-barrel portable grill in a tweed suit and flopped down at their table uninvited. Loudly ordered three cheeseburgers to go. Then sang them a few lines of the old ballad "Fair and Tender Ladies."

He had a fresh crew cut and seemed to be growing a mustache, white like his hair.

As his lawyer, Rannnie should have instructed him not to run off at the mouth around Lazelle. But she didn't particularly care. If he chose to lynch himself that was fine with her.

And of course he could never resist a fresh audience. Set right in on her. "You know I was at an AME church last year and they had a sign out front said 'Exercise Daily. Walk with Jesus.' I've taken it to heart, if you'll forgive the pun. Try to do two miles a day."

Lazelle's antennae went up. Rannie thought whuh-ohh. She had seen Lazelle dressed all in white, a Deaconess of Behold God Army Ebenezer Church of God.

Lazelle looked him right in the eye and said, "I bet that's what you tell your white college kids. Give 'em that little ironic smirk. Everybody have a good laugh about the God-fearing."

"Did you know I'm an ordained Baptist minister?" Gaston asked. A smile was sewn on his face. Trying to charm a snake back into its basket.

"You know, I hear stuff about you. Gaston Garnett the

Demon Coed Lover. But looking at you in the flesh, I'm wondering how many a' them coeds are two hundred pound lonesome doves."

That cut to the quick. Which helped him to look pained. "I'm still grieving the tragic death of my wife. For me there is no closure. We were like two old horses standing head to tail, switching the flies off each other."

Lazelle stuck a two dollar tip under her plate and stood up. "I can't sit here and jaw with you. 'Cause I'm going back to the office and dig out a file and take a much harder look at it." She made eye contact with Rannie. "Maybe it can do us some good all 'round."

"You just might be a public benefactor," Rannie agreed.

Ignorant of the meaning of that, Gaston admired her swiveling buttocks as she went out. "Man-oh-man, talk about your dusky beauty. I'd shore like to get to know her a whole lot better."

"You will when you go on trial."

He ignored that, gave Rannie a squinty grin. Slid the hardback book over to her, sat, hands folded patiently on the table as she read.

Carolina Flame-Out. Then underneath "a novel." Like you needed to be told. Jacket picture of an old Mustang with bullet holes in the windshield and kudzoo growing around the bumper. And a sub-title. "They's nice folks down on the Edisto, but they'll kill you."

She turned it over and read the rave reviews.

"Lewis Grizzard meets Cormac McCarthy. A brutal and dark journey with a high energy humor overlay. These ol' boys would beat Buford Pusser with his own ball bat and gang-rape Eudora Welty. But they fret about bad cholesterol in a moon pie."

—*Boston Globe*

"Cruisin' Court House Square in a '62 T-bird. A Southern fried Quest for Cool. Crank up the Allman Brothers, pour a good hit of Old Setter into your Dr. Pepper and settle back for a wild ride on two-lane blacktop."

—*NY Times*

"At last the natural successor to James Dickey. Except without the bow and arrows or the canoe. These good ol' boys and better ol' gals go on a hoot 'n holler outlaw journey from Calhoun Falls to Red Top serenaded by the roar of Lake pipes and the blast of a .357 magnum."

—*Atlanta Constitution*

"Pat Conroy on steroids. A Down-in-Dixie coming-of-age saga that makes you sixteen, horny and hog-wild all over again. First drink of moonshine, first love, and first car-jacking."

—*Charlotte Observer*

Rannnie asked, "Are these people reviewing the same book?"

"Well, they never really read it. Just write a blurb that says it's Southern, violent and weird. Hollywood will change the whole story anyhow."

"You figure it's destined to be a movie."

"Don't you see the quote? I'm the dead solid natural heir to *Deliverance*. I'll have both author and screen-play credits. Maybe sing the sound track. Play Delta blues on an old Fender electric guitar. It could be as famous as 'Dueling Banjos.'"

"Easy street just around the next corner."

"Are we questioning the piety of the Pope here? I believe in the Muse, her ideals, her basic generosity, her reward for virtue here on earth. A hot tub and cocaine-fueled lifestyle is my destiny. Be driven around in a Lincoln Continental with rolled leather interior and a fold-out bar."

"But just right now you need walkin' around money. Dress and act the Southern writer. Live in a certain style. Maybe fly to N.Y. for good-morning shows, stay at the Algonquin."

"It's smart to buy the bigger ham. The bone in the twenty-five pounder is the same size as the twelve. So you get more meat."

"What you're saying is it doesn't cost much more to go first class."

"You are the tarragon on a dish of cooked carrots."

She studied him. The brush haircut, the clipped mustache. "Are you trying to look like William Faulkner?"

Gaston slapped the table. "What a great writer and professional drinker. Serious? Let me tell you. *Sartoris* is the only one of his books that don't make you feel suicidal. Maybe *The Reivers*."

Rannnie stared at him in silence. She could do silent. The big pauses that made hostile witnesses jabber like wind-up dolls. She watched the cloud of doubt settle on Gaston's face. Big wrinkle between the eyes.

"Don't give me the steely-eyed treatment."

She smiled indulgently. "You figure you'll come in here all buoyant. When *Carolina Flame-Out* hits the best-seller list your credit will be good as gold. I'll get enthused and give you back a big piece of the book advance as seed money for you to make the big score."

His eyes glinted with excitement. "And the upshot is?"

"I think you're trying to sin above your station in life."

Gaston stopped smiling. "This is your 'beggar thy neighbor' attitude? Creativity is not wanted, and hustle and native industry are shown the door?"

Rannie paused a beat. Said, "That sack of burgers waiting for you up at the register—don't try to skip out leaving me the bill."

■ ■ ■

"Yeh-boy!" Gaston roared as he walked into the King Street bar. The larger-than-life Southern novelist answering the Call of the Wild. "Bring me a drink in anything with a hole in the top!"

"Your Daddy's Money" was dark even at midday. A magic kingdom of college students where life and love found their nexus. In such a chamber a man could rediscover his first youth in light like star beams that filtered through the neon Budweiser signs. And illusion will counterfeit heaven in the shapes of coed sylphs who love to talk dirty.

The bartender delivered up Gaston's usual draft Blue Ribbon with a shot of Wild Turkey on the side. Gaston poured the bourbon into the beer like a flow of higher chemistry. Holding the mug in both hands, he drank deeply with his eyes closed, then opened them slowly.

"Praise Jesus, the day's starting to improve."

Three of his slacker students heard him and ambled over. Bill caps turned backwards on their heads. Unshaven. Gaunt from diets of Ramen noodles and Fruit Loops. Competing in describing the size of their hangovers in stoner voices.

"Du-ude, did I tie on one last night. Feel like I woke up with cystic fibrosis."

"Man, I feel—I feel like I hit the wall at 180 mph. Got a broke back and a closed head injury."

"That's nothing, man. I could swear I got pancreatic cancer."

Gaston produced a little jar of Rosemary from his pocket. Told them it was eaten in the Middle Ages for a "heavy head." He never went binge drinking without it. Otherwise he'd feel like he had been gored by mule-crippler cactus.

One of the slackers—Ed or Ted or something—said he heard Gaston had been in prison for murder. Laid-back. Passive about it. Like saying "I hear you once kicked a cur dog."

"I shudder at the memory," said Gaston. "A chicken-shit roust as they say in the business. And I've known some rousts. I been down by law from Natchez to Mobile. In the calaboose from Memphis to Macon."

Whoa, Nellie. Check out the talent. A little cutie-pie was with them. How had Gaston overlooked her fine curves? Miss Bobbi-Jean Honeycutt. Now that was a memorable name. Such a honey of a cut you are. Tight jeans with the V of her crotch showing serenely. Tweety Bird t-shirt stretched taut across capacious jugs. To call her teats huge was a mere recognition of the obvious. I could bounce on them like a waterbed. Your white milky flesh. Oh be my alabaster slave.

He took another drink and toasted her by reciting:

"Pour peanuts down the neck o' my RC
And mix in a whisky dram
The moon is over the outhouse
Cocktail time in old Ala-bam."

Ted or Fred or whoever remarked on Gaston's new 'stash. Gaston stroked it with a knuckle, explained he was cultivating a Faulkner look now that his book had finally come out. He slid *Carolina Flame-Out* across the bar for their admiration. Told them, yes, it was completely auto-biographical. A serio-comic backward glance deep-cured with stale beer and second-hand smoke.

"Hard core," breathed Jed or Fred.

"Heaviosity," admired another.

"Aww-raaht," went the third, doing a fist-pumping routine.

"That is so cool," gushed Bobbi-Jean.

Gaston had them hooked. And bless Bobbi-Jean's heart, she was just as bright and cheerful as a drink of Sundrop soda.

Jed asked if he could have a copy. Gaston said this par-ticular one was promised to a dying buddy in the cancer ward. He admonished him to buy one for his own per-sonal self. It would do his soul good. "Wrap yourself in the sanctity of Southern literature. Avoid Ripple wine, sex with animals and sticking up convenience stores. Be loyal to God and Country and the Consumer Price Index. And don't believe for a minute that eating bacon will cause cancer."

"Oh man, I can't buy this *and* afford to drink." He had his head tilted back to keep the smoke of a cigarette out of his eyes. "I guess I'll have to steal a copy. It's kinda like a dark side imperative."

They all laughed.

Gaston gave Bobbi-Jean the elevator eyes. Those hooters are in stark defiance of all law and logic. Ambrosia for the eyes. Glories of creation. And does your family keep bearskin-rug baby photos of you with that pert fanny up in the air?

Gaston did his full-bore Southern *literateur* routine. He told them how to make hog's head cheese and South Georgia gum "rosin" baked sweet potatoes. He recited his poem "Ginsang Eatin' Man," then sang them a few verses of the old ballad "Wayfarin' Stranger." He did his impression of a Mississippi Waffle House waitress and then Arkansas Bill Clinton saying 'I did not have sex with that woman—Monica Lewinsky.' He told them about living on the edge of the Okefenokee Swamp where the snakes were so evil they'd follow you home and wait outside your door. He described his signal victory in the catfish skinning contest in Loango, Alabama and how it led to a night of life-affirming love at the Motel 6 with a gal with drum majorette hair.

Bobbi-Jean was staring at him with the impact of a midair collision between an Airbus and a 747. You little heart-stopper. Talk about your flight-control malfunction.

It was time for the possum dick toothpick. He got it out of his wallet. Picked at a molar. Held it between his front teeth as he gave them the big grin. And they of course asked what was it. And he told them it was the bone of a possum's dick. One of two creatures of the animal kingdom—the red fox being the other—with such a blessing. In New Orleans they make possum dong necklaces as love amulets.

"That's just so wild," Bobbi-Jean Honeycutt said brightly.

Gaston beamed at her. "Although until I took that biology course in high school I believed mine was a bone. So skinny in those days the only way I kept my pants up was a non-stop hard-on."

She giggled without embarrassment. A woman who would stand against cruel winds. A creature to give poetry its voice. Cat-nip. Sweet Basil. Balm in Gilead. And he had gotten the notion out on the table that Gaston was hung like a hoss. Big ol' peter on the boy.

Gaston accepted another drink without protest. And how virtuous of Bobbi-Jean to pay. Come and caress my bald spot with a big ba-zoom.

Then he noticed that Jed had slid out taking the copy of *Carolina Flame-Out* with him. He paused to get the exasperation out of his voice. The whole world was in a conspiracy to ream him and steal from him. Calm thyself, Gaston Bayard. Let the blust'ring storme be o'erblowne. Forge on and woo this comely critter with the big ga-zongas.

Gaston told them about his Redbone hound Old Rattler who would beat out flaming paper bags in exchange for a sausage biscuit. Died tragically in Savannah when he ate some junkie's month supply of methadone. Gaston put his hand over his heart and asked for a moment of silence in memory of the faithful hound. Then he described his python Jungle Jim and winning a $500 bet in a saloon in Gulf Hammock, Florida, Jim swallowing fifty pickled eggs from the big jars behind the bar.

The two remaining dudes went to take a whizz. Leaving him alone with Miss Bobbi-Jean, the ham hock in a big ol' plate of Hoppin' John. She told him she really hated it when someone would tell her to "have a good one." Looking at him with deep emotion.

Gaston took an audible slurp of his beer and tried to look judicious.

She tweaked one of his love-handles. Just the faintest squeeze.

"Professor Garnett?" she said in a relaxed voice. "If you're like into the lyricism of the dark side of our nature . . ."

Gaston leaned close. "Yes, Miss Sweet Patootie?"

". . . and you're into, like, wild-hogging and moon-baying . . ."

"Yes, you little home-wrecker?" Gaston's palms were sweating. The mating call of the connubial coed. Her spell was cast.

"Then why do you eat yourself into such a big ol' lard bucket?"

13

"It's like Antarctica out here," Rannie muttered, rubbing her mittened hands together.

The marsh stretched out gray and orange with winter. Marsh grass lined by cypress and cedars. Decoys bobbed and nodded. Sitting in the duck blind, Rannie scanned the sky just as the top of the trees split with the first yellow crack of dawn. Rhett's stolid bigheaded black Labrador kept squeezing in between the two of them like the cold was too much for him.

It had been pure joy to get out her hunting clothes and long-johns. Fill the shell loops. Unlock the mahogany gun case and take out her daddy's best Parker shotgun handed down in the family since 1908. Clean its double barrels and wipe the oily rag over the walnut stock until it gleamed. And now sit beside this man screened by the brush.

Rannie had never realized she could think about sex when she was freezing, but she could. Like a porno film running in her head, she imagined Rhett going down on her as she begged for release.

Rhett said, "Did you wear enough clothes?"

"People talk about extreme sports, trying to sound so tough. Nothing can match the sheer wind-driven sleet nastiness of duck hunting."

"Cold are you?"

"The expression 'freezing my ass off' is inadequate to describe the situation."

The dog rubbed his big faithful body against Rhett who in turn stroked his head. "So talk to me, Randolph Ralston, now back in my life. Tell me about the current 'you'."

She laughed. "I've got this new client. Robbed the Carolina First and actually stopped in the parking lot to count his money. Dye pack blew up in his fool face. Woman deputy spots him there staggering in a cloud of pink smoke. Said it looked like the Fourth of July come early. She had him on the ground and cuffed before he could see. Anyhow, I'm interviewing up at County and his alibi, get this, he says he was tie-dying a t-shirt and spilled it on him."

Rhett grinned. Said he was asking for something more in the profound category.

That stumped her. What was the "current her"? Researching the spiritual abyss of a manless state of being. Desperate to be ruled by this aggressively beautiful man. She said, "I guess I'm rad-lib without being it. If you follow me. Yes, that's me. I'm saying it emphatically."

"So what are your behavioral aspects?"

"I work for a living. A real job. No Small Business loans for womyn-fest enterprises. No pottery shoppe or crafts or fern dripping vegetarian cafés and juice bars. I'm not into dykery or single women klatches. I don't hate men unless they're assholes, which unfortunately so many of them are. I don't wear Birkenstocks and hang around a college campus writing journal articles on cross-cultural gender roles."

Rhett laughed. "Sure enough none of the above."

"I think I'm balanced. And I've gotten beyond the past. The old model of English lit major at Agnes Scott who marries an Emory MBA and devotes her time to arranging children's play dates."

"Your sister's persona."

"She should be so lucky. I once saw a domestic turkey sit on an electric fence. Just sat there getting a big continuous shocking jolt. Didn't have the sense to get off. That's the way I think of Moira."

Rhett laughed, but he was back silent and watching the sky again. His hand idly scratched the dog behind the ears. The dog was watching the sky too. With difficulty, Rannie restrained herself from grabbing hold of Rhett. Sat on her freezing hands.

Her nose was running making her sniff something awful. It was about as romantic as having a case of the drizzling shits. She fought to re-ignite her fantasy.

She put herself into a version of transcendental meditation. Sex appeal is a state of mind—a state of the soul. She was a glossy package that could fill a man with heady and overwrought desires. Bodies vertical become bodies horizontal.

Rhett suddenly stood up in the blind, swung his 12-gauge in an arc and let off one barrel right after the other. Two ducks came plummeting down to splash into the gray water. The black Labrador was up, bounding into the icy water.

KER-SPLASH!

"I didn't hear or see them," Rannie said abjectly. God bless it, he had hit a left and a right. Rannie hated being shown up.

"We are here to shoot ducks," he said blithely.

Thanks, Rannie thought. I need some further demoralization. At least her LL Bean boots were old and worn. She felt they lent her some minor legitimacy.

Rhett just sat there scanning the sky like a master of the tease. Melting her resistance. Not that she had any. And she was ready to do him right there in the blind. Pants off in the cold.

How could she get things going? Establish a bodily architecture that sends appropriate signals? Not when you're bundled in long-johns and a wool shirt and a padded hunting coat. Wool cap pulled down over her ears.

Say something wry? Who do I have to sleep with to get back to a hot drink and central heating? Maybe just thrust her tongue in his mouth in lieu of a spoken statement. That would convey the message.

The dog marked one bird and brought back the other. Then jumped back in the water to go for the second one. And of course when he got back he had to shake water and mud all over them. And then drool all over Rannie. Just pleased as punch over the two drake mallards.

Rhett sat there like a glimpse of Paradise. Rannie wanted his tongue running around their edges of her mouth with every nerve crying out. His hand rubbing the inside of her thigh. She hesitated. Swallowed. Leaned towards him to purr into his ear.

He reacted by turning his head sharply towards her,

bonking her a really sharp crack in the nose with his head. It felt like a hammer-blow.

"Ow Goddamit!" she howled, squinting against the pain.

He tried to touch her nose but she smacked his hand away. A rising wind was shaking the trees in a frenzy.

"I've still got the shark's jaws!" she practically shouted, tears blurring her eyes.

He sounded puzzled. "That's nice."

He didn't have a clue. Her besotted memory meant nothing to him. You nincompoop wunderkind, Rhett MacReady.

Rain started to fall in large drops on the gray water. The wind stirred the water and let out a smell like sewer gas.

She was shaking violently with the cold and her anger. "What are you doing with that revolting Tabby? That little moony bitch with the eyes like dark purple pansies!"

He didn't even look surprised. "She's Claitey Pusey's sole heir."

"Sole? What about Gaston?"

"He gets nothing. Claitey had a big cash flow at the time they married, but she lived high on the hog and was paying off three other husbands to boot. So she made Gaston sign a really nasty pre-nup. He had to crawl around her for lunch money."

"So what does the girl get?"

"Not much. Claitie's last book bombed. The publishers will turn on you in a second if you fail them. She gets the house in Ansonborough. But I'll sweeten the pot for her.

I'm going to be suing Gaston on behalf of the dead wife's estate."

"Wrongful death?"

"No, there's no evidence of that according to the Solicitor."

"Well what then?"

"Plagiarism. Theft of copyright."

■ ■ ■

"Do it now
Do it now
Get down sweaty dirty.
And do it now."

The young beauty with the somewhat preposterous name of Susie-Q Infinger read her short poem aloud to Gaston Garnett's writing class.

Gaston, the distinguished creative writing professor planted on the edge of his desk resting on one hefty thigh.

A freezing rain was pounding on the windows. One of the students had brought a wet dog into the classroom which was licking its privates. Others were eating fast food, drinking Starbucks coffees.

Gaston pinched the bridge of his nose. Four lines of quote 'verse'. That was all. And she was finished. This vile sloganeering that she imagined was poetry.

"It seems to lack an . . . um . . . clearly articulated and coherent . . . um . . . theme."

"No it doesn't," she argued pertly.

"Well . . . um . . . help us out here," he urged, striving to draw a minimal performance out of her.

"It's obvious," she continued stubbornly, a bit of a pout on that pretty face.

How does one deal with such aggressive stupidity? What was the measured policy response? He gave her a forced smile. "I don't want to dilute my critical role here. Nor risk the perils of condescension. But pray elucidate."

"Say what?"

His voice was sugar-coated. "Explain your blankety-blank poem in such a way that the class and I may understand it."

Amused ripples went down the rows of seats.

She was exasperated now. "It's about . . . you know . . . doing it!"

The class laughed. She tossed her hair defiantly.

To give her a 'B' seemed remarkably lenient for such writing. Yet he lived in an era of grade inflation where there really were only two grades: 'A' and 'B'. To not deviate from the norm was the common sense approach. Let the little swine go out into an unfeeling world utterly unprepared for its rigors.

"Well, all of your work is subject to ongoing review. I'll peruse it again tonight. It may amplify or dampen my emotional reaction."

Gaston felt a sense of drift among his constituency. The doorway had filled with a slow-witted hulk from some redneck subspecies. Clemson sweatshirt against the cold. Wool cap pulled down over his ears. A crippled claw for a left hand that clutched a long envelope. Asked in the slowest of drawls if he was Gaston Bayard Garnett, putting about fifteen syllables in the name.

After some initial hesitation, Gaston allowed that he was. But couldn't resist performing for his gallery. "Garnett the semi-prominent poet. The beloved mentor of the young, some call me. While others call me pugnacious. Combative. Contrarian. More righteous than repentant. Approach with caution as I breathe fire and eat charred meat."

The claw thrust out. Garnett took the envelope dumbly. Realized what it was. Agog in disbelief. Why had he not recognized a process server? He had met them so many times before.

"Now comes the Plaintiff who complaining of the Defendant alleges and says . . ."

A taste of bile rose in his throat. The paradox of our age. All talent must be punished in public. It was a relentless program. He would be stripped of his new-found wealth.

"Fine day, ain't it," the server said in parting. A comment that went unchallenged and unremarked.

Would nothing save him from total ruin? Had he not suffered more than his share of pain?

By God they were all staring at him like some Greek chorus awaiting a cue to voice the lines memorializing his solemn doom. Did they sense his shame? He had thought to compartmentalize this. Remain the romantic novelist hero on campus. Fight this wretched legal matter in private. Have the terms of the settlement sealed by the court.

"So what are you gettin' sued for?" quipped a wise-acre in the back. "Work evasion?"

Big gale of laughter.

He dismissed the class. Wanting only to crawl wounded to the outpost of his office. Collapse in cerebral solitude out of sight of the health police and sneak a very stiff drink of Jack Daniels Old No. 7.

Susie-Q Infinger stood outside in the hall waiting in open ambush. Expecting fulsome praise. Saints above, I can't face kissing up to her ego needs.

"Good effort," he purred. "I'll be looking forward to future work. Perhaps something more deep and complicated next time. Wrestle with the big themes of life."

"Not so fast," she said peevishly, crossing her arms over her chest.

Low alarums. Caution, Garnett. Look for the small signs of her mood.

"I didn't care for the way you belittled me in class. It made me extremely uncomfortable."

Growing panic. Think, Garnett. What will give you wiggle room? Grovel or be stern? Take a strong hand. Yes, that would set the right tone.

"Let's drop the charade, Miss Infinger. Yours was a very weak effort. Quite aside from the fact you so nearly plagiarized the Nike ad—which I see as both a violation of their copyright and an honor court offense—but quite aside from that, if you're interested in poetry, I suggest you try to write something of greater length."

His attempt at exercising professorial authority failed. She looked ready to snatch him bald-headed.

"That's Ms. Infinger to you. And I'm afraid I'm going to have to report you for harassment."

He gaped in consternation. Not another one. And on top

of the excessive staring complaints. "No need for a titanic power struggle here," he virtually begged. "You know my impulsive mercurial nature. Can't be held accountable for the odd hurtful remark."

She snorted derisively.

Inwardly, Gaston fumed. The rad-lib attack-bitches spread their tentacles and enlist the aid of the sullen and immature. These dreadful little nihilists who believe their own aggrandizement lies in the destruction of all adult authority.

He tried again to placate her. "I know you're intense. Your work heretofore has been . . . well, powerful . . . um . . . deeply compassionate . . . um . . . even in the realm of the heartbreaking."

She rolled her eyes. "Oh puh-*leeze*. Sucking up to me won't save you."

Gaston dug his fingernails in his palms. Strict adherence to the rule of law required he not throttle her on the spot. Was there a viable alternative? Would there be no abatement of his excruciating pain?

She turned to walk off, then paused and gave him a parting shot in her rich Southern accent. "Yew're a ree-eel ice-hole. Yew know that? The way yew stare at me alla the time . . . what a gross-out. Eew."

14

"Claitey would get into her Tabitha Boone persona and write such over-blown prose," Gaston explained earnestly. "I thought I'd lift a line here and there. No one would notice. Her imagery was all so trite."

"And it just sort of got out of hand," said Rannie.

"Only moderately."

"Their complaint says every second sentence in the book has been taken from one—only one mind you—of Tabitha Boone's novels. *Flames of the Carolinas* to be precise."

"I couldn't stand to read more than one Tabby Boone novel."

"But you just copied it?"

"'The moon rode high in the sky like a Spanish galleon,'" Gaston quoted. "How can anyone own that sentence?"

Rannie was not in a good mood. She had broken one of her cardinal rules and accepted a client's check. It had bounced, of course. What would you expect from an embezzler? Guy had stolen from a TV station for five years.

Worse, she had eaten a chili-cheeseburger and then stuck her finger down her throat over the commode. Threw it up like a bulimic teenager.

She said, "You had a few belts before coming over. I can smell you over here. And your eyes have that bright and merry sheen."

Gaston was wearing one of Big Collier's old suits. A double-breasted pin-stripe with a pocket handkerchief and the necktie of the Carolina Yacht Club. "Lawyers are the killjoys of life," he lamented. "Don't you see? I'm a poet. I never dreamed the book would be a success. It was an exercise to cure writer's block. A writer's gymnastics if you will."

"I'll tell you how Rhett will paint you for the jury. Claitey was the magisterial Tabitha Boone who brought joy to the lives of housebound women. You were a shiftless creative writing buffoon in a college only known to the outside world because it has Charleston in its name. So you ripped off her work."

"Yes, yes, I admit it. I'm a literary tart. And I dispatched Claitey because she caught me at it. In the dark of night when the moon had gone gratefully to bed leaving me to creep on little cat feet and blast her with a high-powered gun."

"Sardonic humor won't play real well."

"I know. I'll make a hash of it. My dissolute lifestyle—the cheating, the lying—no one hates it as much as I do. I am a churning mess of terror, self-loathing and grief. Do I sound suicidal? Because I am." He put his face in his hands and sobbed.

Rannie said dryly, "Do my eyes look full of compassion? Because they're not."

His sobs subsided.

He lifted his face from his hands, leaned towards her

earnestly. "Your sepulchral laughter. Your rapacity. The way that dress clings to your heaving awesomes. You look positively lit up from inside when you're in one of these dominant moods. I would crawl on my hands and knees for a taste of your flesh."

Rannie snorted. "I'm not giving you the check, Gaston."

"You can't just take my book money."

"It's in my trust account. I'm billing my services out at two hundred-fifty an hour. That's modest for a big time criminal lawyer."

"So you forged my endorsement on it."

"You authorized me as your agent to deposit it where it could be of use to you."

"I never!"

"That's your story. Mine, as you can imagine, differs."

Gaston twisted his mouth. "I suppose we're into billable hours now."

Rannie said, "You eat pretty well under my roof. What was it yesterday? Ham and asparagus. Avocado out of season and double the normal price. Everything's overbudget in our house. I leave in the morning, you've got your snout down in a huge bowl of blueberries."

Gaston dashed his copy of the lawsuit to the floor. "Women take and take and give nothing in return! They're all the same. The psychobabbler. The moral uplifty busybody. The handmaid of arts and crafts who dresses in peasant costumes with earrings as big as curtain rings. They are positive inventive Einstein's when it comes to stripping you of money. That little amoral wench Tabby suing me! I mentored that girl! I wrote her damned freshman English papers at Hollins! I get the first breath of success and she wants to suck it right back out of my lungs!"

"Tried to get in Tabby's pants did you?"

He pounded a fist into his palm. "I would dearly like to bash her head with a sickening crunch. It would be a heartfelt relief to see her carping tongue choking in blood."

He reared up out of his chair and pounded on her desk in a fury. "You keep abusing me and I'll give you a dose of the same!"

Rannie laced her fingers under her chin. Stared at him with half-lidded eyes. She was thinking she had to bill out the entire $100,000 as fast as she could. Otherwise Tabby was going to take it. The copyright suit was a slam-dunk. She'd wander by the solicitor's office for fifteen minutes, chew the fat with Lazelle, and bill it as three hours.

She said, "You through yet?"

Gaston flopped back in the chair, mopped his head with a big blue pattern bandana. "This is a port city," he said cozily. "I could easily hire a sport fishing boat to take me to Bimini. The court would seize Number 1. Legendre. I'd send you a post card with a coconut palm on it. 'Wish you were here' kind of message."

Rannie chuckled. "I sometimes think I'd love to have that millstone of a house off from around my neck. Mother wouldn't be very happy though once it sunk in what you had engineered. I've often thought her capable of homicide. I'm sure she'd kill you for that. Just come right off a tour boat with a gun in one of those big woven tote sacks the tourists carry."

■ ■ ■

"Fine young men these Citadel lads," said Gaston, sounding like a retired Colonel as he looked out over the parade ground from the library steps. Hands clasped behind his tweed-clad back, bright yellow paisley ascot at his throat. "And a great place for them. Give them a backbone instead of a wishbone."

The library director—Anne Boudreaux Ravenel—beamed and wished him and Moira well in a trilling voice and left them to watch the Friday afternoon parade. A nearly six-foot woman wearing the army uniform of the faculty. She had been quite delighted by their proposed poetry reading. She was old Charleston—a "bin ya" as the Gullahs called it—and admired Gaston's Southern poet reputation.

A late February warm snap bathed the campus of the Military College of South Carolina. White buildings with Beau Geste crenellations around a green parade field with tanks and a jet at one end, a helicopter and cannons at the other. A thousand cadets in shakos and white cross belts paraded to the music of a band. Moira watched with rapt delight.

"I know what goes on behind those barracks walls," said Gaston. "Buggery, circle jerks and savage hazing. Seniors staggering back roaring drunk and brutalizing the freshmen. Forcing them to do push-ups over razor blades. Blanket parties where they slip into a room at night, pinion the hapless victim with a blanket and then pound him black and blue."

Moira didn't know what buggery or a circle jerk was, but she sure didn't care for the sound of the rest of it. "My daddy was a Citadel man. He lived right over in that barracks with the brass plaque with the Robert E. Lee quote. 'Duty is the sublimest word in the English language.'"

"Lee said something more profound than that," snorted Gaston. "It was in his last days when he was the President of Washington College in Virginia. Reporter came by and asked him what was his biggest mistake. Figured he'd say sending Pickett's brigade across the open ground on the third day at Gettysburg. Instead he said 'My biggest mistake in life was getting a military education.'" Gaston guffawed with laughter.

"I don't believe a word of that."

Moira got Gaston into the Lincoln before he embarrassed her in front of campus visitors. She hated cars and had failed her driver's test four times because that ridiculous policeman kept giving her such confusing instructions and getting so upset when she made teensy little mistakes. Charleston was getting so crowded and cars just came flying at you from all directions.

Gaston studied the barracks with their rows of windows as Moira drove the wrong way around the parade field and out the side gate. He said, "Lit up at night, it looks like a damn garment factory up in rust-belt New Jersey."

"Well I think it's just stirring and awesome and everything else good you can say about it."

"I hate uniforms. I hate rules. I hate conformity. I despise all the constricting garrote of the military-industrial complex."

Moira was shocked. "I thought you were a decorated soldier," she said in dismay.

"Oh, that. I was an irregular. A sneaky-Pete. Behind the

enemy lines in the dark of the moon with grease paint on my face and a Commando blade clenched between my teeth. Blowing up things with C-4 *plastique*. Ka-boom! Flames dancing merrily. The acrid smell of charred flesh. Yum." He rubbed his big stomach.

"You're just always trying to shock people. I saw that the first time you came to Sweet Briar. It's the behavior of an adolescent boy with jam on his face."

Gaston hammered the dashboard. "I will not perform before those ramrod fascists. I am not some dancing bear whose chain you jerk to make me cavort about."

"But you must," Moira pleaded in desperation.

Gaston crossed his arms. "I am adamant. I am stone. I am impervious to all pleas however pathetic and heart-rending. Express my regrets when you go on your own."

Moira set her lips in a narrow little line. She was just going to have to give Gaston a little taste of discipline. And the venue was so convenient to the Citadel. Just drive down past the football stadium, turn right, then the Riley Baseball Park with the Ashley River right there looking so pretty and blue. Ibises with their deep curled bills stalking the expanse of lawn. Turn into the big city police station with its buckling parking lot and all the black and white cars with those big light-up things on top.

She parked and got out of the car, knowing he'd have to follow her and he sure enough did. At double-time. Spluttering let's not get carried away. Get the wind up you headstrong. Ass-backward notions. Sho' thing, honey-chile, we can come to some modus-vivendi on this one. You betchore bippy, Miss Piece a'Sweet Patootie Pie.

She felt a bit gleeful as she walked into the big entrance

room where fines were paid at a window and a police sergeant sat behind a big counter.

Moira had known how to get immediate attention all her life. And this time she didn't need to start wailing or screaming. She just stood in the middle of the floor and talked at the top of her voice.

"I'm afraid I'm just all new at this, but this man here is out on bail for murder and I really think he needs to be back behind bars. I declare he just makes the most awful, blood-curdling threats and just carries on about who he's going to choke or stab or shoot with a great big ol' gun."

The whole room turned and stared. Motorcycle cops in high top boots. Lawyers in suits. Teenagers looking for the driver's license bureau.

"You know who he is don't you? Gaston Garnett? The poet? He was married to Claitey Pusey, better known as Tabitha Boone the novelist. And as to this murder business, I can't say I feel any surprise by the charges against him, only puzzlement that she didn't murder him first."

Gaston flashed the room a sickly, frightened grin. "Skittish little filly ain't she?" He did a manic jangling of the change in his pocket. "Prone to these fits of hysteria for years. Her momma begged me to look after her for the afternoon. I'm not really trained in this area."

Moira crossed her arms and patted her foot. "And are we in agreement on other matters?" she said in a sing-song voice.

"Yes, yes. I'm on permanent stand-by. Chaffing at the bit." He took her by the arm and hustled her back out of the seedy building.

"You diabolical witch," he hissed at her.

"It's not my fault you're going on trial for murder. I'm sure you'll deserve whatever's coming to you, the way you carry on so."

"You *can't* believe little ol' me killed his wife," he protested.

"How should I know. But I can tell you one little thing. Rannie only defends guilty people. She takes all their money and then pleads them guilty in some ridiculous deal that she laughs about around the house. How this turkey or that dodo—although she calls them much worse things than that mind you—how they thought they were getting such a deal and they're going off for all their natural born days."

"I feel a sick revulsion coming on. I'm going to barf. Stand back."

"Oh stop it," Moira ordered.

15

"I hope we can handle this in a dignified fashion," sniffed the Dean of Faculty Disciplinary Affairs. An uncompromising mouth set above a weak chin.

So this is what it comes down to, thought Gaston. A hangin' judge in half-glasses.

Outside the high up office in the ancient Randolph Hall, the grass of the cistern was frosty and the gray trees looked like pall bearers. Each spring they held college graduation there, the boys in white dinner jackets and the girls in white prom dresses.

Susie-Q Infinger had just left a neighboring room in a terrible state, copiously shedding tears of anguish. Under the new rules of sexual harassment prosecution, no man was allowed to face his accuser.

Gaston slumped in his chair. A very straight and uncomfortable chair. Once the Dean took endless phone calls making poor old Bocock from the Math Department sit in it until his hemorrhoids bled.

Rannie was there as his attorney, the flame-haired cow. She didn't care if he was fired. Just wanted to run up billable hours. Charging him for the trip to and from the College campus. The girl must wear at least a DD-cup. God, he'd love to lap at those. Suck and savor until her inner thermometer marked high degrees.

For once the Dean wasn't cowering behind his own attorney. He knew he had Gaston by the short hairs.

How he will love to put me in shackles. Chain gang boss in Dean's clothing. Lay waste to my small freedoms. Put me beside the highway in a striped suit with a weed-cutter to chop the rank grass under a broiling sun.

Gaston looked at the deep stain of red wine he had spilled on his shirt front. Moira had caught him imbibing and startled him into dropping it. Like the blood of a fresh wound he thought. An omen of the evisceration I shall sure enough receive.

Outside, a cold March wind was getting up, shaking the oaks around the cistern.

"Ms. . . . um . . . Infinger's critique of you is quite explicit, I'm afraid," the Dean began sternly. "Sexism of the grossest sort. Excessive staring. A constant stream of vulgarity designed to intimidate the female students, objectify their bodies, and marginalize them."

"Textbook language on gelding the male professor," observed Rannie. She sounded quite cheerful as though she thought it a sound policy.

"It's the artistic temperament," Gaston argued weakly. "We tend to shout quite a bit. Dramatic effect and all that."

"Your back-story is rife with similar complaints in small colleges. I believe you were fired from Mars Hill and Pfeiffer before coming here." The Dean shuddered at the thought of those boondocks colleges. "You lied about it to us. Forged letters of recommendation. No one caught it.

No follow-up phone calls because it was just a writer-in-residence position. We figured you'd move on in a year."

Yes, brooded Gaston. A carnival freak traveling from hick burg to tank town. Step right up and gawk at Albino Man as he dances the hootchie-kootchie. See him spin his nipple tassels in opposite directions.

The Dean was reading now from a lengthy statement by Susie-Q. "He would loom over me and bellow. His breath stank to high-heaven. It nearly made me puke."

"I never laid a hand on her," Gaston inserted almost proudly. And it probably was a first for him.

"When I had my period he would sniff the air and smack his lips loudly."

Gaston gazed into space. The faculty all hated him. Students pack the creative courses and leave Milton and Beowulf high and dry. They're not even majoring in English anymore. Droves of them in that silly mix of journalism and PR writing called Corporate Communication. Put the word corporate in front of it and they think they'll get rich writing press releases.

The Dean rapped the desk sharply, speaking to Gaston like a wayward child. "Have we lost your attention? I wouldn't want to bore you."

"Fear not, O Dean," Gaston answered. "I am riveted by the music of my funeral dirge."

A wintry smile drifted across the Dean's face and then was gone. "Is there some defense you wish to proffer?"

"Not really," said Rannie. "It pretty much sounds vintage Gaston Garnett. But help me get clear on something."

She paused, tapped a red fingernail against a tooth. "I

understand you tell your students you served in Vietnam and then returned as a veteran against the war. Flung your medals back in the face of the Pentagon."

"A modest gesture," the Dean tut-tutted. "A heartfelt moral issue. Felt I had to make some small symbolic act to protest an unjust war."

"I'm sure your war stories are quite an aid in that course you teach. What is it? The Dimensions of Moral & Ethical Philosophy in an Age of Travail?"

Gaston ground his molars. Your absurd course where the little morons mouth platitudes about abortion and capital punishment, and everyone gets an 'A.'

The Dean took off his glasses and gestured languidly with them. "We discuss torture. I saw a fair amount of it first-hand. Had to intervene once or twice at risk of my own life."

Yes, thought Gaston. Torture. And how you love to mete it out. Poor old Grimsley from Romance Languages who finally got his sabbatical and then you stripped him of it the day he was to leave for Paris. He meant to spend six months buried in the *Bibliothèque Nationale.* Not my idea of Paris, but then he's into scholarship and all that rot. Had waited twenty-five years for the chance. He was actually weeping when he left here.

"The students," said Rannie, "are quite impressed with your stories of being a Navy SEAL. They call you 'Full Metal Jacket.'"

An unbearably long pause elapsed. Rannie seemed quite serene. The Dean had developed a nervous tic at the corner of his mouth. It became increasingly pronounced, crawling up his face and closing an eye.

"It's funny," said Rannie at last, opening a file and

leafing through some pages. "The Navy doesn't have any record of your service. And your draft board—Peoria, Illinois wasn't it?—their record shows you classified 4-F. Flat feet, allergies and a series of nervous disorders that caused you to . . . well, I don't need to mention that aloud."

A flicker of horror took hold of the Dean.

"I think you need to drop the entire matter," Rannie suggested.

"That's not possible," the Dean croaked. "The process has gone too far. There's got to be at least a token punishment. Sensitivity training at the bare minimum."

Rannie took another peek at the file. "Nocturnal enuresis. You were primarily not called to serve your country because of bedwetting."

The Dean turned white as a sheet. His eyes turned up in his head like he was about to faint. "I'll quash the whole thing," he whispered.

"Susie-Q will not be returning to Gaston's class. Give her an 'A' for her transcript. I doubt she'll object."

The Dean looked aged and shrunken down into his suit. His hair seemed lank and damp from perspiration, his face changed now from white to the gray of a cadaver. "Yes. Of course," he agreed.

"And Gaston will be given a tenured position on the faculty and his salary trebled."

The Dean gagged so badly that he could only nod in affirmation.

Gaston couldn't believe his ears. She had gone in over the horns and delivered the *coup de grace*. Just skewered him clean right to the vitals.

The Rannie girl is stronger than polecat piss! She done beat the Dean so flat they can bury him in a waffle iron. Gaston wanted to spring up and do a victory dance and punch the air. To play the dulcimer in sheer joy. To sing it from the rooftops. I will buy this girl a huge drink with an umbrella in it. She may steal my car and kick my dog. She can lap dance on my face whenever she wishes!

■ ■ ■

"Oh God get out of the way!" Moira shrieked as she sped through the intersection of East Bay and Market Street against the red light. She took both hands off the steering wheel of the family Lincoln and frantically waved her arms in warning.

Cars slammed on brakes and furiously honked their horns. Pedestrians scattered.

Moira hated to drive. All the trees and cars and people were so distracting, and Rannie would just go ballistic over the least little ding on the car. Her sister had no appreciation for the fact that Moira was artistically gifted and not given over to practical concerns. When Moira would explain, for example, that Confederate jasmine could make a post box into a focal point, Rannie would always say something rude.

The sibling rivalry had always been there. Moira had been the pretty one, and Rannie was nothing if not bumptious. So it was to be expected that Rannie would resent Moira's growing confidence.

But Rannie's constant disapproval of Gaston was shocking. She simply refused to recognize his expansive talent and charm. At dinner when he spoke of the "poetic act,"

Rannie said he was "nothing but a pseudo-intellectual slam-dancer," whatever that meant.

Moira liked having Gaston living at No. 1. Legendre because it allowed her to supervise his routine and prevent him getting up to his "hijinks" as she called them. Only one drink before dinner and one glass of wine with it. If he had produced a suitable number of lines of poetry during the day, then perhaps a small cognac.

Moira had been especially productive in recent days. The approaching date of the Citadel reading—the knowledge that it was an irrevocable deadline—had gotten her brain tilling new ground, or breaking new ground, whichever it was. She had temporarily abandoned the pastoral for the heroic.

"The fat's in the fire," she said, although she wasn't quite sure that was the metaphor she wanted. And was that a metaphor?

But she knew the poem she intended to read was perfect for the occasion.

THE SWORD OF DUTY
By Moira Allegra Dewees Ralston, a Charleston Lady

Forged in the flame of purity
Our valiant sword of war & honor.
The blue, pure flame flickers and dies.
    Our sword
Now sheathed in a sense of grievance
Linger it long
'Ere we bid farewell
To States' Rights
    And all the noble panoply.

Hail Citadel.

Hail sword

Hail Duty & Honor & Sovereign South Carolina

She recited it with hand flourishes as she drove. It seemed so stirring. She would carry her father's sword and hold the cross-shaped hilt aloft.

Moira made a left turn, again against the light on Hasell, provoking more honks, and slowed on the quiet tree-lined streets of Ansonborough. She was seeking Gaston's home on Middlesex. The death of his wife was so painful that he refused to go near it.

Moira felt he needed the catharsis—if that was the right word—catheter?—of facing his wife's death scene. It would help him get beyond this pointless grieving and face up to practical matters like the disposition of Tabitha Boone's personal possessions. After all, when he married her, they might very well end up living there if it was large enough to be suitable. She could estimate the size from the outside. And if there were tenants, she would explain her need to come in and look around.

Dear Gaston, she thought. He looked so haggard. Perhaps even suicidal. She knew she was his only comfort. They spent so much time gazing at one another meaningfully that it led her to feel that tying the marriage knot was just as natural as could be.

Ordinarily she confided such romantic thoughts only to her diary. But in this instance she had boldly told Gaston that her honesty as a writer would be at stake if she didn't point out his need for a strong feminine relationship. The poor man was speechless.

Moira looked at street signs. Ansonborough is sixty-four acres platted in 1746 that lies south of Calhoun Street between King, Anson and the old Rhettsbury area. Homes were built by merchants, the prosperous class of tradesmen and the odd planter. The shady streets are quiet, secluded from tourists. Seldom known to tourists, it could exist in a dream of antiquity.

What happened over the next half hour possessed the peculiar quality of a dream, noticeable then and even more like a feverish fantasy as she looked back at it.

The trees were turning to dark silhouettes and mourning doves called balefully. It made Moira uneasy, particularly with all those derelicts in Charleston now. Why you could scarcely step out of your house for a gang of tourists or some seedy character hanging around. And Ansonborough was very close to one of those dreadful housing projects where colored people lived.

As she got out of the car, the gray cloudy sky seemed as though it were about to drop on her head. Moira shivered inside her overcoat. The address she sought was a small Greek Revival style house with double-tiered portico, brick chimneys at either end, and a leaning palmetto,

A light burned inside, giving it an element of phantasmagoria. She approached the door trying to display a confidence she didn't feel. The Corinthian doorframe she could identify. Whatever people said, Moira knew the essential things about Charleston.

When she lived here, she would dedicate the garden to summer-blooming flowers for birds and butterflies. Coneflower and sedum. Bee balm. Butterfly weed. A sourwood tree would lend a nice scarlet to each autumn. Yes, and an Indian corn garland on the door to celebrate the harvest bounty of that festive season.

Moira had just lifted her hand to the bell when the door was whipped open. A dark haired girl stood there, watchful like a cat at a mouse hole. She regarded her visitor suspiciously.

"How now, brown cow?" she trilled.

Moira didn't have a witty retort to that. But what struck her first was how astonishingly pretty the girl was. Like a wan heroine from a Regency novel. With her white, almost transparent flesh, she might have been dying of consumption. And she was dressed in the loveliest burgundy velvet.

Moira introduced herself with a minor excursion into the Ralston genealogy and its place in the history of Charleston. The girl said she was Tabby Boone, daughter of the author.

This news startled Moira a bit. It seemed to clutter things. But she went on and explained her role as "helpmeet" in Gaston's life and her natural curiosity about the house.

"Yes, poor Gaston," said the girl, putting the back of her wrist to her brow in melodrama. "A shadowy simulacrum of himself."

"And here he lived and composed," observed Moira.

"He used to call it 'Hangman's Roost.' He hated it. I think he hated most things about marriage to mummy." She paused and fingered the Virginia creeper that grew around the door. "It's all so distant now. Mummy seems like someone who lived ages ago. Like a dim memory of the Spanish Inquisition."

Tabby invited Moira in without any reluctance.

Moira had to admit the house was tastefully furnished in fine federal furniture and a color scheme of wonderful creams and golds blended with greens and grays. She wasn't quite sure what she had expected. But that brass tray was polished far too brightly. It should never have more than a subtle shine.

Tabby curled up in a chintz armchair, feet tucked beneath her. Waved Moira to a divan covered with needlepoint of bright white and red flower medallions. Moira sat on the edge as she had learned at Ashley Hall teas with her back straight and her knees together. Her feet were firmly on what must have been an Aubusson carpet.

Over the mantel hung a large oil portrait of Claitey Pussey as one of her characters: Crimson Flame O'Rorke in *Fair Wind for the Carolinas*.

"She was not universally loved," said Tabby. "Especially not by her last husband. She called his poetry 'caterwauling.' He said her novels 'blighted all hope for humanity.'"

"Her mouth is certainly . . . prominent," ventured Moira when what she really was noticing was the astonishing décolletage.

"Gaston always said her crimson red mouth was like unto a gash or laceration." She blew a kiss towards the picture. "Ta-ta, Mummy."

A built-in bookcase was filled with Tabitha Boone first editions and numerous volumes by poets she had never heard of. You could tell they were poetry by the titles. *Time's Tinsel. The Ampersands of 'Morrow. Dustmotes in a Snowstorm. Nasturtiums of Dawn.* And there were some

Gaston Garnetts. *Bad Drunk in Natchez. Biloxi Boogaloo Breakdown. Tinhorn Sheriff Roust.*

Moira felt she had to make some insightful comment.

"I think Sylvia Plath is so . . . so suicidal," Moira ventured.

"Like a lamb for the slaughter," Tabby agreed.

And that seemed to break the ice.

"I'm a Hollins drop-out," Tabby offered with a bright smile.

"I quit Sweet Briar," said Moira, relieved at their sisterhood. "I hated every minute of it."

"All those tests," Tabby agreed. "Grubbing for grades just gets in the way of creating."

"It was just all . . . antagonism," said Moira, remembering how the other girls made such fun of her because she couldn't ride a horse and kept a constant cold.

"And I had a famous ribald poet for a stepfather. Why did I need history courses?"

"Ribald?"

"You need to wear a chastity belt around him," Tabby confided. "He would sit real close to me and talk about having his vasectomy reversed."

Moira felt herself turn pink, pulled her dress tight over her knees. Gaston was always up to something lewd, and it seemed as though Tabby were implicating herself in that mode of behavior.

"He can certainly humiliate himself," said Moira. "Begging for liquor. It almost makes him into a figure of fun."

The light touched Tabby's face with the faintest color.

"He is fun though. Like some Silenus who can't get it up for the dryads."

"Get it . . . up?" asked Moira in a little gasp.

Tabby rose and crossed the room to a delicate writing desk on curved spindly legs, a pile of her writings stacked on it neatly. She flourished a poem for Moira's admiration. It had only one verse neatly centered in the page.

THE GAZEHOUND'S LUST
Hommage to G.G.
Poète du Sud Profonde

You howl like a dog
   With longing
To sniff my pink slit
Its dense hair
   like deadly nightshade

Tabby's face held a contented smile. "It's also called 'enchanter's nightshade'. I don't know if readers will catch the unstated *double entendre*."

Moira's lips tightened. "I think it's trashy. And awfully short."

Tabby went to the mantel and deliberately pushed a porcelain bowl with a pastoral scene to the floor to shatter to pieces on the brick hearth.

"You've broken one of my Mummy's favorite things," she accused. "That was very unpleasant of you."

Moira's jaw dropped. "I most certainly did not." All her life she had been blamed for things that were not her fault, and this reminder brought on a near panic attack.

"Yes, you did," Tabby persisted. She edged closer.

Moira leaped to her feet and backed towards the door. This girl was being absolutely vile and weird and not at all nice. But Moira wasn't about to be intimidated. She had put up with too much of this sort of thing at Sweet Briar.

"I really don't think I like you," Moira said. Her hands were trembling despite her anger and she longed to take off in disgraceful flight back to her car.

Tabby's eyes got real wide and round. "I think something bad will happen to you," she said eerily. "Like getting pushed into the abyss."

Outside, a cold rain had begun to fall. And Moira had brought no umbrella.

16

"Sure, I'd like you to slide by with two years too," said Rannie Ralston. "But the folks in the Solicitor's office aren't real sympathetic to my point of view."

"Den we jus' go to cote an' blow up they shit."

"For that you're going to have to come up with ten thousand more."

"Well fuck that shit."

The client made his self-important hoodlum's way out of her office. His gold teeth gleaming and his pants hanging down to show his underwear the way they do. Corn-rowed hair and gang tattoos. Fake ruby rings on four fingers of the left hand. Like something heaved into her office with a dung fork.

She had only clipped him for three grand. Figured it would be an easy plea. Now he was trying to jerk her chain. Maybe she'd get the bondsman to pull his jacket. Get him focused on reality. He'd respond better than her family.

Moira had been somewhere yesterday she couldn't quite explain and totaled the Lincoln. Just wrapped it around a tree and walked away without a scratch on her. No one cared. It was just something for Rannie to worry with. They were preoccupied with Dale and the historic three o'clock dinner.

Historic because the tradition had long died out. Main meal at three p.m. because the summer heat was so bad. Also the servants could clean up and go home to some minimal lives of their own. The men would come home from Broad Street, eat, take a quick nap and go back to work until seven. Air conditioning and the dwindling of the servant class had pretty much killed it.

When Mary Canty announced they would do this for Dale, Rannie protested: "We haven't had three o'clock dinner since I was six years old."

Mary Canty drew herself up. "We will have dinner at three o'clock because that is when we have dinner."

Meaning Dale had best accept that Ralston ways would rule her marriage.

Agreement on anything by Moira and Mary Canty was so rare that they were simply reveling in their hatred of Dale. Mary Canty made herself agreeable to Moira by reminiscing about every marital disaster in the history of Charleston, or at least as far back as her girlhood. Moira made herself useful to Mary Canty by nitpicking every mannerism that Dale had revealed. Their loud and penetrating tones echoed through the house.

Fortune hunter. Social climber. Nonentity. Dresses like a tramp. Probably a slut. Marriage won't last a year. Why oh why couldn't Collier have gotten interested in that nice Gervais girl?

Rannie reminded them that Celeste Gervais had sued Collier for something unmentionable.

Rannie took a nip out of the desk drawer Jim Beam bottle.

Perhaps she'd just sit there at her desk and drink herself insensible. Say she got tied up in court and couldn't make the festive gala. She couldn't permit herself to eat anyhow. She was down five pounds and starting to see it in the way her clothes fit.

What a cat-and-dog family. Moira the drama queen. She would always voice her opinion the second it popped into her head. And just demolish a car and have no memory of it.

Her mother accusing Rannie of practicing law like an act of defiance to Southern womanhood. "You'll never get married now," she moaned. "Not a chance. Men just seize up around you."

The scary thing was it was probably true. Beat them in a game of racket ball and they look like they just had a vasectomy. She made an inventory of the men in her life. Cotesworth "Cotey" Kershaw in high school. That was certainly disgusting. The SAE her freshman year in college. He made her read a paper he had written entitled "Copulation Before Conversation." A real romantic lead-in. Then Rhett. Well, she'd stop right there. What came afterwards was a mediocre mix of neurotics and momma's boys.

What was she supposed to do about male fragility? Nervous dinks. Throwing quick glances around the room as she talked to them. Looking for an escape route. She was a careerist. It was not unknown, even in the South.

Everyone says criminal lawyers just plead their clients guilty and strip them of money. Well, there was that aspect to the business. But it still made her see red when they said it. Because when her back was to the wall, Rannie would DO a damn trial.

She could cross-examine an eyewitness with a spirit of terrifying vengeance. Raise a point of evidence like the wrath of God, and leave assistant solicitors flummoxing. She could distract a jury during the prosecution's closing argument. Dismiss damning evidence with an indulgent smile. Paint a Sistine Chapel fresco of innocence that placed her client among the saints and angels.

And put a dirtbag back on the street. But that was her job. She didn't invent the system.

Collier was so worthless he would make their daddy dance with fury. Knocking up a high school aged Senate page. Confessing to it on the morning Daddy was to start a death penalty case—the Toogoodoo Road Root Medicine Murders.

The shock had been serious. It hit Big Collier like a chimney falling through a rotten roof. He weakly told Rannie he had to go lie down. Staggered down the street. Collapsed. Had to be carried to the house by passers-by.

Rannie was stolid. Ralston & Ralston had taken on the case, and she had to see it through. She stepped up to the plate and did the defense in Daddy's place. Her first jury trial and a man's life hung in the balance. When the "not guilty" verdict came in at midnight five days later, Big Collier was a half hour dead in Roper Hospital. She had never gotten to tell him how well she had done.

And there was that burning hunk of love Rhett MacReady across the street in the window with the masonry sill. Painting. Daubing out a $30,000 pig. With a big piece of twelve million in the bank. While she sat over here filled with longing and an engine on her like a locomotive.

A second nip from the bottle drew her attention to her old birdwatcher binoculars in the back of the drawer. They lay there with her daddy's gun from the Korean War, an army Colt .45 automatic. She had yet to need it, but you never knew when a client would go psycho on you.

Rummity-tum. Little focus adjustment on the binocs. And there was Rhett.

Lawsy what an exhibition of male bonanza.

He turned, looked right at her. The impact zapped her like an electric shock of shame. He saw her spying on him!

He nodded. Gave her a little wave. A little beam of recognition.

That pretty much settled her misery. Satisfied that her life was an absolute pile of dog poop, she closed up the office and headed home for the dreaded encounter with Dale. And what the hell. She'd have something to eat for once. They were having lamb that would be cooked so tender you could cut it with a fork.

■ ■ ■

"This is the Randolph family silver," Mary Canty said coldly. "It has survived earthquake, fire, hurricane and Sherman's marauders. Please treat it with respect."

A sheepish Gaston ceased picking his molar with the fork and set it down on his plate. Yes, and one day he just might sell a sack of it in some upstate flea market. The paraphernalia of their pride melted down in one of those little mobile smelters the thieves carry about in their vans.

Insolent tyrant sitting up there at the head of the table reigning supreme. He gave Mary Canty his winning smile which she could never resist. Her ruthless scowl softened slightly, satisfied that he was playing his proper doormat role.

It was not a happy dinner for the family. Dale's first serious sit-down with the pack of them. And of course she was heartily disapproved of. And then two days before, that pompous twit Collier had gotten carried away in front of his supporters at a rebel flag rally and referred to the NAACP as the National Association for the Advancement of Retarded People.

A collective media chorus had gone up of "Uh-OHHHH. You said a bad thing!"

While he could largely ignore it due to the voting majority of his constituency, the state-wide Republican party was not pleased. Plus, his fiancée Dale seemed not as mired in the past as the Ralstons. She appeared to be raising some valid questions about what she was marrying into.

But all this was an endless source of mirth for our Gaston. Like they say, it's N'awlins when you're busted, but it's Noo Or-leens when you're flush. He had a larger college paycheck coming in, even if Rannie had demanded the newly added two-thirds for her fees. He was just beside himself with joy and laughter.

It had been a plu-perfect dee-light to tell everyone about the Dean's youthful bedwetting—after the charges had been safely dismissed and he had been granted tenure in a totally irregular proceeding that had faculty governance fanatics in an uproar. The dear man could scarcely cross the campus without someone cat-calling at him. "Old pisser-roo" was one of the better ones.

"This is awfully good lamb," Dale ventured.

Mary Canty's cold eyes wandered over Dale, contemptuous even of social pour-parlers.

"You will note," said Moira primly, "that stemware goes to the top right placed in the order of use. The water goblet should be one inch from the point of the dinner knife. A cup and saucer are only brought to the table after the last course."

She gave her tight little smile, being just oh-so-helpful. Moira was simply reveling in talking down to Dale. Letting her know how out of her depth she was in presuming to marry into the august Ralston clan.

And they had put on the dog all right. Cold curried squash soup. Butter beans and okra. Rice. Pickled shrimp. And the ambrosial, cooked-to-death lamb.

Gaston stretched out across the table for the claret. Filled his glass to the brim. Praised its down-home *terroir* quality with that touch of ploughed earth. Wondered aloud if he should fetch another bottle from the larder. Couldn't help but remark it was the rich red of menstrual blood.

"When women live in a house together, do they all have their periods at the same time?" he queried the table at large.

Moira flushed a deep crimson matching the wine.

Rannie barked in laughter.

And the leggy Miss Dale suppressed a grin, appreciative of his efforts to puncture the pomposity of the Ralston clan. God the gal was a hum-dinger. She'd set off car alarms just walking down the street.

Making no attempt to hide his interest, Gaston crinkled

his eyes at her and gave a big wink. No dry intimations from him.

The little sidewinder Moira shot him a reproving look. She always had that wary eye on him. Noting how fast he drained his wine glass, the gravy he had just spilled on his shirt, the way he wiped his sleeve through the mint jelly when he reached for things. She had forced him to read her dreadful poem "Sword of Duty" and it had left him dumbfounded. No vocabulary existed to describe such utter dreck and drivel.

Conversation was strained. They learned that Dale was a Gamecocks fan, had majored in English at Carolina. Mary Canty was from the generation that had at most a year of college—one married an established doctor or lawyer or heir to a business right after the debut. So to her, a Southern woman with an actual college degree was in itself a bit sinister.

There was an uncomfortable pause. Forks clinked.

Collier volunteered that both of Dale's parents were public school teachers. "They say they make so little money, that anything she does would outclass them. So they'll always be proud of her."

The Ralston women glowered at him.

Collier yammered on. "That's why they had no objection to her whacking around the modeling world in New York. Or . . . or getting hitched to an attorney who's starting out."

"Yes, she certainly has a fine eye for the main chance," Mary Canty said.

"You've been starting out for the last seven years," said Rannie, sticking the needle in Collier.

"Well, I *am* a senator," he huffed.

"It's a magician's cloak to conceal your fumbling the card-up-the-sleeve trick."

Collier laughed shrilly. "My sis is a one-girl fan club."

"Well you certainly have a fine cook," said Dale gamely.

"Oh the coloreds," Mary Canty. She rolled her eyes to heaven. Ordinarily around guests she acted like they were slavishly devoted darkies. Relating this and that cute just precious thing they said all mangling the English language Amos 'n Andy style.

"Well I think the gravy is very poor," said Moira. "And I'm convinced they're doing it on purpose."

Dale gave her a look. Opened her mouth to say something, then thought better of it.

"Tell them the story about the boa constrictor," Collier urged.

"It's nothing," Dale murmured.

"Oh please. They'll love it."

"I had to find a boa for a shot. Put an ad in the *Times* offering a hundred a day boa rental. Amazing how many people in New York keep boas in their apartments. Must have gotten forty calls. A vet told me once if an animal will fit through the door, someone will keep it in an apartment."

Collier laughed appreciatively. "Isn't that incredible?"

The Ralston women did not join in the mirth. The dinner continued, following the convention of making things as dreary and miserable for a social interloper as possible.

Moira explained to Dale that the word "coin" on the

reverse side of the Ralston silver meant that it was made just after the American Revolution. The U.S. Mint dictated the amount of silver in it at the time. While it was two percent less than sterling silver, the age and style make it worth far more than American sterling.

When at last the meal was finished, Dale insisted on getting up to join the maid in clearing away. Gaston made a great show of dumping wine down his shirt to give him an excuse to follow her. As he hurried out mumbling about mopping himself up, he heard Mary Canty mention a Yankee neighbor who had bought into the street. Drove a Rolls Royce.

"Well, I think it's a vulgar put-on," said Moira tartly.

The door swung behind. And there was the scrumptious Miss Dale scraping plates in the little butler's pantry between the dining room and the kitchen. She had legs like a Rockette and the raw sex appeal of a Dallas Cowboy cheerleader.

Gaston reached into her work and forked a hunk of lamb fat into his mouth. The drinks he had managed to swill over Moira's strong disapproval had given him that old strung-out impulse of recklessness.

He talked with his mouth full. "Now what is it you do? A model-stroke-actress?"

She gave him a look. Went back to scraping. "I'm a set designer. Pull together props. Figure a theme. The photographers are not but so imaginative."

"I've got a thing for women in the fashion industry," he confided.

"So does Collier," she replied coolly. "That's why he's marrying me."

Gaston worked at that troublesome molar with his finger. His first wife had hit him in the jaw with a frozen t-bone steak, and the dental repairs had never been satisfactory. "Don't misinterpret the ice-age reception. It gets far worse once you've been here a bit." He laughed at his own wit and selected a sugar lump from the tray with the coffee. "God knows they should be grateful for anyone who would take on the project of settling Collier down. Not a candidate for high rank in the Salvation Army that boy. They're all the time bailing him out of this and that scrape. Making good on checks that have bounced. Sweeping skeletons into the closet." He plopped the sugar in his mouth and sucked.

"Okay," said Dale. "I'll bite. Tell me the most deplorable thing he's done."

Gaston transfixed her with his debonair stare and wry grin. The rogue poet who had now written a novel with such a big advance that the publisher would guarantee its success. "Oh, probably that Senate page he knocked up. Technically it was statutory rape, not that anyone pays much attention to it today. But it lends leverage when you lay on the big money demands. The sum in question led directly to Big Collier's heart failure. Mary Canty can give you chapter and verse on that one."

"Yes," Dale agreed. "Collier's a stud. He walks into a room and you can hear the panties drop."

Gaston liked the sound of that. The raffish come-on. This girl knew what was between her legs all right. Just pure-t hedonism. His face took on a look of amiability and that utter desire to be helpful. "He will flaunt his women. Which leaves the open question of whether he's over-compensating."

"Because?"

"Oh surely you've thought of it. All that dressing up in the costumes of the *gay* Southern cavalier." He pointedly stressed the word "gay."

"What complete nonsense," she said—over her shoulder as she left—but in a tone that was quite stifled.

Touché and thrust home, thought Gaston, and he was so pleased with his success that he decided to celebrate with a little nip out of the brandy bottle he knew was in the low cabinet. One led to three, and Gaston returned to the dining room feeling well pleased with himself and the general state of the world. One hand thrust into a jacket pocket, the other swinging carelessly at his side. Situated himself, breathing a bit heavily. Looked about the company. Wondered why he hadn't reached the wine while he was standing up.

Dale put her hand on Collier's arm and spoke directly to him. "Were you wondering what was going on in there? Gaston took time out from poetry to speak frankly about your history of bad behavior. The old Dutch Uncle lecture. From that rabbity-looking grin on his face, I'd venture he either wants to get in my pants himself or he was put up to rupturing our engagement by parties unknown."

Mary Canty's jaw seemed to have fallen out of joint.

Rannie gave a long slow clapping. Bap. Pause. Bap. Pause. Bap. "Thank *you*, Miss Dale," she said in a tone of admiration. "And welcome to the family. I think you'll fit in just fine."

17

Moira had written a line of poetry today and was quite content. "Exuberant colors mark the spot." Rhyming with 'spot' had stumped her, blocking the second line. All she could think of was 'flower pot.' Or 'colleus pot'. But then colleus didn't have exuberant colors. But all the same, the line was a true gem. The effect was ethereal yet strangely compelling.

Though her work was capable of great subtlety, her style would be recognizable to the devoted following which she knew would appear. Unlike her family, they would understand the poet's toil. How she spent her day struggling to convey her most precious thoughts and feelings, bringing the world a brightness and joy it so sadly lacked.

Moira had become accustomed to giving a quick once-over of Gaston's room, pass things under scrutiny to make sure he had been at work during the day and wasn't up to anything she disapproved of.

In accordance with this program she lifted the pillows and the edges of the mattress, the usual places he childishly hid things. Here was his much dog-eared copy of *Catfish Delight*. He did like to go back and re-read his own work.

Folded inside was a pink paper that held a faint smell

of perfume like warm peaches. She held it to the window in the falling sunlight.

THE GAZEHOUND'S LUST

Hommage to G.G.

Poète du Sud Profonde

I catch you gazing on
my handwashed dainties
gossamer strands
    hung to sun dry
my demeurities

You howl like a dog
    With longing
To sniff my pink slit
Its dense hair
    like deadly nightshade

It was two verses long now. She distinctly remembered only one. The disgusting one about the pink slit. And now there was this demeurities part. Demeurities. What a silly, made-up word.

As she stormed downstairs, Moira determined to get things ironed out once and for all. Gaston could straighten up and fly right or he'd just paddle his own canoe off into the sunset.

What she found was like a scene of desolation. Mary Canty passed out snoring, her highball glass fallen at her feet. And Gaston sitting there awake but in a reverie, red with the afterglow of the liquor he had swilled, his forbidden glass on a side table with a marble veined top.

Moira squared her shoulders, thrust the poem in Gaston's face and demanded the meaning of it.

He grunted at her. Actually grunted. Topped up his drink from the open bottle of Jim Beam.

Gaston was brazenly drinking. Even though she had repeatedly forbidden it.

He raised his glass in a toast. "I am drinking to your health. And now I unleash a rebel yell of big time loyalty. Yee-ha."

Moira was bewildered for a moment. "You're making fun of me."

His face was expressionless. He squinted one eye and stared balefully with the other, eyebrow lifted. "I am putting the evil eye on you. A curse I learned from a gypsy crone in Sicily. She gave me the clap, the runs, and kidney stones."

Moira could not control her venom. "You're . . . you're taunting me! Explain the meaning of this!"

Gaston looked down his nose, pretending to study the poem. "Well, the pink slit is . . ."

She snatched it from his hands and tore it to shreds. "Don't you dare use gutter language around me! Or those profane hand gestures you're so fond of. I want to know the exact nature of your relationship with Tabby—God what a ludicrous name—Boone!"

He waved a hand airily. "One more of my 'sweet thang' conquests. Coveys of little comely quail. I poach at night in the darkling wood."

She began to splutter. "I'll put the icing on your cake! I'll fix your little red wagon! You'll go to jail so fast your head will spin like a top!"

"I am looking forward to Death Row with evident pleasure."

Her voice started to break. "You think you're some kind of snake charmer who can get by with anything. I have caught you in poem swapping *flagrante* with that nasty person. You are . . . you're rancid!"

Gaston got down on his hands and knees on the floor, wagging his huge rump from side to side. "I have been a naughty lad. Take me to the woodshed and spank me hard. Put me to bed early and crawl in with me. Make me a mommy's-only boy straight out of Tennessee Williams."

He ran his hand up and down Moira's calf. She shrieked and jumped back.

"Yes, I am the gazehound in question." He began to growl and bark at her like a dog. Lunged forward and nipped her on the ankle. She kicked out at him, and he toppled her over, wrestled her to the carpet.

"Show me your pale gold beaver. You can't keep it shut up like a clam."

"Stop it stop it!" she yelled struggling with his hand that was clawing its way into her underpants.

"Lemon yellow. Parsnip yellow. Yellow of ripening wheat."

He ripped open his sweat-soaked shirt. God his fat belly was covered with a pelt of white hair almost like fur.

"Give me those thrust-forward breasts. Rut with the beef bone up your jeroboam. Or let me religiously suck thy clit like a Jerusalem artichoke."

She fought him frantically, releasing one piercing shriek after the next.

"What in the name of God?" Mary Canty demanded indignantly. She had been awakened from her Delta-level sleep. She loomed over them, hands on her hips.

Gaston rolled off of Moira and lay on his back panting, viewing Mary Canty upside down. "She asked to learn some basic self-defense moves," he lied glibly. "I had mastered a rare variety of judo in the Orient. She got a bit carried away with the role-playing." He paused, studied the imposing Mary Canty with her hands akimbo. Laughed nervously. Tried on his engaging smile. "This doesn't have the makings of an *Entente Cordiale*. You look like you'd cheerfully snip off my willy with pinking-shears."

"You're such a crybaby," Mary Canty told Moira in disgust.

Moira staggered to her feet and fled up the stairs to her room.

She stood feverishly rubbing the portions of herself which Gaston had pawed. Her face was beaded with sweat, and her breath came in heaving gulps. All of her upbringing and position in Charleston society seemed totally inadequate to the situation.

She had come close to being ravished. Just like in a Tabitha Boone novel!

■ ■ ■

"You don't seem to have learned any new tricks," Rannie observed.

"Say what?"

They were sitting in the little interrogation room in the county jail, him in the orange jump suit and shower shoes.

Her potential client was a skinny, no-account white boy with a goatee and thin mustache. No chin. Dragon tattoo on his neck.

"You do a year for purse snatching. Now you get busted for mugging tourists."

"Well, I used a knife," he said defensively. "That moves me up to armed robbery."

Rannie shook her head in disgust. "You cruise around, hop out of your truck and hold a knife to them. Then drive off. But they get your license plate number."

"Yeah you know how it is. One minute you feel you got things really rolling, the next you're down on the asphalt with your hands cuffed behind your back."

"You're not moving up real fast in a life of crime."

"Well, career-wise, I was thinking of doing something in the area of sticking up gas stations with those snack areas in them. My old dad always said I'd never handle the pressure of using a gun. But from what I seen, I think I'd like that line of work."

"Well, you tell old dad to come up with ten thousand dollars, and I'll see about representing you."

"Now let's not get carried away with this here fee. I plan on being back on the street. You'll be getting return bid'ness if I like your service."

Rannie looked at her watch, stood up. "You got the fee? Ten big ones."

"You don't think much of me do you? Well, I'll have you know folks in here appreciate my talent."

"Talent?"

"I jail good."

"That'll be useful where you're going."

Rannie drove back to her office in a cold wind that shook her rental Buick she was driving since Moira demolished the Lincoln. She really wanted that Land Rover. A deep forest green. Spare tire bolted down on the hood. Or bonnet as the Brits called it. It whispered to her in her dreams.

Her mother had been shopping for wedding clothes, bought out the store at Elza's. The bill brought with it the usual collateral damage of frayed finances, stress and bickering at the dinner table. Mary Canty arguing that luxuries were really necessities.

Saying bills were nothing that couldn't be cured with a check book.

She took the interstate into the cross-town past the string of garish fast-food places. Ring billed gulls flocking in the McDonald's parking lot squawking and fighting over discarded fries.

Down Lockwood past the yacht basin with its forest of masts. Two crank-heads had been arrested there running a floating methamphetamine lab. She had one for a client. Brewing their stew with ammonia and ether. With the waves rocking the boat, the whole thing so unstable they could have blown themselves sky high. Now an environmental clean-up crew was in there with the boat yellow taped off.

Rannie drove by Rhett's old house on Tradd Street. A 1773 classic single house—one story wide and placed to catch the breeze. Little wooden historical plaque beside the door telling its history. It was owned by Yankees now. Rannie remembered when the widowed mother had sold it.

Their daddies had been partners from when she was born. But Rhett was always the older boy doing older boy things. He had kept a rescued egret in his back yard. The thing sure liked to go shrimping and crabbing with him. Perch on the bow of a John boat and watch him cast a seine net.

She stopped the car and gazed down the long piazzas at the carriage house out back where they had done the infamous portrait. And he had reduced her to helpless moans. A coming-of-age summer idyll.

She drove on filled with nostalgic longing. A lone raindrop spattered her windshield, signaling the coming storm.

In her office, the violent gale rattled the windows while the gloom of nightfall crept in. Rannie flopped down feeling the seizure of money anxiety. The strain had taken its toll. Looking across the street, she first thought Rhett's office was empty, but then saw him moving about. No more binocular spying for her. She'd just sit and succumb to the soothing influence of the office bottle of Jim Beam.

She looked miserably at the files and law books stacked on her desk. The only reading Rannie wanted to do was a bodice-ripper where the girl gets raped in Chapter One by the dark stranger she later learns to love. Kind of an outreach program for a horny girl. Or one of those Harlequin romances where a stud like Rhett would bicker with her at first and then come to adore her spunk and grit as she learned to handle the copra schooner or the rubber plantation or whatever. And put an iron in her fire.

Then she impulsively did the act of bravado. She'd invite Rhett for a drink. Do the bold thing her mother always deplored and swore got a girl nothing but spinsterhood.

Rannie wouldn't have done it without that first drink inside her, but she figured at least it didn't require three. As she ran across Broad Street in the rain, all her thoughts were centered on her mission.

Battered in spirit, but unshaken in courage, the lone girl attorney rides in. It was a modern age, and she would be the prime mover in kick-starting this romance.

And lo and behold it paid off. Rhett greeted her with a just-the-girl-I-want-to-see effusion.

"I'm hunting wild pig on the weekend. Get some photos to work from. Going out with some pro hog hunters from down in Red Top. Right rough ol' boys. But nobody you can't manage."

Rannie wanted to sing her 'yes' like an Aria. The air was filled with heavenly sweetness and the sound of celestial chords.

She had found the man she had been waiting for. A man to stir her blood. A man who could kill wild pigs and paint them and sell them for $30,000 and win multi-million dollar tax cases taking a third and still have the energy to bang her bow-legged.

Just as Rannie was preparing to grab Rhett's head and mash her mouth against his, a new dimension to the scene was added. Tabby Boone walked in, a wan smile on her bloodless white face.

Rhett made introductions.

"We've met," Rannie said flatly.

Examining Rannie, Tabby's face held a mask like quality, but when she turned it on Rhett, it conveyed a current of raw sexual suggestion.

Rannie thought goo-goo eyes little strumpet. I live in a world of lying insincerity, but I would sincerely like to put your little noggin straight through the wall.

To make matters worse, Tabby and Rhett seemed to have some silent understanding. Rhett cleared his throat uncomfortably.

"We need to prep for the deposition. Afraid I've never read *Flames of the Carolinas*. Tabitha is going to give me a tutorial on it."

"I'm sure it'll be a lulu," Rannie said, trying to curb her fury.

Tabby stood there, arms crossed in a little non-verbal order to Rannie; just get the hell out and go play with your law books.

As she re-crossed the street, the woebegone Rannie felt like she was on a boat slowly drifting away from diminishing figures on the shore. Her clothes fitted too tight and her shoes pinched.

Back in her office, she kept the lights off, barking her shin on the edge of the desk and knocking over the trashcan. As the sunset was fading into deep purple, she took the binoculars and crouched at the bottom edge of her window.

Tabby had both hands feathering through Rhett's hair as she kissed him passionately. Just devouring his face like a red-lipped conflagration. She had . . . yes, she had one foot off the floor.

Rannie was transfixed.

The predatory little weasel. Why couldn't she stay in her socio-sexual age grouping? Leading Rhett down the oh-poor-little-sensitive-me lovers' lane.

Without removing Tabby's hands, Rhett reached behind him and pulled the blinds.

"You sorrier-than-white-trash scum-bag!" Rannie yelled in the darkness. Although under the circumstances that seemed too mild an epithet. Rhett MacReady was a crude, ignorant, insensitive, treacherous moron. Two-bit, two-timing, two-faced, half-assed . . .

She slammed the door and stalked out for home. Combative instincts came to the fore. She set her teeth. Rhett MacReady with his damned big-time tax appeals. By God she'd show him some lawyering that would put him flat on his patootie. She'd have Gaston primed and rehearsed for that deposition. Man with a mouth on him like his, he'd talk circles around them. She was going to win this case if she had to bill the whole hundred thousand to do it.

WHERE ARE THE OTHER TWO HUNDRED??

18

Rannie had gone over the rules of the deposition until Gaston thought he would scream. She said they're entitled to ask any question even vaguely relevant. She could object only to the form of the question. Told him to answer succinctly, don't ramble and for God's sake don't tell your usual whoppers. At least pretend you're an adult.

Rannnie led him down Broad Street, nagging him and putting him in a foul temper. It was all a blur. He gestured aimlessly in the air and recited:

"Oh horse reiver Pete
Quivered and quailed
As they dragged his sorry ass
To the gallows."

The pompous offices of Dombey, Trouche & Makepeace on a brass plaque. A room with a long mahogany table, two tall windows and shelves of law books. Court reporter setting up her little tripod typing machine.

The lawyer for Tabby, Rhett somebody. Rannie for him. Lawyer for Gaston's publisher Farrar, Straus & Giroux, another one for their insurance company. That pair were there to hang the whole thing around his neck, absolve the publisher of liability. They regarded him critically. He could feel bad vibes. False smiles. Yellow power ties. Yellow legal pads. Yellow vipers every one.

Gaston had permitted himself the luxury of a half bottle of Glenlivet before coming down. A good single malt to get the fine words trilling off his tongue.

What? He had been asked his name by that Rhett person. Gaston placed a hand over his heart. Looked enquiringly at the reporter who nodded.

"Oh yes. I'm on. Name? Gaston Bayard Garnett, man of parts. Peripatetic poet. Southerner by birth and by the grace of God."

"Are you under the influence of drugs or alcohol or anything that would prevent you from answering these questions accurately?"

He laughed heartily. "I am most certainly under the influence of alcohol. Have half a bag on you might say. Which is the way I teach my students, and the way I faced daily dinner with my obnoxious wife Claitey, and the way I wrote that abominable novel. Drunkenness is my preferred milieu."

Rannie sighed deeply. "You'll never catch him sober," she said. "You may as well go forward."

All that balderdash out of Rannie about not embellishing on his personal history. He kept them spellbound for over an hour describing his Dickensian childhood, his education at Oxford and the Sorbonne, and his multiple marriages to sexual contortionists. Along the way, he touched on his war record, his career as a drag racer and the stint in prison for moonshine running.

Finally Rannie jerked him out in the hall. Belligerently and in forceful language explained to him:

(a) all these "lies" as she called them would be used to impeach him at trial, and
(b) none of the lawyers particularly cared how long he rambled.

Other than Rhett, they were all billing by the hour. If it wasn't this, they'd be working elsewhere. Ergo, lawyers for insurance companies have been known to drag out depositions for days under the guise of being thorough.

"Time has no meaning to them," she snarled. "And they aren't beguiled by your bull!"

Gaston took a mild restorative from his pigskin covered hip flask, a gift, he always claimed, of NASCAR racing legend Richard "The King" Petty. "The irrigated landscape of the mind is my past. They must see the outermost possibilities of my imagination. Only then can they grasp the sheer inanity of Claitey's novels, and that her puerile language may be used by one of my talent without it being a theft."

Rannie actually rammed Gaston's huge bulk up against the wall. God she had an arm on her like a baseball pitcher.

"Don't you dare go in there and admit you lifted the language. 'Moon like a wheel of white cheese.' 'Moon like a ghost ship scudding on a frozen sea.' Anyone could have pulled those images out of his own head."

Gaston straightened his tie. Whack-a-doodle-doo he'd like to bounce on those pneumatic tits like an inflatable sex doll. He strode back in and seated himself with the dignity of a distinguished man of letters.

"Despite my attorney counseling me to lie through my teeth, I am prepared to continue with the whole truth and nothing but."

Rannie closed her eyes. Moved her jaw from side to side.

Rhett went forward. "You are the author of numerous volumes of poetry: *Good Old Boy Ramblings, Catfish Delight, Bad Drunk in Natchez* and *Whiskey Hoedown.* Correct?"

"Author? I am the explorer in back-country roads. I am the seeker after shimmering mirages on the two-lane blacktop highway of life. Writing poetry is a going forward not backwards process. You leave behind the empty and shuttered mansions of your past among worn out cotton fields and seek the Beale Street Blues on a Saturday night."

The lawyers seemed to be examining the statement for logic. Well Gaston knew there was none. How does one explain the creative act? An escape from the dreaded hinterland of suburbia? A search for perfumed poontang that's always denied by real life women?

Rhett asked, "You are familiar with *Flames of the Carolinas*?" He held up a paperback novel. The cover had a muscular Southern planter stripped to the waist and brandishing a whip. A mulatto girl clung to his leg while a white girl looked over her shoulder at him in a sultry way. Behind them all, sat a Tara type mansion with flames licking out the windows.

"Yes, it's some of Claitey's tripe. Writing as Tabitha Boone, hothouse plant of the female novelist set. The woman needed to be raped by a tribe of pygmies. She couldn't take much length, but the abundance of it might have actually given her an ecstatic vision."

Eyes swiveled. The lawyers for Farrar, Straus and their insurance company seemed taken aback.

Rhett held up another book. "And you are the author of *Carolina Flame-Out*?"

Gaston leaned across the table confidentially. "Why don't you just cut to the chase? Virtually every sentence in that book is lifted from Claitey's so-called novel. Where there was a horse, I substituted a '56 Chevy or a hot-rod Lincoln. A Greek revival plantation house became a double-wide trailer. I called a dick a dick when she would have said 'his throbbing manhood.' Her 'blossoming rose' I properly interpreted as a wet pussy."

The Farrar, Straus and insurance lawyers huddled mumbling in incredulity. There was no way Gaston could be risked on the witness stand. Plus he had admitted his guilt. Summary Judgement. The only thing to determine was damages.

"You don't seem to think much of your wife's writing," said Rhett carefully.

Gaston began in an almost caressing voice. "No. And I thought of her as little as possible." He looked to the ceiling gathering his thoughts. Spoke to the ceiling. "To know true love while nestling one's nose in twat hair. Such are the fair dreams of youth . . ."

Brought his eyes down to lay a steely glare on Rhett. ". . . that run smack into the reality of women who lie beneath one's efforts like inanimate objects. Headaches. Fatigue. PMS bloat, cramp and whine. So one substitutes for them a figment of imagination. A lost South of Burma

Shave signs, Bull Durham on the barns and See Rock City. A tale of moonshine runnin' good ol' boys who take you on the cross-country jaunt of a lifetime."

His face had become shiny with tears. His voice rose. "And one strives mightily in a world of booby-traps, groaning like Atlas holding up the heavens, each day kicked in the balls by the jackboot of Fate!"

WHAM came both ham-like fists down on the table, making the Parker pens jump.

The Farrar, Straus pair edged their chairs back.

"And after years of anathemas from the stillborn ghouls of the English department and mockery from arrogant little student swine . . . one fine day a large contract comes in the mail and a promise of three hundred thousand dollars. 'Is this original work?' they ask. Oh, Claitey contributed her jot and tittle. No problem, they reply. You're married after all. Can't steal from one's distaff side. Oh yes, they knew all about it although they'll deny it now."

Big finger thrusting at the cringing pair as he swung round in fury.

"Because now Tabby Boone and her lawyer have gathered like carrion crows to pick the eyes of the dead."

WHAM the fists landed.

"You vultures! You jackals!" he bellowed in a torrent of abuse.

And then Gaston simply went berserk. He reared up, and in a frightening display of strength, flipped the long table on its end and then slashing down through the window in an explosion of wood and glass. His jacket and shirt split all down the back as he flexed and lifted again, ramming it through the shattered glass and sending it hurling down to crash onto a parked car on the street.

Trial lawyers are not ordinarily men of physical courage. They wound with words. They trap helpless schnooks in the toils of judicial procedure. Confronted by real violence they quail. The lawyer for the Farrar, Straus & Giroux insurance company was close to weeping in his terror and despair. Never in his experience had he seen a defendant so utterly throw away his case.

"I'm sure we can arrive at a settlement," he whined pathetically. Pin-points of sweat had popped out on his forehead.

"It'll be a record one," chortled Rhett making no attempt to mask his delight.

Rannie pulled her head back inside the window from looking at the hub-bub down on Broad Street. She told Gaston: "I gotta confess to being a learner in the law of copyright. But I know for a fact this won't help your murder case worth a tootle."

■ ■ ■

Leaving Mary Canty in mid-rant over Collier's coming wedding, Moira walked down Broad Street in the late day gloom seeking Gaston Garnett who she believed she'd heard was doing something with Rannie. Which must mean something silly and pointless.

Moira had so many things on her mind that she was all a-tizzy. She would just have to take Dale in hand if the poor girl expected to make any headway at all in Charleston. So much for her to learn. Jezebel sauce goes perfectly with pork, beef or venison. And the American Beautyberry with its rich magenta berries can just add a perfect touch of color to a faded winter garden. And many annuals like geraniums should be brought indoors for the cold weather.

Moira was so absorbed in her thoughts that she failed to hear the huge crash of a table coming down from the offices of Dombey, Trouche & Makepeace on Broad Street. At the moment, walking intently towards the People's Building, she was filled with a sense of the rightness of things as she was handling them. When the Citadel library director complained of what she termed Moira's "persistent calling" to check on arrangements, Moira had replied with a new edge of authority to her voice.

The *Post & Courier* had obliged her to go all the way to the top before they would consent to cover the reading. They seemed to feel nothing went on at the Citadel except crude violence, and she had had to put them straight on that. Well they'd learn soon enough. Once her talent was recognized, all those nondescript little people who got in the way of great things would just have to—well—eat their crows.

All the hostility she had endured from those Sweet Briar girls who rode show horses and reveled in dressage was far behind her. Her thoughts spiraled down the Yellow Brick Road of fame and applause. Her mood was breathless and excited with the possibilities of life. She was a leaf swept up and whirled about by the Wind of Destiny.

Goodness, that would make a good title.

In the lobby of the People's Building she punched the elevator button with particular vigor.

She needed to see Gaston because she had sorted out

some important matters and had to tell him. While pondering the writer's role in society, she had begun to question whether Gaston's work really dealt with matters of significance. And then there was the need of rewriting. His verse held promise, but a little touching up would not hurt. All those vulgar words he used, for example. They should be struck out in the interest of returning to the values of a more civilized time. With her blue pencil they would reject trashy modern ways and manners.

Gaston was just going to have to sit up like he had good sense and submit to her editing. Perhaps—and as the thought struck, it seemed very sound—he should stick with writing novels and leave the poetry to her. If he wouldn't see it her way she'd just stamp her foot or go into a long fainting fit. And if he cut up nasty about her plan . . . well, he'd get plenty of gross material back in that filthy jail.

Moira opened the door with the frosted glass and the Ralston & Ralston lettering. The room was lit only by the pale glow of a computer screen. Moira's feet tangled in articles of clothing which for no good reason had been left on the floor.

A hunched figure was opening computer files, searching for something. Bare milky white back with faint ladder of spine. She looked up. Stretched like a cat. Tabby Boone in the altogether.

Her flesh was quite pale in the failing light. Her lips seemed wet as though smeared with cherry jam. Violet shadows beneath huge languorous eyes. The long dark hair. Breasts like small apples. She seemed to grow in ethereal beauty under the sudden orange lighting of the last gasp of the sun over the rooftops of Broad Street.

Moira stood there endeavoring to produce articulate sounds.

Tabby had no difficulty achieving speech. "I'm feeling rather radiant. It was utterly satisfying."

By that, she indicated that Moira had arrived post and not pre-revelry. And that she—Tabby—was completely unfazed at being caught in the buff. That smile of contentment. Like she had awakened from a long and delicious sleep.

From Collier's office floated a voice of good ol' boy jubilation. "Woo-eee, Miss Tabby. Yeh-boy. Bait a trap with pussy and I'll fall in it evah time."

Pause. Double-take. Face set in horror. Both hands clapped over his privates.

"Moira!"

"Holy Moses!" Moira gasped numbly.

"Get out of here!" he gulped without authority.

Moira felt as though some sort of waking nightmare had her by the throat. And with the ghastly spectacle came a new sense of the harsh reality of life.

She leaned against the wall and shut her eyes. She was beginning to tremble all over. She hadn't seen her brother naked since . . . since . . . well, she had NEVER seen him naked! Or any man for that matter.

19

Rannie Ralston all decked out in red wool shirt, leather chaps and work gloves was telling the hog hunters, "So this dirtbag tells the judge he's in a 'growing process' and trying to 'handle responsibility better.' He wanted anger management counseling. And then—get this—he hoped to go to college and major in criminal justice."

They laughed. Asked what had he done?

"Not much. Beat a woman with a sock full of fishing weights, then bit her on the arm."

Another round of laughs. Rannie had always preferred mixing with men.

For a moment the clouds broke and sunlight glided across the silent woods and then was gone again. The dogs ran back and forth, heads to the ground, an eager pack of ferocious, rangy mongrels. Pit bull flat heads. Spotted coats like hyenas.

Your feral hogs are a true nuisance, breeding multiple litters, tearing up the forest rooting everywhere. Invading suburbia. So most folks are real pleased to be able to turn loose some pro hunters who will go anywhere anytime to "hoag hunt."

Rannie and Rhett had an unspoken truce. She wasn't

going to say a word about seeing him spit-swapping with Tabby, and he wasn't gloating over what would be an obvious victory over Farrar, Straus. Today they were out to raise merry hell with a shit-kicker band of good ol' boys who eat deep-fried everything. All were dressed in khaki overalls and steel-toed work boots. Lariats hanging from Western saddles. Horses stamping their feet.

Fortitude, she thought. Blood and guts. Carnivorous heroes in a world of salad-eaters. Chest-thumpers in a nation of mall rats.

A couple of them wore pistols. Rannie had brought her .45 but left it in the Land Rover glove box. Yes, she had lashed out and bought the deep green gleaming beauty with the brush guards and the spare tire on the hood. It was part of her new persona of outdoor girl. Side-kick and future wife of a major wildlife painter. And Rhett had seemed impressed as all get-out when she picked him up.

They mounted up, the hounds were cast, and then they were off wending among the trees.

A swish of dead leaves. Landscape of bare trees. With a flash of total insight, Rannie suddenly knew herself. The Amazon Queen who could hold her own in the world of men. Finding beauty in the brutality of a slam-bang jury trial. Skill, poise and the heady joy of running down wild animals. And in her button popping confidence she was a hard-core fan of male resplendence.

She would be the bride and consort of Rhett MacReady. Look at him just sitting casually on his horse doing irremediable damage to her heart. High price camera hanging across his chest. Alpha-male masculinity coming out of him in a slow ooze that she would have liked to lap like a thirsty bitch dog. No thinking woman—hell, no woman with an ounce of libido could deny he was an anointed stud bull.

Suddenly the dogs were up and running on a scent, yowling and barking as the riders whooped after in vehement joy. Rattling down meandering trails. Ker-splashing through standing water. Trees flashing by. Chasing down that vicious calamity on split hooves.

Reins shortened, Rannie posted in the saddle, leaning over the horse's mane. Thorns ripping at her wool shirt, overhanging branch lashing her face and whipping away her cap. She pulled in front of them all without the slightest fear.

Down in a muddy palmetto slough the dogs had the hog held snarling, jaws clamped on his legs and ears. Rannie leaped off her horse, about as exuberant as you could get, shoved in among the dogs and grabbed his two rear legs to flop him over on his side.

The men were pitching in now. Hog-tied his feet with the handcuffs they used. Wrapped his savage jaws together with twine. Hog squealing and dogs barking. Dragging the dogs off him.

Rannie let out a long breath. "It's your real convivial camaraderie," she grinned, wiping mud off her face.

All the men congratulating her on her guts. Being just fall-down amazed she had dove in and body slammed a three hundred pounder. The pig stench took on an ambrosial air.

Rhett came up and she felt a sudden fear she was a sweat-hog. Calamity Jane in a head-on collision with a natural disaster. And he was giving her that crooked smile.

Looking trim, worked-out, totally relaxed. But he took up his camera and snapped her picture with the captive hog as the men heaved it up in front of her saddle for her to ride it back to the trailer on the dirt road.

Gusto, she thought. Audacity. Vitality. Manifest authority. And afterwards the smile of repose. A pregnant pause. God what a thought. Rannie Ralston waddling around carrying a little Rhett in her womb. Conceived when her mouth was wide in groaning rapture.

And so it went for seven hours of riding and endorphin euphoria. Six pigs and a dozen piglets all caged up in the trailer to be taken to a farm and fattened for the butchering. A day of furtive glances with Rhett. Physiology, she thought. Maleness.

Rhett said he had to break it off before the last drive, and they put their horses into a trailer while the good ol' boys left in a profusion of so-longs and y'all come out again sometime.

As they got into the Land Rover she breathed in the savory odor of Rhett sweat. Virile. A menace to any girl's chastity.

She didn't start the engine. Just sat there thinking deep biological need. Hard-wired lust. All alone in the woods. Putting herself at serious risk. She went feverish. Her half-lidded eyes said I am your vessel of longing.

"Your boy Gaston was a real treat yesterday."

She flipped her hair. "No comment. Other than he's a malevolent stinker who killed his wife. But the cops can't prove it. So he'll walk if I can get him to clam up and not convict himself."

"He's right entertaining when he gets up a head of steam."

"He'll talk the hind leg off a billy goat, but it has no connection with the truth."

"He's almost a type you find on college faculties. The fake gonzo outlaw. Represents a raffish world the kids can explore with no real possibility of danger."

She was thinking, God bless it, shut up and kiss me.

But Rhett kept talking. "So you doing okay with your career? Statistically or whatever?"

She shrugged. "It started out with your basic searing scrutiny from the bar. I've got a short fuse. People whispered I was erratic. Now it's settled down. I get some grudging respect."

He laughed. "Ever think about moving out of your family house?"

Was that some kind of come-on? She rapped a knuckle on the dashboard. "Life with that crew of weasels is sho' 'nuff a disillusioning experience. Mother plays sleight-of-hand tricks with credit cards. Eventually she'll have me on the street corner with a cardboard sign that says 'Will litigate for food'. Moira has never believed you have to live in the present. Collier's got a wastrel gene in him. Every day I just want to give them a big family hug."

"Family's a bitch," he agreed. "The old man died with the offshore bank account numbers in his head. I've been scuffling ever since. Some kids have a parent die of cancer, want to grow up and be doctors. My daddy imbued me with a big interest in tax evasion."

Rannie said, "When we were teenagers I figured adult

life would be kind of a wild, sweeping freedom with a broad sense of mission."

She rested her gloved hand half way across the seat towards him. A little subtle semaphore.

Rhett said, "You're not for the tassel loafer kind of guy. Lofty snoots. All those big firm lawyers strutting with their tailored suits and air of manic energy. They need the hostess and career booster kind of wife."

She put on a smile she figured was a mite wicked. Thinking how about some sexually assertive moves. God, wife. He actually said the word.

He said, "What it is, you're fetching."

"What?"

"That's a little antique a label I guess. Maybe you're a paean to something."

He tugged a piece of her shirttail out of her pants and ran his bare hand up under it, kind of posing the question. His tone shifted to a lower octave. "Your summer-girl freckles used to drive me nuts."

What she was remembering was how he had told her her hair was like a blaze of ecstasy.

His hand was cupping her big breast, mouth inches from hers. He slid his hand out of her shirt and down to her crotch, laying it lightly on what was central to the entire enterprise.

She said, "You sure took your time that summer. But once you got going, you were certainly relentless."

"You liked it?"

"I think I kind of conveyed the idea."

That was preamble enough because he was kissing her now. She felt the inner throbbing of need coming all over her. He slid his hand into her jeans.

This was it, she thought. The end of the long and feverish quest for man. Whups, there went the snap on her jeans. Zipper coming down. Nice problem solving style.

She closed her eyes as he shoved her jeans down over her round hips. Validation. She was woman. And she would show him some steam heat he wouldn't forget.

Frantic yowling of the dog pack coming towards them at a ferocious clip.

She opened the door to see what was . . . and a huge boar leaped in! Big ivory tusks flashing right at her face. Her mind processed it in quick bits like snapshots.

She grabbed an ear in each hand and wrenched the vicious head to one side just as his three hundred pound bulk landed smack on her. And then came the dogs in a hell-broth tumult.

She wrestled with the thing in a kind of wild-ass havoc. Insane eyes, froth flying from his mouth. Vicious hooves and tusks. The stench. Dogs writhing all over her head and body.

Finally Rhett seized an ear and slashed its throat with a k-bar knife. Blood spewing everywhere. Hog thrashing and squealing a death peal.

The world was back into a strange clarity. Her clothes were ripped. Body a mess of black-and-blue contusions from the hooves kicking her. Face sticky with the steaming blood.

Dogs still howling and barking to beat the band and ripping at the beast.

Rhett was biting off a grin like he was having the last laugh about something.

Rannie flung a dog out of the car. She felt like she had fallen down a chute into a slop bucket. She was pissed at fate and furious with the stinking pig and she wanted to kick Rhett MacReady in the shins.

She spat dirt and fur and used a lot of salty language. He looked at her unfazed. "You look like you got stirred up in a tornado with a bunch of farm animals, li'l dahlin'."

He wiped the blood from her face with his hands. And leaned over the now thoroughly dead hog and kissed her. And God-almighty it made her intoxicated. She'd probably break out in a rash from all the testosterone leaking out of him.

He had called her 'little'. He was big enough to make her feel small and shy and vulnerable like some red-haired Pre-Raphaelite maiden. Or a Botticelli sylph.

"You don't have any trouble with your sexual identity," she breathed.

"I can do macho," he said.

Yeee-haaas! split the air. And there was that gang of leering rednecks leaning on their saddle pommels. Big ol' mule-eatin'-briars grins on their faces.

And her pants were down around her ankles.

20

It was on the day after Rannie went hog hunting with Rhett that Moira got creative about Collier's wedding plans, ultimately convulsing the house from top to bottom, dividing them into armed camps and very nearly wrecking the nuptials with her "good" intentions.

Outside, the temperature was rising faintly under the influence of a weak morning sun. Moira ran her fingertips over the window swags of Collier's bedroom. "I trust you have recovered from your excesses," she sniffed.

"You haven't the faintest idea what you saw," Collier said defiantly. He was dressed for work. Returning to the office like to the scene of a crime.

Moira smiled spitefully. "You think I am so naive. You were out on a spree. Or whatever you call it. Sowing wild oats."

Collier had been drinking in his room until late in the night. Moths had drowned in the dregs of his whiskey glass. He was listless and seemed to be suffering a pounding headache. His hands quivered.

"I'm not feeling well," he confessed. "Why don't you go play with your doll house?"

"It's post-Tabitha remorse. And don't imagine that you

can banish me." She strolled about the big high room papered in scenes of colonial Virginia. Lightly touched his cabinet painted with birds and rococo fruit.

"I'm going to read poetry at your wedding. Following the success of the Citadel reading, it should really bring it all together."

"No, you're not."

"Yes, I am." Pause. "And you know why."

"Do you imagine you're going to bully me?" he said indignantly. "I am a state senator."

"I'll teh-ell-l-l," she said in the familiar kindergarten sing-song.

He straightened his tie, somewhat shaken but still hanging in gamely. "Dale won't believe a word you say. She knows you and Mums spend glorious hours bitching about her."

"I'll tell Mummy."

"You know Mums will side with me. I'm the man of the family. She hates Dale anyway. So what difference does any of this make?"

Moira conceded this grudgingly. "What's wrong with me reading a poem?" she pouted. "Lots of people have special vows, and it's just going to be a big old Methodist mess anyhow."

Collier looked at his watch. "Because your poems are abominable."

Moira's head snapped like he had slapped her. The change in her was both sudden and phenomenal. She was absolutely snarling. "I'll tell Rannie that Tabitha was plundering her computer files. In fact I'm so furious and put out about your behavior that I'm thinking of writing Rannie a big long letter so you can sit around and dread its arrival."

Collier seemed to be turning a faint shade of green.

"Everyone thinks Southern girls spend their time polishing silver," she boasted. "Well, I have a mission here on this fair earth. And I intend to carry it out."

Collier collapsed into a chair. He stared at her like he was facing a one-woman lynch mob. The sweat from his armpits was visible.

Moira paused before a painting framed with tarnished gold leaf. The house had its share of Confederate portraits. This was Major Chadwick Rantowles Ralston who fell off his horse at Five Forks and got dragged to death. Up until Collier was rejected by the navy, the Ralstons had always been a big military family.

Chadwick here in martial resplendence was handsome, valiant with far-seeing blue eyes. Double-breasted gray tunic with yellow cavalry facings and yellow neckerchief. Jaunty *képi*. Cavalier's boots over his knees. Just standing admiring it filled Moira with a luminous beauty. It was so different from Gaston in his permanent state of potbelly and disarray.

And then Moira had an idea.

"I think," she began tentatively, "that your wedding should have a theme."

"A what?"

"Well, if they're going to ruin it by being Methodists in Irmo, we need to enhance things a bit. Put a stamp on it that will live in infamy. I mean in memory. It's developing in my mind, but I'll tell you when I've got it all straight."

Moira left smiling. Oh Collier would huff and puff with disapproval and probably run to Mummy. He always was such a crybaby. But she held the trump card.

Their mother would be vastly relieved as well. She was so loud about how worry and fret was creasing her face with anxieties and she really had to see a plastic surgeon about an eye tuck. Mary Canty had always held such iron control of family matters. She could go off and try to preserve her fading beauty while Moira ran things efficiently and with the utmost creativity. It was time for the child to become the parent.

On the verge of panic, Collier chased after her into the hall. "What kind of theme for God's sake?"

"No hints now. But you'll like it," she said reassuringly.

■ ■ ■

"What I remember most about Ashley Hall," said Rannie, "was an undefeated volleyball season senior year and then winning the state championship."

From up on the stage, she looked out over the sea of faces. Ashley Hall. Where Girls are Champions. It was the slogan on their purple and white bumper sticker. The all-girls private school in an old mansion on Rutledge Avenue.

Rannie was the third featured speaker in the Women in Leadership program. Before her, a surgeon and then a cute little TV news gal who told a cute little story about capturing a runaway kangaroo. The auditorium was rows of very upscale girls whose parents could afford the tuition for three and four kids at a time.

Rannie hadn't just done her share of rebelling. She

had been nothing but trouble at Ashley Hall. Smoking and drinking and sneaking off campus. And that little nastiness over the BMW tires that the Headmistress had alluded to in the introduction. The faculty had been only too happy to see her graduate. But with the passage of time and the possibility of alumni gifts, she was brought back transformed into a model product.

"I'm reminded of volleyball daily," she said, "because I developed big thighs from five years of digging balls." Pause. "And I fight cellulite daily."

Laughter.

"And I learned how to put on a game face. Just look absolutely sullen and threatening. Which is a big help when you're in the criminal lawyer business. You're on your own. Every case a Lone Ranger job.

"What it is, you get a client who's busted through a road block, run down a sheriff's deputy, smacked over mail boxes, side-swiped parked cars. You have to plead him guilty to assault and battery with intent to kill, felony driving under the influence. He'll get at best twenty years suspended to fifteen. Have his burglary sentence probation revoked. Maybe get that to run concurrent. And you've got to make him see the plea as a good thing.

"Well, you can't be all chirpy, perky sparkly. And sincere empathy doesn't cut it either. Because this animal thinks he should get community service. Maybe even an apology from the cops for how rough they were jamming him into the squad car.

"He'll swear he never put a foot wrong in his life. Want to revisit the burglary conviction because he was framed on that one. Give you a big lecture on his civil rights.

"So you've got to give him the look." And she did it. Giving the room the dead pan glare like you'd see in a prison yard. The zombie eyes that put chills in the opposition back court when she got up to serve for the Ashley Hall panthers. And could shut up a hardened sociopath in mid rant.

"Then you kind of sigh and get a tired sound to your voice. Like you've had enough idiots for one day. Tell him, look, Bozo. Your clown act is going behind bars. You can take the twenty or you can shuck and jive around and try for thirty."

She paused. "Do the look right, and he'll take the twenty and feel grateful."

She went on to talk about college and law school. Reminisce about Field Day, Junior Kidnap, the Latin Club slave auction, the senior lawn, all the old traditions that were still alive and linked her to the girls.

She knew most of them were spoiled doctors' daughters planning a future of car-pooling and garden clubbing. But out there somewhere was a scrappy little girl who felt no attraction to Junior League fashion shows. And Rannie was talking to her.

She said, "In college I was told by a psychology professor that I was a classic Artemis archetype. The Amazon. The woman warrior. Combative. Competitive. Which is an interesting insight and probably true. He had a Ph.D. in that kind of thing. But I don't think about it a lot. I don't worry about what makes me tick. What I do daily is handle dirtbags who rob a Captain D's Seafood up on Rivers Avenue; put the whole staff in the freezer."

Afterwards, she greeted her old teachers, the

Headmistress, her volleyball coach. Laughed about the time she told the English teacher Holden Caulfield was a whiny loser in a dumb red cap who wasn't worth reading about.

The mob flowed out onto the green lawn with the live oak trees and the great mansion that had been built by George Trenholm, blockade runner, Treasurer of the Confederacy and model for Rhett Butler in *Gone with the Wind*.

Tea, little sandwiches, and cookies were the next stage, but that had never been Rannie's thing. She slipped away past the "shell house"—the gazebo with big conch shells embedded in the stucco that by privilege belonged to the seniors. Remembering how she used to lounge around in there between class with the two Katies and Regan and Millie and Carson gossiping about boys.

Moira had gone here. Their mother. Both grandmothers. All Randolph and Ralston women going back to the founding in 1909. You started in kindergarten and went through twelfth grade. Like all the "been-heres"—or "bin-yas" if you had had a Gullah nanny.

Newcomer Charleston wealth—the "from-offs"—typically sent their daughters to the mixed sex private school Porter-Gaud. Which made for a really nasty athletic rivalry between the girls of each school, and volleyball had been the key sport.

The Porter-Gaud boys were strutting little snots convinced they were going to own the world, and no rules applied to them. They'd pack the gym cheering their girls on, but being really vulgar and crude and often with male teachers joining in. Which was what had caused the little fracas that had nearly got Rannie expelled.

The senior game had been particularly intense because the two schools were clearly the top among the state's private schools, and one of them would be state champion. The enemy boys had been particularly savage whenever Rannie was up to serve, and it had made her so mad that she scored the final five winning points—just blistering the ball in like a missile—without Porter-Gaud able to get under a single one.

Afterwards out in the dirt parking lot with the shady trees across the street, she had spotted the ringleader, Ashmead Cotesworth "Cotey" Kershaw III, in his BMW with his smirky pals. She had gotten a buck knife out of her purse and slashed all four of their tires. The boys just sat there frozen with the doors locked, too scared to get out as the car collapsed onto the ground.

To put the icing on the cake, a florid-faced Porter-Gaud teacher—a man no less—who had done nothing to control the boys in the gym came huffing over. Rannie put the blade flat up against her thigh and told him, "If you don't believe I'll use it, just jump on me."

It hit the fan the next day. Loud bellowing out of the Porter-Gaud Headmaster. Threats from parents. Rannie hauled to the Headmistress' office to "explain yourself, young lady." What a mess that had been.

Incredibly, though, her daddy had stood up for her. Had taken out criminal warrants against the boys for trying to run over her with a car, charged the teacher with attempted sexual assault. Then watched real amused as some of his lawyer buddies jacked them all up for staggering fees to get the charges dismissed.

That was the first time Rannie had realized how a creative lawyer could turn a hopeless situation right around.

He told her nothing was going to stand in the way of his little girl going to college and law school if that was what she had her heart set on.

Rannie wiped a tear out of her eye. It had been the only time she had felt sure he loved her.

21

Dale's family was not thrilled with Moira's projected Old South wedding. Particularly when it hit them over the phone and out of the blue. They hemmed and hawed about the expense, but Moira overrode that easily. Collier's reenactment regiment had their own uniforms. There'd be no need for morning suit rentals like regular groomsmen. All two hundred of them.

Dale's school teacher daddy gagged at the thought of the catering cost for a herd of rebel ya-hoos. He sounded like a dog with a chicken bone in his throat.

Moira laughed gaily. "Collier is in complete agreement."

"Yes," Mary Canty chimed in from the phone extension. "It will bring a cultural sanctity to the union of the Upstate and the Low Country."

"You're mixing up a wedding and theatre," Dale's mother protested.

"Marriage is a theatrical art," argued Mary Canty.

Finally Dale's mother got her back up and said she didn't know what she objected to most, the tackiness of the idea or Moira's smug self-satisfaction with her plans.

Moira told them a Methodist wedding fell somewhere on the taste scale between Holiday Inn and K-mart.

More personal comments were exchanged before Dale's parents hung up.

Moira was unmoved. She lisped some distorted lines from *Gone with the Wind* about the "last barbecue at Twelve Oaks." Mary Canty's eyes were alight with a genuine interest, and she made numerous suggestions that Moira agreed were just divine. They really should have Taittingers and not that cheap bubbly in plastic glasses that so many people use. And a wedding cake iced with all the flags of the Confederacy was just perfect. "Beauregard" sweet potatoes at the wedding supper. Cream of curried peanut soup because rebel soldiers practically lived off goobers.

Moira in turn was delighted by Mary Canty's broad-minded approach to the matter of a rifle salute by Collier's entire reenactment regiment, the avenue of crossed sabres and the drum and fife serenade.

Collier nodded his apparent approval in Moira's presence, but privately whimpered and moaned to his mother. Mary Canty of course thought the whole thing a hoot. For once, Moira's foolishness had produced an unintended but fully desirable result. Dale would end the engagement, and Collier could get on with finding a suitable girl with money of her own. The break-up would not even be an eyebrow raiser in Charleston.

Collier protested her failure to understand his feelings for Dale.

"What do you mean?" she demanded archly. "I've seen dogs swarm around a bitch in heat before."

In an agony of fear, Collier delayed phoning Dale who

was back in New York closing up her apartment for the permanent move back south. There was nothing he could say to her that would make it palatable, and he dreaded what she would say to him.

The suspense was broken when she called, having learned the dire news from her parents. When the rather one-sided conversation was finished, he sat in a state of shock, clutching the phone, his ears ringing with four-letter words he had not known were in her vocabulary. He stared at the family portraits that suggested Moira's planned ceremony rather than a more modern event.

After multiple calls to an unresponding answering machine in New York, Collier screwed up his courage to confront his sister.

"I'm not going to do it, you sorry little twinkie!" he raged. "Tattle to Rannie and be damned!"

Which Moira promptly did, or at least the first part.

Rannie was sitting morose and mopey over her Jim Beam, disgusted with a wasted afternoon trying to coach a junkie prostitute to provide an alibi for an armed robbery client. She said she had a huge craving for Brunswick stew with a big dollop of flaming hot chow-chow in it. Wipe the sides of the bowl with sweet potato corn muffins.

Moira's voice was quite tart. "Collier had Tabby Boone in your office, and they were both not fully clothed because they had been . . . living together . . . and she was messing in your computer."

Collier froze, a foot from Moira, his hands reaching to cover her mouth. He turned white to the lips when he saw Rannie's blazing eyes.

She half-started out of her chair. "You dildo-brained ding-a-ling!" she began in the mildest part of the ensuing tirade. "You are an arsenal of pure-t stupid plots, plans and misbehavior. You live in transit from debacle to fuck-up!"

Mary Canty breezed in, arching her thin penciled eyebrows. She seemed unnaturally sober. "Rannie, Rannie," she chided. "Is this some era of hostility and bitterness?" She patted Collier's cheek and made kissing noises. "My poor little wounded puppy dog." Turned back to Rannie.

"Sure, I admit to some hesitation about this marriage. Any mother would when her precious and only son is marrying what is virtually trailer trash. But I feel sure Moira's orchestration will make this a momentous event both in Charleston social history and in . . . in serendipity. It will be nothing short of magnificent."

She flashed a genial smile of pure treachery.

■ ■ ■

Moira thumbed a Thesaurus and wrote trial words on scrap paper.

Cartiledge. Cartridge. No, those weren't floral words.

Castigated. That was something her family did. They lived in perpetual ire and disarray. But here in her room a restful quiet always prevailed. How she liked to sit by the window and watch the clouds change their shapes above the harbor. It was such a comfort to her. Her mother said she wallowed there in gloom and self-pity. Or something more cutting. Like 'You're the wet hanky of my life.'

True, Moira was fretful at times. But a wonderful sunset, the moon coming up, the strong Charleston sun—all cured her despair and filled her with romantic yearnings that just buoyed her up and up like a great big old red helium balloon.

Her moment of fame was just round the corner. The author tours would be tiring, but she would reward herself with a holiday afterwards. Perhaps take the occasion to plan a coffee table book of her work with photos of her beloved Charleston. Her home would be pictured, of course, but not the family. Poor Rannie. Photographs had never been kind to her.

Excluding her mother would be tricky. Mary Canty was always lurking. It was as if she had the knack of being drunk in several places at the same time.

Was it such a terrible thing to want to sanitize the present? Modern times seemed so blighted. Moira decided she was like a dromedary in search of an oasis. No, that wasn't a nice image. Well, never mind.

She had made a list of flowers she thought might work in a poem but they made rhyming very confusing. Poppies. Valerian. Irises. Orchids. Buttercups. Marsh marrow. Daisies. Hare bells.

What knell the hare bell? What sorrow the marsh marrow?

The title had come easily. *Champ fleuri.* From the French. Flowering field. Moira had failed freshman French at Sweet Briar, but that was because she was expected to memorize those nasty irregular verbs. French was easy when you just plucked phrases out of a dictionary.

She read what she had done so far:

CHAMP FLEURI

"In full & glorious flower
The stately marsh marrow
While above trills
The vainglorious mocking bird
Intoxicated with dew
Imprimatur of daisies"

When finished, it would all be nicely written in a leatherbound book, a most suitable setting for her work. She practised her engaging smile in the looking glass. Held the book in various poses.

She only had the two poems, "Figs in Season" and "Sword of Duty." The burning question of the hour was which should precede in a reading.

An ominous gravity settled on her as she pondered this.

Followed by a faint frisson at the nape of her neck. She was touched by a premonition. Something was amiss. Cautiously she opened the book.

Desecration!

Someone had ripped up figs; put the scrap between the pages stuck down by a thumbtack.

Her mind flew back to Ashley Hall days when the other girls would tear up her homework and smirk at her.

Hideous superstitions flashed in her brain. Vile tales told her by gullah maids just to terrify her and make her cry. Tear up something precious and say the owner's name and death soon follows.

"I must be calm," she said to herself. "I really must be calm. I am thinking of plants in a bright tapestry of color."

She ran screaming down the stairs.

Rannie was reading a deposition, getting ready for a trial. She told Moira to do please button her lip. Moira didn't. She seemed to run in place, twisting her hands, shifting to torture a button. And all the while her yelps, squeals, wails and trills came out in a ceaseless torrent.

Rannie sighed, "I try to lead a quiet and regular life. But I'm locked up with a perpetual crisis. What I'd like is to lounge about in a mauve satin wrap. Sip absinthe. Have an organized sex life."

Moira began to weep bitterly. Her sister's dreadful green eyes that tracked her and trapped her, never leaving her face. Like she was one of Rannie's helpless victims in a courtroom.

At last her voice came. "Everyone is looking at me like a goose that lays the golden eggs. And they're getting out their carving knives."

Rannie laughed in despair. "I wish I could put you on fast-forward and get through this psycho-drama."

"She's a murderer. Tabby Boone is a killer. I know it."

"Like everything else around here you're exaggerated. It's not enough you're a hysteric, you have to be a gibbering idiot. Mother can't just be a lush; she has to achieve dipsomania. The house can't just be a grind of maintenance. It has to be a black hole down which Fort Knox pours its gold."

Moira was sobbing now. "You're like a fly in the amber. Or in the ointment or something."

22

"Shit," Gaston muttered.

It was not the word that Moira would have chosen, but it more or less described the situation. Driving Rannie's Land Rover through the front gate of the Citadel in the dark, Moira had knocked over the 'dim your lights' sign on the wooden sawhorse.

A Citadel cop jumped into his cruiser, flipped on all the lights and siren in a cop onslaught. Thoroughly rattled, Moira bumped one front wheel up on the sidewalk as she pulled over, leaving the Rover lurched at an angle. She simply couldn't understand why Rannie had had to go out and buy this unsuitable vehicle that was impossible to drive.

When the cop did the little air sniff around her face to see if she had been drinking, the sodden odor of Gaston wafted over. The cop asked her to step out of the car. Which meant he got Moira out to walk a straight line. She told him in no uncertain terms that her daddy was a Citadel graduate, and the President was going to hear of her shabby treatment, and if need be the Board of Visitors and the Alumni Association would be involved as well.

The cop made her touch her nose while standing on one foot.

And Moira being Moira, she fell down and began shrieking.

Gaston got out of the car to inject himself and make a bad situation awful. "There's no rational explanation for what we are doing here tonight," he bellowed. "Miss Moira is my consolation prize for failure in a bibulous life."

He stood on one foot, missed his nose and fell down as well. Lying supine he asserted that he was the tippler, the riotous *bon viveur.* That Miss Moira would sooner say "damn" than let liquor pass her prim lips. That she was the missing link between the Carrie Nation teetotal past and the Hillary Clinton nanny state present.

The cop gave Moira a ticket for careless driving. She felt like tearing it up and throwing it in his face, but figured she'd attach it to her letter to the President.

And if Gaston's behavior now was anything to go on, he was likely to get worse as the evening progressed. She had walked in, head held high, through the main room of the library with all the murals of Civil War battles fought by Citadel graduates. This was her night. She was to read her poems and find her triumph.

The few cadets who ever use the library had turned to gape at her fragile bright blonde prettiness. Hunched over at the long tables muttering behind their hands.

Gaston had paused to admire a glass case of brightly painted lead soldiers. Then he had loudly demanded the men's room leaving her to stand outside and wait while he made the most dreadful noises behind the closed door. He emerged wiping his mouth with the smell of liquor even stronger.

"Don't have the runs?" he asked crudely. "I figured I wouldn't be able to get you off the pot. Butterfly bowels and all that."

Moira refrained from pointing out that he was drunk, sweaty, smelly and disgusting. And he looked like something that had been dredged out of the harbor. Instead she put him in his place with an imperious glance. Lifted her chin in the air. Swiveled and walked toward the Rare Books room.

The Director—Anne Boudreaux Ravenel—was old Charleston, born and raised on Water Street. She would give an appropriate introduction. Explain that the Ralstons threaded their way through the history of the state like a vein of gold. For those who in the 17th century had sought to bring aristocratic structure from England to the New World, the Ralstons were frequently cited as justification.

Even the occupying Yankees in 1865 had conceded the Ralston supremacy and were amazed at how the family was beloved by their faithful slaves who refused the freedom that Lincoln granted them.

In the years following the dreadful Reconstruction, Ralstons were pillars of the Democratic Party, their counsel sought not just in Columbia but Washington as well. Collectors and patrons of the arts. Leaders of scientific inquiry. And so many Citadel graduates, all patriots and citizen soldiers.

The small rare book room was packed with a sea of cadet faces running from eggplant black to *café au lait*. Moira stopped, a puzzled look in her wide blue eyes.

Anne Ravenel seemed in an excellent mood as she

introduced Gaston Bayard Garnett, Southern Poet extraordinaire to African-American Cadet Club night at the library.

Moira digested this like a wet fish slap across the face. An agonizing tension spread through her. In an unsteady voice she asked if they had come on the correct date. Anne Ravenel didn't seem to have heard. Numbly, Moira sat down, trembling.

"Well," said Gaston. "No tedious orations tonight. We must improvise madly."

Incredibly, he loosened his belt and lowered his trousers until his underwear was visible. This seemed to arouse the interest of the audience.

Then he began to dance and juke about as though hearing celestial jive music. Step forward. Clap hands. Step back. Side slide. Clap again.

"Do the doo-wah dap," he chanted.

Moira was rigid with horror. From the remote recesses of his sodden brain he was extemporizing doggerel.

"Do the doo-wah dap." Side slide. Clap.

The cadets joined in, swaying left and then right, clapping in unison.

"Do the doo-wah dap."

He stopped, turned, extended his arms. Broke his wrists downward and made strange signals with his fingers.

"Do the doo-wah dap
Catch the clap
Mercury cure
Gotta endure

Bap bap
   Do the DOO WAH DAP!

Bitch say no
Fuck that ho'
Thigh on thigh
   Bye-de-bye
Slap slap
   Do the DOO WAH DAP!"

On and on it went for numberless verses incomprehensible except in their lewd suggestiveness and blatant trashiness. Moira became acutely conscious of her clothes and the perspiration that was oozing in dreadful half-moons in her armpits.

And suddenly he was finished.

Wild clapping and foot stomping.

"You de P-Diddy!"

"You de main mutha!"

Anne Ravenel applauded tepidly, fingers against a palm, a wintry smile on her face. Maintaining her poise and a sense of ritual in the teeth of this low pantomime.

Gaston mopped his face with a red bandana. Said he was hotter than a two dollar pistol. Moira stood up unsteadily, trying to steel herself. He said to her, "Whew! Did your deodorant fail? Your reek would knock the buzzards off a gut wagon."

He turned to the audience, arms raised in benediction. "And now, my lollapalooza cotton patch 'ho, the humdinger herself . . . Lady Moira Ralston."

Cheers. Whistles.

Trying to steel herself, Moira clutched the hilt of the sword until her hands hurt.

"Don't antagonize them," Gaston warned her *sotto voce*. "And whatever happens, don't give them a flash of tit. Your negro has an uncontrolled libido and the thought patterns of a child. They're liable to gang-rape you right here."

In her mind Moira had taken several big steps forward, but in fact she had hardly moved. God the faces. Jet black to chocolate brown. One of them seemed genuine African with an enormous spread nose and ceremonial cuts on both cheeks. He grinned at her showing a gold tooth.

Moira gripped the sword, rigid with terror. "Sword of . . . Sword of Duty," she croaked.

"Cain't heah yoo!" a cadet sang out.

"Southern cross o noble escutcheon," she bleated. And then fell silent, unable to remember the words.

"She's kind of a tight ass-hole," Gaston explained loudly. "You know how white bitches can be."

And there was another voice inside her head, louder yet. Her mother's. "I so dislike failure in a child."

Gaston's face goggling at her in a gibbering grin. Slobber at the corners of his mouth. "Gotcher panties in a twist?"

"You are sooo . . . *unsuitable*," she said firmly.

And then she stabbed him deep in his thigh. Just rammed the sword in half way to the hilt.

Gaston paused a beat, gaping with contorted features.

"YEEE-AAAHH!" he squealed as the pain hit him.

The blade slid in like it was going through butter but

curiously resisted being removed or she might have done him far greater damage. Unable to pull it out, she jerked at it futilely while Gaston bellowed in searing agony.

The cadets erupted in cheers, clapping and catcalls.

"Yoo go, bitch!"

"Cut him ass good!"

"Slice an' dice that muvva!"

Fleeing the room, Moira blundered into the glass case of soldiers and sent it shattering over. Little colorful lead warriors spilling everywhere.

Gaston came flailing after her like some dire yowling Caliban. He got the sword jammed up in the turnstile at the entrance while Moira glided out. He flailed there and fell down.

His shouting faded as she drove away, side-swiping three parked cars and heading back the wrong way on a one-way circle to get to the front gate. The Citadel cop came out of the guard post waving his arms, and she bounced him off the hood, creating another casualty for the Cid to cope with.

■ ■ ■

Rannie told Rhett, "So I'm pleading this lowlife, and I find I'm asking the judge for a sentence that'll allow the boy to 'amount to something some day.'"

"You didn't."

"It just came out."

"Not that it matters. Judges hand out what they've

already planned. You're just up there snowing the client. Making him think you're working for your money."

"And get this. That lame brain tells the judge he didn't know driving a getaway car in a holdup was the same as armed robbery. He says if they want to reduce crime they should put up posters in the high schools telling young folks the prison time they face for this or that."

"Civic minded young man."

They sat at the oyster bar in "A.W. Shucks" just off the long covered market where the tourists congregated to buy junk out of the stalls. They were getting through a dozen on the half shell, lemon juice and hot sauce, and drinking vodka tonics.

They had spent an afternoon on the wind swept beach at Sullivan's Island, holding hands, reminiscing. Saw oyster catchers and Forster's terns. A few hundred yards off shore a huge raft of common scoters and scaup floated in the frigid Atlantic. Thousand of birds.

Rannie squeezed lemon across the oysters and said, "When our daddies were practicing law it was like all the crime came out of one or two families. You knew all the players. Not many guns. Still using those pearl handled straight razors. Other than that was just domestic violence. Maybe a crime of passion now and then."

Rhett nodded in agreement. "It's like Charleston is getting crushed down by all the industry piling up around it. On the news they had North Charleston trying to 'enhance its image' by bringing in a massive transportation hub."

"I heard that," Rannie laughed. "The mayor said it was visionary. And he said—what was it?—'All roads lead to North Charleston.'"

"You got your crack shooting galleries all along Line Street now. Your weekly drug murder. One dead and three in jail. Hard to figure where the trash all comes from."

"A couple of minor delinquents like us, we wouldn't even register with folks today."

Rhett chuckled. "I always did wonder about the story behind you slashing the tires on Cotey Kershaw's BMW. With him and his buddies sitting right in it."

"I made a mistake of dating him. And letting him get to second base. They were telling the world about it during the game."

"That would tend to make one a mite tetchy. And prone to use a buck knife."

"That was when I learned something valuable. I mean other than keeping my blouse buttoned around a rich snot. I confessed to my daddy. Not the you-know part, but the knife and the tires. And he said, 'What I'm hearing is criminal assault on their part.' To which I reply that's not precisely true. But he said—I'll never forget, I was so amazed—he kind of struck that pose he'd do in front of a jury and said, 'There's a larger truth in the law that transcends some petty facts that are all open to misinterpretation.'"

Rhett chuckled. "Which is to say they had it coming to them."

She slurped an oyster out of the shell, thinking how suggestive it seemed. "I do recall you ripping up Porter-Gaud's lawn in your daddy's new Cadillac El Dorado."

"There were mitigating circumstances. I was blind drunk. Anyhow that was the media's take on it."

"You becoming a tax lawyer kind of lends retrospective

legitimacy to your chequered past." And she was just dying to ask him about his cut of the twelve million and had to bite her tongue not to do it.

"I was pretty poorly brought up. You can say that at my guilty plea. Thrown out of Porter-Gaud for that aforementioned wheel work. Finished at a public high school where the kids wore key chains that hung down to their knees. Got into U. Va. somehow, but that didn't help. A man's not considered drunk there unless his head's down in the toilet so sick he's trying to drown himself. The army was mostly playing in the dirt."

"What about me? I never learned how to comport myself socially. No guidance out of my mother. She's the closest thing to what used to be called the town drunk without actually being put in the stocks with a sign around her neck."

"Society ought to come naturally to you. You were born a 'lady'. Not that one was calling it that by then. And you've got all those illustrious ancestors."

"Notorious maybe. Slews of them died violent and sordid deaths. Hanged for consorting with Blackbeard. Shot down in a duel. Flayed alive by Yemassee Indians. Dragged out of the county jail and lynched by a mob."

Rhett signaled the bartender for a refuel.

They sat there waxing nostalgic for the days when Charleston was littered with tiny groceries with wood floors, screen doors and slow moving fans. Display coolers with cool drinks. When you could hear the roosters on the corner of Tradd and King Streets because the man who lived there raised fighting cocks. When folks would stroll the streets in the evening, hear someone yelling to come on up on the porch and have a drink. More folks would amble by and pretty soon a front porch party would be in full swing.

It got them feeling really close, and Rannie's heart jumped up in her throat when Rhett kind of leaned into her and laid his hand over hers. Said, "You know I been reading that rip tides are pretty predictable. Not quirky at all like we once believed."

She tilted her head so her thick red hair curtained one eye. Nose about four inches from his. "You're saying we can know when they'll strike?"

"Hidden under the surface, but hanging around for weeks, even months at a time."

She half closed her eyes. "Just sucking the unwary under."

Then her cell phone went off.

Moira was hysterical, calling from the city jail on Lockwood. Incoherent. Something about stabbing Gaston.

Rannie yelled, "If you've bent Daddy's sword I'll skin you alive!"

23

Gaston lay in a three patient room in the wretched County Hospital where all the welfare cases were stacked. Rannie had refused to sign for the bill at a higher class establishment. There is no veneer of civilization at County, the halls groaning with the razor slashed, the gun-shot, and the fargone meningitis cases of folks who used the emergency room as primary care provider.

Gaston groaned in agony, begged for pain-killers, and aired his complaints. His thigh was aflame. The nurses wouldn't come when he called. He needed a therapeutic bed and not the sack of rocks he lay upon. Rannie changed the subject.

"So Moira wasn't popular with the cadets?"

He closed his eyes and shuddered at the memory. "Her poetry lacks a . . . shall we call it 'intellectual rigor'?"

"But she does so like to help out. Enthusiastically. She's oodles of fun. I'd urge you to consider marriage except I won't have you in the family."

One of the other room denizens shouted in delirium. "Gone cap yo' ass!" He had been shot in the chest in a drive-by.

"Security at the Citadel is far too lax," Gaston huffed. "I'll expect you to sue them for me. We'll make a bundle."

"No can do. It's my daddy's alma mater."

"Then I'll haul my business elsewhere," Gaston said indignantly.

"No you won't."

"But she skewered me! I'm permanently disabled. I'll spend my life in bed doing embroidery."

"The Citadel is not just famous, it's notorious for violence. Anyone who sets foot on the campus embraces the risk."

"They let some crazed harpy run amok like Jack the Ripper. They have to pay the damages. Anyhow, I know you won't let me sue Moira."

"True. She's family bankroll. And I'll be having enough trouble with the cop she ran over. The Supreme Court's new ruling on how we can't execute the mentally retarded will always keep her from the electric chair. But I don't know about life in prison. I'll need you to say the cop suddenly appeared out of the darkness and virtually leaped in front of her."

"I was fainted on the steps bleeding to death. I didn't see a thing."

"Yes you did. Refresh your memory."

He pulled himself up in the bed. "I need a drink. A life enhancer. My alcohol intake has been reduced to zip. I feel like I'm at Betty Ford."

"Can't help you."

"The nights are interminable here," he pleaded.

Rannie responded with some sharp remarks about him

malingering, trying to arouse pity. He needed to be up and around. Walking on that injured leg. That would get him back to the bourbon bottle, the chalice of his true faith.

His face contorted in desperation. "Smuggle it in a coffee thermos. Or a walking stick. Or pig's bladder."

"Nope. You just lie back and enjoy a nice attack of the jitters. Do you good to dry out. Your body's like a jug of fish-house punch."

He didn't take the refusal well. "You merciless reptile!" he bellowed in a crescendo of protest.

Rannie stood up. "Well, I always enjoy a passionate exchange with you, but money grubbing calls. Mummy's trying to get lined up with the face-lift doctor, and they refused her charge card. I got an abusive phone call on that one."

Gaston fell silent, pouting like a stubborn child. "Tell me about the nature of the bail bond posted for me."

"Why?" Rannie asked.

"As I understand it, if I fail to appear at various proceedings you lose the sacrosanct No. 1 Legendre."

"Where would you go? Off to forge a brilliant career at some other provincial college? What exactly are your job prospects these days?"

"I could deal blackjack on an Indian Reservation casino. Then I'd be outside the sovereignty of the United States."

"It doesn't work that way."

"I would say your really crucial problem is keeping me within reach of the long arm of the law."

Rannie shook her head in disgust. She felt tired,

overweight, and weary of the creeps she had to associate with. "If you try to pull some stunt, I'll . . . well, let's just say I won't be mounting a charm offensive."

"Catch me if you can," he laughed triumphantly.

On the way out, Rannie ordered the security guard to handcuff Gaston to the bed. Said Gaston had homicidal tendencies and a court ordered psychiatric evaluation was coming shortly. And to tell the nurses to double-check the drug inventory. The man would stick anything up his nose or down his throat.

■ ■ ■

Not half a mile away in the expensive overnight room of a plastic surgeon, Mary Canty was trying out the bed and the decor. Never one to be denied the slightest creature comfort, she had to be certain she could tolerate the lone post-face-lift night she would have to spend there.

"I can't believe there's no kleenex in the room," she said in dismay.

"It's easy enough to bring your own box," said Moira.

"I can't be expected to handle everything. I'll be the patient."

The room was banked with flowers Mary Canty had ordered for herself. In identical rooms down the hall other plastic surgery cases lounged abed, faces all purple or if still bandaged, their eyes popped out and staring. To Mary Canty, they were such indolent Country Club bores. Going on about memorable lifts and tucks and lipos.

And they were old. Someone needed to be planning their memorial services.

She looked appreciatively in a hand mirror as though she could sense the perfection that would soon reflect there. A minor bit of surgery and she could walk away from the past.

There was no mini-bar and in fact a shocking rule against alcohol at all. Accustomed to falling into a stupor that would take her through the night, she figured she would have to make do with smuggled booze and sedatives.

And with smoke alarms everywhere, there was no way she could sneak a smoke. Moira was grateful that her cigarette breath might be at least partially cured.

To fight the boredom, Mary Canty took a keen pleasure in pulling willy-nilly the name of every hack politician she could find onto Collier's wedding invitation list. The church was already packed to capacity, but she was greedy for more. It was necessary for Collier's career. She particularly liked the idea of the Black Caucus showing up to find the Confederate uniforms. The ensuing ruckus would be sure to attract media attention.

"Collier is becoming such a nuisance," she said to Moira. "Ungrateful. Moping. That hangdog defeated look. Here this wedding will be a major achievement for me. Men are so unmaleable."

"You just have to take them firmly in hand," Moira put in from her armchair.

"You don't start out apologetic. 'Fact you never apologize."

"You tell a man to just stop his tirade, and that is that."

"Keep them on the hop. A little torment is never misplaced. And if they ever are so foolish as to confide a weakness, you tuck it away in the memory to use later."

"So true." Moira's little stabbing incident with Gaston had been gruesome, and yet there was something deeply satisfying about it. A lot of events had passed after that, but she had absolutely no memory of them. Moira had long developed an ability to zone out when things got too unpleasant. A psychologist she had been seeing in the last fretful days at Sweet Briar had called it a 'waking dream.' Seemed quite amazed at how she could enter it at will.

Mary Canty said, "Of course the minister in Irmo is not being cooperative about the gunfire salutes. Very chilly reception on that one."

"Methodists view things so differently," said Moira.

"I told that man I was the most reasonable woman on earth as long as he understood he would do as I said."

"We take so much abuse and insult," Moira sniffed.

"I don't need a gaggle of critics," Mary Canty said complacently. "Dale's family is quite enough, thank you. I had the strangest phone call from them yesterday. Abusive? Let me tell you. Ill-tempered. Nasty. I'm starting to wonder if they drink to excess."

"They do seem very bitter about something," Moira agreed. "Probably quite insecure about their daughter becoming a Ralston."

"I told them I had had a Road-to-Damascus conversion on this matrimonial union and was just whole-hearted behind it. A splendid wedding, I think it's the least I can do for the two love birds. See they get the right send-off in life. And Dale—not that I had anything against her personally—but she needs to brush up on her etiquette a bit if she expects to be a senator's wife."

"No one appreciates our efforts."

"I'm so even-handed, it's like I have no opinions of my own. Always striving to please. So much of my good works are completely anonymous. I detest people fawning in gratitude."

Moira cautiously broached her concern. "But Collier . . . I'm uneasy about him."

"Men are nothing but status symbols," Mary Canty scoffed. "I've long given up on them being providers. But women feel they must have one. It's like a territorial urge to own one."

"But Collier and Tabitha Boone . . ."

"What for God's sake?"

"He was . . . escorting her."

Mary Canty's lips pursed peevishly. "I have to be a realist where Collier is concerned. He's always up to some shambles of a seduction. Just like his father. At least until Big Collier fell impotent. Prostate the size of a grapefruit. At last I was delivered from the nuisance of his demands."

Moira spoke in a tragic voice. "Men with their ungovernable passions." When Moira found she had an expanded vocabulary it was usually lifted from an historical romance novel.

"Oh I shed the occasional tear," said Mary Canty. "But still . . . well, I shudder at the memories of sexual intercourse with him."

"But Tabitha . . . she's like a chicken before the egg or something."

"Well, the most unlikely people seem involved with sex

these days. In my time, men were taught to leave you alone. Unless you wanted something immediate from them.

"Your father was a lush. The horror stories I could tell you. I got to the stage where I was beyond embarrassment. Still, no point in sitting here brooding on the past. Having a dark night of the soul." She pressed the button and held it down relentlessly to summon the nurse. She needed her bed adjusted and more mixer for her toddy.

"We really need to throw some more money around," she said with relish.

24

Rannie said, "Moira doesn't have much sense of time. Or of anything else. Or sense period."

"You're serious?" said Lazelle, the assistant Solicitor with the mahogany skin. "She doesn't remember anything of the cops arresting her? Being in the city jail all night? She was in the drunk tank with a coupl'a ho's and a mental case."

"They leave her alone?"

"After an hour they begged to be put in another cell. Even some of the matrons—you know what hard-asses they be—one of thems as big as a telephone booth—they were threatening to quit their jobs."

Rannie casually roamed the tiny office. Her food obsession was entering a stage of near-dementia. She found herself thinking of the strangest food. Chicken pot pies. Ice cream sandwiches. Cracker Jacks. She said, "So what kind of a legal tussle am I in for?"

Lazelle shrugged. "Whatever I choose. They've thrown it to me. Whole Solicitor's office is scared shitless of you. Every time you give one a hiding he develops grave doubts he can cut it in private practice. A couple of them have gone into therapy. The county health policy has mental health on it now."

"Men. What can you do with them?"

"Moira acted mighty strange. Drug cop guessed PCP. Maybe high-grade crank. They tested her blood for drugs and booze. Nothing. But she seemed like she needed to be resuscitated from something or other."

"Moira doesn't need hallucinogens. Her brain produces them under ordinary conditions. Did she talk?"

"Oh she talked all right. Real animated."

"She didn't confess to anything, did she?"

Lazelle looked at some notes. "She talked about the last barbeque at Twelve Oaks. And some Confederate wedding she was planning. What a blockhead a Methodist minister was. How you and your mother didn't appreciate her refined sensibilities. How a climbing rose was a perfect combination with clematis. The spider lily is a real fine persimmon-colored flower that always pops out in September. Your brother was 'knowing' somebody. Is that 'knowing' like out of the Bible? And some girl she hated in college who was fish-faced and bug-eyed."

"How long did this go on?"

"Four hours. She was like a wind-up zombie. They finally gave up. Direct questions she didn't hear. Just listening produced, well, all that." She slapped the report with the back of her hand.

"She kept talking all night, didn't she?"

"Would not shut up. Not a poster child for *compos mentis*. Real wearying for all involved."

"She's what you call anachronistic."

"You old Southrons got my sympathy."

"So tell me the worrisome news."

"Our man Gaston's theoretically going on trial for Murder One. Mind you, it's still under my consideration. But nobody cares he got shanked. The Citadel cop poses a problem though."

"Why?"

"You might have noticed, the prosecution and cops are on the same side in this business. Cops get right bent out of shape if we don't take up for them."

Rannie looked out the dirty window where a starling sat on the sill staring at her with beady eyes like a witch's messenger. She said, "We might be willing to plead to a driving offense. Pay a fine. You take her license. Moira ought to stay out from behind the wheel."

"She broke his collar bone. Dislocated the shoulder."

"I've got an eyewitness says the cop lurched out of the dark straight in front of the car."

"Is this the same eyewitness you been telling me was so drunk he done impaled himself on the sword back in the library?"

"No. It'll probably be about fifteen Citadel cadets who never liked that cop in the first place."

"I got to tell you, Rannie, you got the reputation of a legendary bitch. Even among your fans."

Rannie shrugged. "I've got a feel for balance. Act like I'm in complete command even if I'm not. By the way, can I have the sword back? It's sentimental. Belonged to Daddy."

■ ■ ■

Mary Canty said, "When this surgery ordeal's all over, it'll be good to be back in my routine. I like to get my work done in the day, then relax in the evening. Maybe have a toddy with friends. Play a rubber of bridge."

She sucked deeply on a cigarette and stubbed out the butt in a brass ashtray.

Rannie closed her eyes and sighed. Mary Canty's "friends" were the more malicious drunks who bunkered into the back bar of the Yacht Club from eleven AM until pass-out time.

And she was only going to take out one day and a night to go under the surgeon's knife, come out looking thirty-five. Her suitcases—five of them—were packed and waiting in the hall. At five thousand dollars, the price was pretty typical of one of her days.

"I don't care how they gussy up those private rooms," her mother said, "it's still a place of dread disorders. The nurse kept asking me if the furnishings were suitable. It made me feel violated."

Rannie closed her eyes and rolled the chill glass of Jim Beam along her forehead, figuring and reconfiguring her life. Rhett was playing some sexual cat-and-mouse game with her. She wanted to be a smoldering eyed beauty and all she got was interruptions. Jumped on by a boar hog and gaped at with her pants down. Nice tête-à-tête going in a smoky bar, and Moira chooses the moment to maim Gaston.

Mary Canty touched the edges of her face that would soon undergo damage control, then fixed Rannie with her small staring eyes. "So, tell me about your day.

Whatever it is you do. Trip people up on alibis. Ferret out ulterior motives. View cadavers."

Rannie thought what is this little mother-daughter moment? Trying to leave me a fond memory if you expire under the knife. She said, "Oh, I pass the hours living up to my reputation for volatility."

Her mind drifted to an outdoor crab boil. Black iron cauldron of boiling water over a wood campfire. Smoke sweeping this way and that in the wind. Toss in the big Jimmies as the adult males were called. Tong them out and dump them on newspaper on a wooden table. Crack the claws and dredge them through melted butter. Heaven on earth.

"You're always so closed-mouth," said Mary Canty. "Well, I've been busy. I've decided to invite Tabby Boone— is that her name?—so strange. Well I'm going to invite her into our home."

"Someone else for me to support with my manic energy," Rannie said distantly. "Swell."

"She's an orphan now. All alone."

"By definition."

"What?"

"Orphans are all alone. What made you think of this? You've never met the girl."

"Truth be known, it's Gaston's idea. He feels responsibility as the step-father."

"Is this going to be like some permanent undertaking? Bring her out as a deb at St. Cecilia's? Set her up a trust fund? Drape her in heirloom jewelry?"

Mary Canty missed the sarcasm. "I haven't worked out

the details," she said airily. "Anyhow, it will do Moira good to have a companion her age. Improve her mentally."

"Let's stick in the realm of the possible."

"I have to live with hope. Despite my lingering frustration at Moira's shenanigans. Stabbing poor Gaston through the thigh. Just unsuitable ferocity. Men should be dealt with much more subtly."

"The Tabby girl is weird," said Rannie. "Morbid. Morose. Withdrawn. Dropped out of Hollins, and they don't even have a math requirement there."

"Well of course our Moira abandoned Sweet Briar. The shame of that is deeply engraved on my soul."

"You only did a year there yourself," Rannie reminded.

"Yes, freshman summer I married your father at his insane insistence. He was just out of law school and wanted my family connections, this house, all this." She waved her hand at the room. "Oh yes I fit the bill nicely. So I gave up a chance to be informed on so many subjects. But I've always had such hopes for my daughters."

"I do have a law degree. That sometimes gets overlooked around here."

"My my. Do you think I don't know that? You're always overcompensating. I probably should have breast-fed you as a child."

Rannie blew out her cheeks. Asked her mother just what "work" she had been doing today.

"I've been reading *Carolina Flame-Out*. Wonderful book and wonderful to think the author is staying under our roof. Gaston said it allowed him to exercise his passion for unusual friends and interests."

The bookmark indicated she might have gotten as far as page 5.

"He copied it almost word-for-word from Tabitha Boone's *Flames of the Carolinas*," Rannie said dryly.

"I don't believe it," Mary Canty scoffed.

"It's in litigation."

"Well, I myself have frequently been the subject of vicious rumors. Poisonous people will sue you whenever they find an angle."

"He admitted to it in a deposition."

"The man is so forthright."

"Did he tell you it was Tabby who's suing him?"

"That doesn't surprise me. You don't understand ingratitude until you've had children. But Gaston's such a dear. If we could just get him beyond his little drinking problem he'd be a paragon."

"Good luck on that one."

"I gave him a lecture on sobriety."

Rannie rolled her eyes. She was thinking *I get her in the car, drive her over to the surgeon, and I'm rid of her for an entire day and a night. Maybe have Rhett over for a diner à deux by candlelight. Something light. Crab-avocado. Pears poached in champagne. Persimmon pudding. Just a mouthful of that. The merest dab of cream on it.*

"I do so love putting Gaston in his place and then watching him grovel with that chastened tone of his." Mary Canty waved a torn open envelope. "Oh, this came in the mail today. Dear man sits there in a hospital bed writing me poetry. So romantic."

A kind of unease began to set in as Rannie read the lines of doggerel.

A wringing of hands
o'er cigar butt clues
the chicken has flown the coop

lark on the wing
con on the lam
drunkard off on a toot

cleared out
run out
Hauled ass away
leaving Miz Rannie
    . . . the poop to scoop

Off to the land of Boudin-eaters
just for the hell of it
Carolina Flame-out

"Have you read this?" Rannie asked.

"That Gaston. His eye for the offbeat and zany."

Rannie made a quick phone call to the hospital. Her fears were realized. "He wriggled out of the handcuffs and took off."

"Who could blame him? County hospital is so wretched. When I visited him, I had to hold a handkerchief to my nose to stand the smell."

"We forfeit the bond. The court will take our house."

"That's absurd. I'll speak to the judge myself."

25

Mary Canty was no more than forty-five minutes out of surgery when she had gotten the word on the bond forfeiture hearing. Barely out of the anesthesia. But she got galvanized in a second. Just stormed out of the surgeon's office stiff-arming a nurse on the way and got Rannie from home.

Rannie thought her mother looked like something from the mummy's tomb with her face swathed in bandages as they sat on the benches in the courtroom.

But nobody was in any hurry to get to them. They had to sit watching some punk named Jalonzo something up before the bench having bond set. Corn row hair and branding iron scars on his biceps.

"Well, I unnerstan' I been acoosed of chasing a woman 'round a car an-uh shootin' at her."

"It's called assault with intent to kill," said the magistrate.

Rannie thought they always try to argue their case and it makes no difference. Bail would be set based on the charge.

"I didn't unnastan' at the time that the safety was off. When the gun started going off I just panicked. That's why I fled the scene. Realizin' that what I had done was life-threatenin'. It's had a deep effect on me. Really put me under a cloud. Here I am an honor graduate of Burke High School and all. I'm thinkin' what I need is teen grief counseling."

The magistrate set a $200,000 surety bond. The price would be ten percent. Jalonzo argued he couldn't afford that and it ought to be lowered to something more in his price range. The magistrate said that was the bond.

"Well, I mean what about all that improper touching that goes on back in the cells?"

The magistrate looked bored. Processing the detritus of humanity in a dingy room of beige walls.

"I know all this will be cleared up. So do I get to keep the clothes? Like a souvenir t-shirt?"

The bailiff brought in another line of the rank and rotten. A long-haired drunk pulled off Folly Beach for public intoxication said out loud to the room, "I got back surgery scheduled. Got a herniated disc. I mean that's a contributing factor in all this."

The mood was tense.

And God the stench of them. Smell of toilets and cleansers, sweat and dirty hair. Mary Canty kept demanding to know who were these despicable people and why was she forced to sit among them. Muttering through the gauze that wrapped her face.

The bailiff didn't care for her carping. But he figured she was some crazy Rannie was maybe having committed.

And so it went. Five dudes who beat and robbed a man and stuffed him in the trunk of his car. All of them glowering. Mumbling incoherently.

Drug deal.

Drug deal.

Drug deal.

All of them with crime sheets like rolls of toilet paper.

Lazelle, Rannie's only hope of a lifeline, was nowhere in sight. Instead the solicitor himself was strutting, unfamiliar with doing any real work. Talking too loud, all good ol' boy heartiness, to the bailiffs and cops. He was there to grandstand. Maybe take the mandatory press conference afterwards saying Gaston the dangerous fugitive poet was out there on the loose.

The entrance of Judge Peasley Chitwind did not brighten Rannie's outlook. A nemesis throughout the years she had been in practice, the passage of time had made his bad-rulings, insults and temper tantrums seem epic. The solicitor had wanted him in for a reason. Heavy artillery to evict her onto Legendre Street.

"I would like this to be low-key and non-confrontational," said the judge. His face was well seasoned by years of high-end Bourbon. He gave them a smile that was too placid and tranquil. Like he was all set to enjoy what was coming.

"Don't think I don't know your reputation . . ." Mary Canty began. Rannie grabbed her arm, shook her.

Mary Canty had alienated so much of the town over the years. Just working at it tirelessly. A perfectionist honing her craft of insult, slander and back-stabbing. Totally dedicated.

And this was Judge Chitwind who took unholy delight in cutting Rannnie off at the knees at every opportunity. He didn't like women lawyers and didn't care who knew it.

He'd ogle her, say things like "If I told you you got a bodacious body, would you hold it against me?" Then slap his knee and laugh. Or act serious, wanting to be educated on the wars of the sexes. "I hear gals don't like men with technique. What is it they want? Just dive in and do it like minks?"

"What we're here for . . ." the Judge began.

Mary Canty butted in. "You'll have to excuse me if I have a healthy dose of skepticism about all this."

The Judge stuck his tongue in his cheek. Rolled it thoughtfully. "Everybody's got a beef with the system. Saying there's shortcomings and loopholes. Parents wanting tougher sex predator laws. The death penalty quandary. We got to educate the media when they don't know diddley-squat about what we face daily. Ad-hoc this and that all shrill and blasting that and the other. But getting the ball rolling here, Mr. Solicitor, let's read the letter that was I believe addressed directly to you."

The solicitor began to declaim like he was at a poetry contest.

"Wrappers on moon pies
and tire tracks on skivvies
cold Blues and corn dogs
and '56 Chevies
beer cans that litter the side of the road
these are the things that lighten my load

"Chittlins and cheese grits
Nehi and cornpone
lashings of fatback
and poontang that moans

beer cans that litter the side of the road
I piss on you like a poisonous toad

Off to the land of Boudin eaters
Carolina Flame-out!"

There was a note of pure-t triumph in his voice. "Yo' Honor, you don't get much mo' clearer than that. It's like the windshield been fresh cleaned with Windex. The man Gaston's done lit out for parts unknown."

Yes, Rannie thought. The self-destructive baboon was going to convict himself through flight. Maybe get gunned down at a roadblock. Lie on his back, bubbles of blood coming out of his mouth.

The judge looked like he was watching some terrible fate coming at them like an avalanche. A disinterested spectator viewing a moment of truth.

"I am in total shock," said Mary Canty. "I've been lied to by everyone involved in this including my own daughter."

Rannie knew she meant Moira. But since Rannie was the one standing there it seemed like her. "Your Honor . . ." she began.

"Just stay out of this," Mary Canty ordered. "It's my house, and I know what's what. Ridiculous little man sitting up there like he's God-a-mighty. I've been told—and I've heard it from more than just you—he's been so drunk he slid down in a stupor behind the bench."

Rannie tried to maintain her composure, fighting an urge to knock her mother to the floor and wedge a shoe in her mouth.

The judge gave Mary Canty that serene, self-contained

smile. "You are one sure 'nuff aggravatin' circumstance. I suppose we could spend an hour trading barbs. You feeling like this is some all-star moment. Got the spotlight on you."

Rannie wondered if she could reinvent herself as a bag lady. Just get a shopping cart and disappear into an alleyway.

Mary Canty fumed, "If you think you can barge into my house . . . !"

"You are clearly angry and disappointed," the judge said. The condolence that was really a deft jab to the solar plexus.

"Judge, she's had surgery and is not herself," Rannie pleaded.

"I am perfectly fine," Mary Canty insisted.

"Will you clam up before he holds you in contempt?"

Mary Canty crossed her arms. "Fine. If you're going to get all in a lather with me trying to inject some common sense into this legal hoo-doo, I'm not saying another word."

"This is progress," the judge rasped.

Rannie reminded him that bondsmen were allowed time to bring the fugitive back.

"One part of me wants to give you a break," he mused. "I'm just trying to sell the rest of myself on it." He rapped shave-and-a-haircut on the bench. "Okay, go track him down and bring him back hog-tied. What was that old Steve McQueen TV show? 'Wanted Dead or Alive'? Yeah. Miz Rannie Ralston bounty hunter. Sawed off shotgun in a holster on your hip."

"Thanks, Judge."

"Now for the caveat."

Rannie knew there'd be a catch.

"I'm giving you two weeks. Then the bond is forfeit. And of course you'll be in open competition with various law enforcement agencies. If they should get to him first, then you haven't provided surety. And the sale value of your house goes to all their expenses and whatever else they want it for." He chuckled. "Optimists—Lord love 'em—might say you had just a prayer of a chance."

As they went out, Mary Canty said, "It's up to me I guess. As God is my witness, I have to take charge of everything for this fractious family."

■ ■ ■

Moira sat trying to breathe regularly and think of a lily pond with gold fish swimming in the shadowy depths. Little darting slivers of gold. It gave her a sense of calm.

Her mother had come tearing home from the plastic surgeon, face wrapped up like a mummy. Screaming into the phone. Rannie bulled in and they both went off having a hissy fit. Something about a court hearing. Snapping at each other. Oh well. She couldn't possibly understand what they did. It was easier to just accept.

But then the plastic surgeon kept calling and demanding her mother return to the post-op room, and Moira had gotten all in a dither and taken the phone off the hook.

And now she was seeing the white blossoms of water lilies. White and green and gold.

Then Moira began to think of the lifestyle that should go with an acclaimed poet. It was a pleasant reverie of pruning roses and watering exotic herbs. Deepening her expertise on the ironwork of Charleston. She would be interviewed by ladies' magazines here in her ancestral home on Legendre Street.

It filled her with a sudden and almost irrational optimism which followed her all the way to answer the door bell.

Tabby Boone stood there, eyes staring defiantly. "I'll come straight to the point. Your mother has invited me to become a part of your family. Gaston is my stepfather, but he's a fugitive from justice and unable to make a home for me. And since we're now family, I've come to sell you Chop-slice knives. I've become an area sales rep. As I am naturally obstinate, a career in sales is my métier. An antidote to the dreary, defeatist depression of my lot."

Moira opened her mouth, but Tabby cut her off. "Let me anticipate your first objection. You are very busy writing. Yes, I'm sure that's true. We're all busy beavers, but you need a break. That haggard look taking hold of the edges of your face. A bit of rest and the satisfaction of owning a fine set of cutlery are just what you need. And Chop-slice knives are full tang, stainless steel with a lifetime sharpness guarantee."

Het-up was the word. Her insistence was so intent that it seemed her entire future depended upon her being able to make her pitch. Tabby watched the indecision on Moira's face. And then predictably, Moira caved.

Tabby strode into the dining room, opened a big cloth roll of knives and laid them all out on the table with brochures and catalogues. She lectured on the toothed edge and the lifetime guarantee and the various price options and easy payment plans for those who were financially not up to the task of paying cash. She proclaimed them heavy duty, functional and oh-so-easy to use. To demonstrate this, she cut neatly through a small piece of shoe leather.

It was such a rigmarole that Moira couldn't follow it and said so.

So Tabby said, "I've made up a verse to aid your comprehension. I know you'll want to hear it, you being interested in poetry and all.

Chop-slice knives are the very best
Chop and slice may your hand be blessed
Chop chop here
Slice slice there
Chop-slice knives are everywhere."

She stopped and smiled expectantly. "Are you piqued? Does that make you want to buy?"

"I . . . don't know."

"You're not just nice but clearly sensible as well. I think you should take the entire set for two thousand dollars. For that price, you join the Chop-slice Family with a monthly newsletter to help you plan creative meals both gourmet and for those on the go." She held up the newsletter. "This issue for example focuses on car interactive foods for those long week-end get-aways."

Moira was speechless.

Tabby leaned forward confidentially. "I'm so glad you put a sword through Gaston's fat thigh. It shows your appreciation for a fine blade. And Gaston's a complete fool."

"Totally," Moira agreed.

"Deserved every iota of the pain."

"And more."

They exchanged little smiles of understanding. Like sorority sisters. Or two gossiping maidens out of Jane Austen.

"You certainly put a spoke in his wheels," continued Tabby. "Or a bone up his ass. Or whatever."

"What?"

"He certainly got what was coming to him. He's always so rude about you. Says there's not the slightest connection between Moira's brain and mouth."

"Oh."

Tabby put a forefinger to her chin. "Oh dear me. I am perplexed. You're still showing sales resistance. Hmmm. That cup seems quite fragile and valuable."

"It's our best bone china."

And it was fine china. Wedgwood with rural English scenes in sepia brown. It came from the Randolph side of the family. Bought when cotton was still king.

Tabby's eyes were unnaturally bright as using the "Petite carver" she sawed through the rim of it with the knife. Sawed and sawed, just working away. Cut it into two perfectly matched halves.

"There," said Tabby, with evident pride in her work. "These knives are so sharp my nerves are in ribbons."

But she didn't seem nervous. She stared fixedly like she was contemplating some new act of vandalism or cruelty. She said, "The set includes paring knives, trimmers, carvers, a cleaver, boning knife, fish filet knife, and shears that will cut through the toughest bones and gristle. Plus fifteen dinner knives for a great long table of guests like this one. You get a hickory block to hold them as well as this durable velour travel bag. Your name and a pleasant kitchen homily will be burned into the wood block in a script of your choice."

She paused and pointed the blade at Moira's chest. "Is it okey-dokey time?"

Completely petrified, Moira agreed to buy the entire set. She chose Pallatino for the script. Tabby said she'd send a bill and left.

Moira was still looking very shaken when her equally formidable mother and sister came in snarling at each other.

"I work for a living," Rannie railed, full of indignation. "I have to face that judge more times than I want to."

Mary Canty gritted her teeth behind the bandages. "Those spiteful little eyes. And such belligerence. After keeping me sitting for hours with smelly social undesireables. Wonder I didn't suffocate."

Rannie said she dealt with subhumans like that every day. Welcome to her world.

Mary Canty said something about Rannie's money-mad schemes, smiling cynically at the folly of her daughter's life as an attorney. Barked at Moira, "What's wrong with you? You look like Death eating a soda cracker."

"Tabby Boone came by. She was . . . menacing."

"Nonsense," said Mary Canty. "She's quite harmless. I hope she'll be coming by a lot. What are all these common looking plastic handled knives?"

Moira owned up to buying them from Tabby.

Rannie laughed mirthlessly. "Whatever brainless thing you do, it's always something no one has thought of yet."

Everyone stopped and stared at Collier as he waltzed in with his own velvet bagged set of knives. He said he thought it charitable to help poor Tabby out. She had lost her mother and now her stepfather a fugitive. She had come by the office and done a really top-notch sales pitch. The hickory block to hold them was coming by Fed Ex. He had chosen Times New Roman for the script.

Real deliberately, Rannie said okay how much?

Collier said two thousand. But you get quite a deal. Along with all the kitchen knives you get carvers and fifteen table knives.

Rannie looked forcefully at Moira who ducked her head.

Rannie whispered four frickin' thousand dollars and something about the phenomenal degree of insanity and unhinged personalities in the family. Called on the Lord God Almighty to strike them with dengue fever.

Moira gulped resoundingly. Suddenly overcome with utter abject misery. All the lurid swearing.

Unable to restrain herself she began Tabby's patter. "A sharp knife is far less dangerous than a dull one."

She demonstrated with the little piece of shoe leather that Tabby had left behind.

Watched in slow motion as the blade sliced into her finger.

So cleanly that at first she didn't feel a thing. Then it hit!

"YAAAHHHH!"

Moira began squawking like a chicken. Clutching

her wounded hand. Amazing amounts of blood running down her arm.

"If your hysteria could be harnessed . . ." began Rannie.

"Hey! Who cut my cup in half?" demanded Mary Canty.

"Eee! Eee! Eee!" Moira squealed, buckling at the knees.

"That's my best china!" declared Mary Canty. "It came from my side of the family."

Moira floundered through the door and out to Rannie's Land Rover determined to drive herself to the emergency room. But of course she didn't have the keys. And passed out in the front seat, wiping blood in big smears on the upholstery.

She didn't hear her mother say, "I'm going to start keeping a strict account of what Moira costs me. Dock her trust fund for it. Teach her to be realistic about money."

26

At ease in the Ansonborough home of Claitey Pusey, Gaston Garnett lifted his glass and recited:

> "The woebegone wretch
> Swung in the wind
> As they stretched his neck
> From the hanging tree"

He lay back in his chair and stretched luxuriously, waggling his sock feet before the nice wood fire. The snug house was not polished to perfection as it had been when Claitey was alive. Tabby treated the place rather like a dormitory room. Clothes and magazines strewn about. Still, it was his refuge from the bloodhounds of the law and the menace of the wind outside.

For close on a week he had holed up here like Clyde Barrow in a cabin in the Minnesota woods. Safe with his partner Tabby. Him the brains of the gang. She the promised poontang that would come across once beyond her girlish inhibitions.

The food had been both paltry and inedible—all bean sprouts and hummus and plums. Rutabaga-carrot mash. But Claitey's liquor cabinet was still well stocked. And it had the added attraction of being free. Daily proof of his redemption.

"I feel like forty miles of bad road," he proclaimed. "That hospital was not what you call your congenial boudoir. I lay abed like one on whom doom had come."

He sipped his single malt scotch with a leisurely zest. The ambrosial Speyside brew crossing his palate. Such a deep down doozy of a delight. And him with the innate capacity of enjoyment.

Snooze and be pampered. No Moira to turn a reproachful eye on his imbibing. Nothing he hated more than reforming zeal. That girl was boundless in her censure. God but his leg hurt.

He had had to take the risk of ripping open the wound. The dreadful pablum they served in hospitals. Stewed prunes pretty much said it all. He needed navy bean soup and chicken fried steak with white gravy. A whole platter of corn on the cob. A plate of chocolate brownies and a quart of tutti-frutti ice cream.

Tutti-frutti, oh rootie! he sang inside his head.

If he could just get the lithe little Tabby Boone over to Harris Teeter to make the necessary purchases. Using the charge card he knew she possessed. And then whip up some sautéed veal chops and oyster mushrooms.

"You are just a sweet indulgence having me in the house like this," he said, waving his glass in her direction. "But on the off-chance," he ventured, "might you want to think about our dinner?"

"Oh but I am thinking about it," said Tabby dreamily. "I see yogurt and a stalk of celery. Perhaps braised chestnuts. I am purging myself as I do once a month. I emerge cleansed and so light I could float. And gloat. Feeling so superior to the gross who feed upon dead animals."

Gaston had been living off grain bread and jello, absolutely wasting away. He had a wild craving for chittlins of all things, and he hadn't eaten them in ages.

"It's only been the last ten thousand years we've eaten grains," Gaston argued. "Before that it was all red meat. Our very souls are grounded in the sinews of animals. No man can versify without such protein succulence dripping with juices and running red with blood."

"I think," she said, "that if you want dead animals you should close your eyes and wish very hard and perhaps brownies and elves will come and bring it in the night. Roast rack of lamb. Hickory-smoked bourbon turkey. Great links of sausage. Game pies. Liver puddings. Mmmm." She rubbed her stomach. "Do you think they'll come tonight?"

Gaston was stymied by that. Like so many "honey college" students she had only the dimmest sense of reality.

But she did look like a nymphet stepped out of the pages of boarding school erotica. Black leotards and short plaid skirt with the big gold safety pin holding it together. Definite compensations those little apple teats behind her white blouse. Make up for the lack of decent grub. And imagine that nimble tongue going over all his surfaces. He used to fantasize daily over her when he was married to the stone-hearted Claitey. Like a women's prison warden that wretch. And an iron-willed, no surrender type when it came to giving up nookie.

But the daughter was a different slice of cake. Used to rub her toes up his trouser leg under the table at family dinners. And only sixteen at the time. Any night now she'd come through his unlocked bedroom door and slide that slim body next to his. She'd turn volatile beneath his stroking.

Inflamed, I reach for my prey, he silently composed. Thrust randily and jolt the jism. Then lie surfeit, the lust departed, leaving me full of fine thoughts. "Wha . . . ?" Tabby was shoving her mauve stationary at him.

"I've been at my escritoire today. I call a poem newly-fledged when I've just finished it. I want you to get this one published."

> Pssst
> Hypnotic moon shadows
> creep through the mist
> my passionate hiss
> brings rising clouds of steam.

Gaston turned the paper to look at the back. Blank. "That's all?"

"It's enough."

He felt he was dealing with Suzie-Q Infinger. "The poetry journals are a bit choosy, you know."

"'Kublai Khan' was short."

"Coleridge had others to his credit."

"You know, my initial girlish enthusiasm for you has begun to pale. I can picture you in old age. Drooling. Wearing an adult diaper. It's not a pretty image."

He made deprecatory noises. Said, "Aw, come on, my little pecan tart." When that didn't work he shifted to placatory. "That first verse is always the agony of childbirth. Tomorrow the others will flow like milk from the mother's swollen paps. You're all wrung out now. The whup down hiatus of the poetic spirit. Come sit upon my lap and let me soothe your spice cake soul and silken back. Curl against me like the Tabby that you are and purr."

"I'm not attracted by middle-aged spread."

Gaston huffed. "Well sure. I'm stout. But so were Alexander Hamilton and Samuel Johnson. And both were extremely attractive to the ladies."

"What you are is unsanitary. Your belly's so big you can't see where you wee-wee, and it's usually all over you as well as the toilet seat."

He gave a loud snort. "Calumny and cant. My fiber is wholesale unabashed. And unleashed it extends near most to the horizon."

"I've seen your tool. You were always pissing in the yard when you were drunk. It's . . . well, paltry."

She said this without a glimmer of a smile.

Gaston went red, smarting under the insult. "I must upbraid you here. Insolence in a young whelp is not an attractive thing. I'll have you know that when I served on a navy aircraft carrier my equipment was widely recognized as the most prodigious among the hundreds of men on board. And navy men see a lot of long dongs in the showers."

"So when were you on a carrier?"

"Not for long. I fell overboard one night during a Force-10 gale. Miraculously made land without a life jacket. But I caught beri-beri on a desert atoll living off shellfish and rainwater. Put out on a medical discharge over heavy protest on my part."

"You did no such thing. My mother saw through you the first year you were married. Couldn't keep your lies straight. Always tangled up in time-lines. If I hadn't hated her so much, I would have seen through you too."

"You don't know nothing, lil' bit. And until you get some smart in you and accept guidance you'll never be a bring-down-the-house writer with her name in the nation's bloodstream."

The corners of her mouth went down. Positively mutinous look in those eyes. She gave him a rude gesture. The well-known middle finger. Her sleek straight hair took on the look of snakey Gorgon locks.

Dog-dookey, he thought. She looks like a ring-leader in a femi-nazi hit squad. The cold eye and sharp voice. You try to give harpies a wide berth and end up in gridlock with them.

Suddenly her eyes brimmed with tears. "I'm cruel and I don't know why. My inheritance from Mummy. Iniquities are all I've got."

Gaston tried to be comforting, stroking her arm. Letting his hand slide down to her thigh. "Claitey's history now. My unholy alliance ruptured. Dead as a doornail, if that's not putting it too crudely. A mere digression in the trajectory of our destinies."

She gave him a shy, glancing look. "Perhaps we should go upstairs and turn down the sheets."

Gaston gaped, his imagination easily taking wing. Her miff was subsiding. From miff to proffered muff. She had wanted it since she was sixteen. Gaston, the unregenerate debauchee, would open up her crack and teach it to juice like a ripe peach. When the female babel dies down they're all hungry for the bone. From Jezebel and Sheba to Traci-Lee and Misty. It's that old common denominator once more.

He put on his tom-cattin' smile. "Are you . . . offering me . . . harvest home?"

"Yes," she whispered, her eyes bright diamonds. "A dignified rapine. A consummation long desired by us both. We were always accomplices in longing and lust."

Well let the big dog eat. Jauntily he took the stairs two at a time. Humming a lively tune. Whole lotta shakin' goin' on. Show the critical little bimbo that he had stamina despite the gut-rending pain shooting up from his leg.

Aww-right. Prime cut. Honey school chicken. A ready-made hard-on would put them both to rights. And he would ride her hard and put her up wet. She could bet her sweet bippy on that.

In the doorway of his bedroom he turned to welcome her with wide arms. Had she peeled off articles of clothing and left them strewn upon the stairs?

He felt the premonition of disaster too late. His mouth went wide in fright just as her foot connected viciously with his testicles. He felt like he had a rupture and a double hernia all at the same time. And pitched backwards into the room.

Jesus Mary and Joseph! God the excruciating pain! His eyes misted in a red haze.

She slammed the door and turned a skeleton key in the lock.

Gaston lay writhing, clutching his jewels until the pain subsided. He breathed in great gulps. Crawled to his knees to scratch against the door.

"Let me out, Tabby," he pleaded. "I haven't finished my drink."

"I don't need you anymore. I've become my own person. I'm selling Chop-slice knives, and I find I'm quite good at it. I made two sales in the same day of two thousand dollars each. And I've written an ad jingle which I fully expect to sell for big money. Not to mention the bundle my extremely handsome lawyer Rhett MacReady will make for me suing you."

He tried to put a genial note in his wheedling voice. "But we had an understanding. Partners in enterprise. The Gold Dust Twins. Golconda Kate and Klondike Dan."

"Yanny-yanny boo-boo
Stick your head in doo-doo."

"What is that supposed to mean other than the obvious? If you jeopardize the . . . um, project, we could both wind up in the clink."

"I really like my lawyer. He's real handsome and has a body like Apollo. And he doesn't smell like a compost heap or grovel in pathetic appeal like somebody else I know. I think you can just sit in there and dream of rosehip jam and scones. Or your filthy old burgers and hot dogs if you prefer. They say dehydration will get to you before you starve to death."

Gaston pounded furiously on the heavy door blaspheming bitterly. "May you get gingivitis and all your teeth fall out!"

Her voice was pure malevolence. "The knives I sell are extremely sharp. I'm holding one in my hand now. It could slice through your blubber like a . . . well, a knife through butter. I know that's not a very original image. But it does hold a certain truth."

Her feet tip-tapped down the stairs.

Gaston bashed at the door, nearly dislocating his shoulder. Cataclysmic ruin. The little minx had turned on him.

He looked frantically about the room. Framed book reviews from Claitey Pusey's earliest successes. Romance novel reviewers fawning over her. A bizarre painting of her as an ecstatic saint with a crown of thorns on her head. A book case with each of her novels lined up chronologically.

He grunted at the window and found it jammed from years of paint and weather swelling. He could smash it out with a chair. But he couldn't leap without imperiling his life.

Gaston flopped on the bed knocked dumb by fear and disbelief.

No one knew where he was. No rescue party would come searching.

Where was Moses when the lights went out?

■ ■ ■

Moira had come out of her swoon in the Land Rover freezing cold with blood dried all down her arm. Forced to bandage herself in the bathroom with no one to help and no one to care. And sleep curled in a ball weeping.

Worse than the pain was the humiliation of admitting her mother was right about something. The Chop-slice knives *were* tacky. They couldn't possibly be used at the table.

She refused to come down for meals. Hearing the shouting through two floors. Something about Gaston's bond that she just didn't want to know about.

It suddenly struck her that she lived among oglers or ogres or whatever the word was. A kind of Cinderella story. Evil tempered mother and sister in a barren and desolate emotional world.

She sat in her room alone, sniffling. When the spark of genius took hold of her mind.

Cinderella was a romantic heroine. Romantic heroines suffered but finally triumphed. Like LaValle "Flame" O'Rorke in *Flames of the Carolinas.*

The pattern of recognition had begun to emerge when Gaston tried to ravish her and she fought him off. Next her natural ease with the sword. She toyed with those two elements. Pictured herself on a rearing stallion wielding a sabre against Yankee scallawags. Decided she was perfectly capable of writing a historical romance in the deathless style of Tabitha Boone.

Her ancestry, her instinctive creativity—really, everything pointed in this direction. All of her varied thoughts and scrambled memories came floating together like a jigsaw puzzle magically assembling itself. And suddenly she was all afire to test her theory.

With pen in hand, the words simply flowed.

"The mists of morn floated in feathery boas across Charleston harbor."

She paused. Boas was not quite right. They dated to the 1920s. And she was writing a Civil War story. But Mists of Morn would make a fine title.

She sat back in her chair. The Mists of Morn by . . . by whom? . . . by Margot . . . McBride. Or Philippa DeCanterville. Or Adriana de Villeneuve.

She felt so uplifted.

She had so much detail to organize. True Charleston egg nog uses only Barbadian rum because the Middletons and other early settlers came from Barbados. The snapdragon, foxglove, periwinkle and alyssum were brought from England by Charles Pinckney while the dogwood, cassena and yellow jessamine were all native. A firkin was . . . well, what exactly was a firkin?

She stopped abruptly, hearing a noise in the hall.

"You can't live in this house," Collier was shouting. "I'm getting married."

"*Excuse me?* But I'm having a bit of a block here. I recall you saying you loved me." It was that little sautéed shrimp Tabby Boone.

"Did not."

"Well, you said I was adorable and irresistible. And that's true. I have a micro-sized waist and patrician good looks."

Collier was really hedging. "I hardly know you."

"Well allow me to tell you a few things about myself. I'm not some bulimia stereotype. I don't tolerate pandering. I don't crawl away and write letters to Ann Landers. I sue for breach of promise."

"Don't make me laugh," Collier scoffed. "Go to a bereavement lecture or something. Or have a long talk with an imaginary friend."

Moira went out into the hall. *"Puh-leeze,"* she said with hauteur. "I am trying to write."

"Trying is the word," Tabby answered derisively. "You can barely read."

"You couldn't write your way out of a paper bag," Moira snapped back.

"Wow. That's a lame image."

"Well, I can write better than you with half my brain tied behind my back."

Tabby shook her head. "Half your biddy brains."

Moira put her hands on her hips. "Well, you're a Hollins College drop-out. And they don't even have a math requirement."

"Well you're a Sweet Briar flunk-out. You failed everything as well as math. And your dippy poems don't get beyond verse one."

"As if yours did. 'My demeurities.' My left foot!"

Tabby rolled her eyes. "'I snip with main and might.' That's virtually retarded."

Moira answered, "I will have you know I have advanced beyond poetry to prose. I have begun my first novel." She looked around as though expecting to find literary agents lurking behind the door.

"And what is this so-called book about?"

Moira actually stuck out her tongue at Tabby. "Corn bread and shoe tacks—None of your beeswax."

"Well I," smiled the cat-eyed Tabby "have written an ad jingle that I will sell for a lot of money. And your mother has invited me to stay here where I will find a refuge and be safe from the gazehound's lust. He won't be sneaking up on me and springing out with his 'great jumping Jehosophat' routine. Saying 'what a spectacular vista you are, sweet baby cakes. You are the sauce piquante on a po'boy of oysters and shrimp.' All the jokey small talk and the hugging and the arm grabbing and hand holding. Every excuse to rub his gross bod up against me."

"Gaston lives here," Moira argued. "He'll see you even more than ever. It won't be long before your little tail wags your dog right on out of here."

"Gaston is safely locked away someplace only I know about." Tabby took hold of Collier's arm. He tried to tug away. "And anyhow, I have a protector," she said. "Collier will break off his engagement, and we'll just become a little rhapsody in blue together."

Collier's face went white as a bone. "No," he croaked.

Tabby said, "You think you can just wander the highways and byways of no responsibility. Well, you better get yourself a conscience transplant, Mister. After the sweet lies you whispered in my ear, I'm just indignant remembering them. And I bet I could fill a notebook. And show them to a certain fiancée whose name is Dale."

This made Moira furious. "You think you can sashay in here and spoil all my nice work in progress for Collier's wedding? I'm putting my foot down on that. You can just go walk a mile in your moccasins to somewhere else. And if you don't I'll drop a few little hints to Dale myself. That girl is whip-smart, and she'll know who the bluebottle fly person is."

Tabby looked at her with bright angry eyes. "I wouldn't do that. It might be suicidal."

27

A brisk cold morning wind cut the harbor in little choppy wavelets and ruffled the palmetto fronds in White Point Gardens. It was a gray, dank backdrop totally in keeping with the condition of Rannie's tortured soul as she trudged across the little park. Ancient oaks dripped moisture onto the gnarled gray roots digging into the soil. Behind her, the Spanish Colonial design of the old 1920s Fort Sumter Hotel, now expensive condos.

Fish crows cawed in the trees. Double-crested cormorants floated out in the harbor.

Then up the East Battery beside the cold white-capped sea. To her left, the monumental Greek Revival houses the same as they were in the old 1831 Barnard painting. Huge Ionic columned porticos. Sitting rooms on the second floor so the doors could be thrown open in summer to catch the sea breeze.

Breakfast had brought out the worst emotions and basest instincts of the family. Finger pointing. Reviling each other in their permanent state of feud.

By the time Collier had coughed delicately and announced he was required in Columbia, Rannie was all out of wrath. Just told him as a law partner he was beyond price.

She was walking the long way to Rhett's office, rehearsing conversations, figuring how she'd beg for his help. He had been an airborne ranger. It would be child's play for him to track Gaston down.

At first glance, the outlook wasn't good. Gaston had twice proclaimed he was off to the land of *boudin*—a form of cajun sausage found exclusively in Louisiana. But that had to be a deliberate ruse. He was probably hanging out in bars, sleeping under cars at night, newspaper stuffed in his clothes for warmth.

Rannie wore an old hunting coat and carried a hickory billy club. She had considered taking her Colt .45, but Gaston's blood pressure was so high he might have a stroke if she even wounded him.

She puffed up the stairs to Rhett's office. You could spend hours a week gutting yourself in an aerobics class and still not get back your high school stamina.

Rhett answered the door, putting down the newspaper he had been reading next to a cup of coffee. Another completed boar and cur dogs painting sat drying on an easel.

Rannie said, "You've got the talent, but all I can think is $30,000 with no overhead and no sleazy client to cajole, coax and bully."

"No art for art's sake," Rhett agreed. "I do it for the filthy lucre. It's more low-stress than having some irascible judge tear strips off me."

Rannie got right close to mentioning the twelve million tax judgment and how she scrapped for a living with low-net-worth clients but didn't. Instead, she explained the mission, said she needed him now if ever, and to shake a leg and make like Galahad. She said, "I need a man you can bust a chair over his head and he won't blink."

Rhett said, "If you can contain your impatience, I'll get kitted out here. Should I dress like a militia fanatic? Black t-shirt. Camos. Jackboots a-gleam. I'll have to pack a gun in a shoulder harness."

"We don't need guns; we'll use tact," she said, smacking the billy club in her palm.

"That's the stuff," he said. "Raid, ambush and sharp hand-to-hand encounter."

She caught the amused half-smile and the faintly cocked eyebrow. Old wonder boy here would condescend to her.

"Well," he mused, "I guess we could drive around all day and not find him. End up in a bar for a warming hit of scotch. Let our eyes lock and finally wonder why we had wasted all those hours. Or . . ." the teasing pause . . . "you could get undressed and climb in my bed now."

Somehow, he seemed to be standing closer. She put her hands up against his chest. "That first scenario . . . you're right. The script's abysmal."

Rhett MacReady was a luscious hunk o'male. He could talk a coon out of a tree and any girl out of her underpants with bewildering speed. And she had the relish of long suppressed hunger.

She gave him a thoughtful look with a lot of memory behind it. Sitting with him in the sin-bin of Captain Harry's Blue Marlin drinking beer. Her first love. After a teenage agony as an object of derision by all the Porter-Gaud snots.

"You do create a certain ambiance," she said, shrugging out of the hunting coat and letting it slide to the floor with the swish of Hedy Lamarr's negligee.

His hands circled her waist, thumbs touching in front. Of course they nowhere near touched in back. But she felt lithe and willow thin and all her guts were in turmoil.

"By gosh by gee, you are put together," he said admiringly.

"Compliments are good. No cries of protest out of me."

He unsnapped her jeans. She thought eat your hearts out, love-lorn maidens. This is a once-in-a-lifetime payday.

Rannie sagged up against him. "I'm all a sudden fearful of releasing powers beyond my control."

Then the phone rang. And to Rannie's complete dismay, Rhett answered it.

There was a long one-sided conversation with Rhett only giving the occasional grunt. He hung up looking real pleased.

"That commotion was Gaston. Full of virtuous outrage. He's locked in a bedroom in Tabby Boone's house. Seems Red Riding Hood has turned on the wolf. He spent the night without food or drink, and he's hit the panic button. Broke down and used the phone which was there all along."

Rannie's heart leapt. "He's locked up? For true?"

"Honest Injun. The boy's in durance vile."

Rannie exulted. Frabous day! Caloo-calay! Now she could enjoy an intense hour without a care in the world. Mesmerized by the hard, hot male bod.

"Hoisted on his own petard," Rhett chuckled. "Back-stabbed by his little partner in crime."

"Partner?"

Rhett raised an eyebrow. "You mean you haven't figured it out?"

She said, "Figured out what?"

"The whole scheme."

Rannie didn't like the feel of where this was going. "Oo-kay . . . tell me."

"He has no money. Claitey was in debt."

"Are you talking about when Claitey was alive?"

"Yes. They cooked this up together. He'd plagiarize one of her books. They'd separate in a huff over it. She'd sue. Get nothing from him of course, but clean out his publisher."

"After Claitey's murder, he cut little Tabby in on it?"

"Way to go, Sherlock."

"You know this for a fact?"

"I'm guessing."

"And you're representing Tabby?"

Rhett shrugged.

"But that's totally crooked. I mean beyond the normal lawyer crooked."

"It's an ethical gray area of course. I've only guessed all this. No firm evidence. And my duty is to represent my client. Farrar, Straus's lawyers can look after their interests."

Rannnie stared, belted right in the ego. She thought she was ahead of Gaston all the way. But he had thrown his own case in the deposition and she'd been clueless. Rannie hated being beaten with a passion, but making a fool of her was over the top.

And there Rhett was looking at her with what had to be skepticism and amused disbelief. Calling her Sherlock. Mr. Big League Tax lawyer Pig Painter. Rolling in income while she fished for change in a storm drain with chewing gum on a stick.

She snapped her jeans back. "I'm wondering where racking out with you would rank on your curious scale of ethics."

"*My* ethics? You pay bondsmen to run you cases. Everyone in the bar knows it."

She jerked her coat on. "Everyone in the bar *does* it. Or at least the criminal lawyers do."

"Well, your daddy did anyhow. But I guess that was one of his larger legal truths that transcends petty facts."

And that did it. Nobody insulted her daddy. Certainly not the son of Daddy's thieving law partner! He could have sweet-talked her five seconds before. But not now.

Not that he was even trying. Standing there in a maddening calm.

While she was getting a big enema from Fate.

Rannie was coming to suspect Rhett of being an asshole. She didn't know what kind of an asshole, but of the general category, she was pretty confident.

"I am parting without rancor!" she shouted, slamming the door as hard as she could. And realizing just how much she sounded like her mother.

■ ■ ■

"Am I some skulker?" demanded Gaston Garnett, framed by the bedroom door. "Do you think I wanted to be locked up in here? My anguished cries of rage and grief stifled by unfeeling walls!"

The effrontery of it hadn't dawned initially. He had phoned Mary Canty who had come straight over to the Ansonborough house to his rescue. And he had tried to show gratitude. But she lit into him, accusing him of hiding here to her detriment.

Women only think of themselves. Here he was weak with fatigue and dehydration confronted by a ghoulish vision. He was looking at the eyes of a homicidal maniac all swathed in bandages.

He asked, "Are you suffering a rush of blood to the head? Can I get you something? A drink? God *I* need a drink."

She began advancing on him. He dodged around her and stumbled backwards down the stairs. Clutched the railing to keep from a bouncing prat fall. Steadied himself in the sitting room. Cast an envious eye on the scotch bottle. Reached for it.

She smacked it to the floor. The blow was incredibly sharp and well aimed. Cracking into the varicose veins on the back of his hand and making him yelp. The bottle fell with a 'thunk' and rolled.

"I think there are wider lessons here," she said. "For both of us."

Gaston tried to get to the bottle, but she had him cut off. "Sure, I'm no angel. I could use a good house-breaking. But you gotta mix a carrot in with the stick some time."

"Stick? I'll stick a two-by-four up your ass!"

God, he had no idea the woman had such a mouth on

her. He smiled faintly. "I gotta confess I'm leery of where this is leading."

"Where you've always been heading. To hell in a bucket."

"True, my life has had a few amalgamations and even a few inventions. Truth and fiction do mingle in a briar patch of tangled ways. I'm a rough diamond with a genius for complicating things. It gums up my career now and again."

Mary Canty hefted a vase, pulled out the dried pussy willows and dropped them on the floor.

Gaston assumed a solemn pose, hands clasped prayerfully in front of his big gut. "This is the murder house you know. My late wife died here. It's something of a shrine to me."

The bandages quivered. It was her nostrils flaring. "Then it'll be a double-murder house. Because I got the urge to flip off your light switch!"

Gaston fled out the front door. She sounded like Rannie. Could it be Rannie wrapped up like that?

The vase flew past him and shattered on the walk. "I will stamp on you like a poisonous toad!" she yelled after him in a quote from his lighting out poem.

Gaston sprinted, then slowed to a fast walk. Breathing heavily. He truly needed a drink. A jelly glass full of head-jolting raw Barbadian rum with a bright green lime to squeeze down his gullet behind it. A boiler-maker of Old Setter and Blue Ribbon beer. Or wine *spotioti*, that deadly mix of crud whisky and muscatel that would throw you right to the floor.

Mary Canty hadn't followed him. No, she had gotten

into the big green Land Rover. She gunned the engine. Clashed the gears into reverse and squealed out of the drive. Braked and whipped it into forward laying a swath of rubber.

Gaston tippy-tapped down the sidewalk and turned the corner, his mind working frantically. We've got to stop this stampede. Sheer hysteria.

She drew up beside him, hunched over the wheel, her glare turned on him full-bore. A madness had taken hold of her.

Bellicose witch. Evil residing in her like a worm. Smoke curling out of her ears.

Gaston couldn't look at her directly. Her eyes were too insane. Practically rabid. How did his path cross these female monstrosities? He could vividly recall his reading at a New England girls' college. Home of all those rad-lib diesel dykes.

Yes, he had lubricated himself a bit too freely. Stood up using his orotund Southern voice. They had wanted a Southern poet after all. It was in the contact. Began:

"Ye-ahs ago, I was in the E-ss-o restroom in Vir-gi-lina."

Pause.

"On the Vuh-gin-yuh side."

Pause as though that had some deep significance.

"And among the wall graffiti, I found the mem-ruh-ble lines—pause—'Joyce Carol Oates'—pause—'can take an en-ty-uh telephone pole.'"

That was when one of the beasts hurled the cup of ice at him. Followed by the others picking up every available missile in the room and letting fly. Books, chairs, a cut glass punch bowl. It had taken fourteen stitches to close his scalp.

He walked on rapidly, muttering to himself, justifying things. Am I perfect or all-wise? No, I be a rip-roaring Southern poet. A brisk and riveting read. Moving with the thunder of NASCAR. I wear Spanish moss in my lapel. I live on shoestring potatoes and pickled hog's feet and RC Colas spiked with bust-head rye. I cuss and spit and belch. I rut with jelly roll negresses with blue dragons tattooed across their mammoth jugs. Ram ten inches of country boy pecker up them until their eyes cross and they moan for Sweet Baby Jesus.

Teaching morons with their caps on backwards. Failures at basic skills exams. Ignorance-is-bliss mob. No one could be a writer having to read their drivel every day. It was like a lunatic asylum for kindergarten I.Q.s.

Why had he chosen such a career? The horror of that breadloaf writing school where he got his paltry M.A. His unheated rat trap student apartment. Drunks breaking bottles in the street at night and junkies fighting in the hall. Kansas winters got so cold that the water froze in the toilets. He'd lie shivering under thin army blankets in a codeine haze from chugging Robitussin to still the ache of longing. And masturbate into a sock.

Claitey gave him no relief. Always on him about his career slump. Carping and belittling. Giving him the most rotten shake in matrimonial history.

Had to take the battle to the enemy. She was just a leak in my canteen. Plugged with chewing gum. Plugged. Plugged indeed.

God he was hungry. Tabby had nearly starved him to

death in that locked room. He had to navigate the streets. Find a congenial café full of raucous and friendly regulars. Sit down to a plate of red beans and dirty rice and fat bursting greasy sausages. Fall upon them like a ravening dog.

Mary Canty was staying right with him in the Land Rover looking like a major catastrophe. Goddam Rannie and her SUV lifestyle. This is a public safety mandate.

He clenched his fists and waved them over his head, shouting at her. "Get thee behind me, Satan's spawn!"

The Land Rover slowed to a crawl and fell behind his frantic pace.

"Piranha!" he bellowed defiantly, wheeling in a circle and forging on. "Man-devouring Orca! Salt-cured, dry-skinned *gris-gris* woman!"

Now if he could just get across the intersection and into that patch of spangled sunlight that beckoned like some Promised Land. It led to pit-cooked barbecue and cole slaw with mounds of crisp hush puppies. A sweaty pitcher of beer that he would kneel before and adore like a votive shrine.

Gaston took a deep breath and sprinted across the street. Heaved up against a decorative iron fence with spikes running along the top like a Macedonian phalanx at parade rest. Bent over hacking as though he might die in a paroxysm. Straightened up, lungs heaving.

"Goodness gracious great balls of fire!" he sang. Pounded his chest to get the oxygen flowing. Yes, he could make it now. Find his way to King Street and a long neck Bud and a fried catfish with a mouth big enough to swallow a soft ball. Six chili dogs lined up for him to devour like a contest at the county fair. Afterwards sit back, lick his fingers and belch. Choose between the banana cream and the rum raisin pie.

The engine roared in fury, a demented thing on wheels.

Gaston's mind clicked like tumblers in a lock.

Mary Canty was coming at him. A deep green aerial smart bomb.

Her eyes were pinpoints of pure malice.

He froze there pale and petrified. No gambits left to play.

The Land Rover ploughed in a big loud BAM through tendon, bone and jagged iron. Gaston's jaws flipped open like they had come unhinged.

A pedestrian coming late on the scene said afterwards that Gaston's face had a glassy expression.

28

The morning after Gaston went through the fence, Rannie saw maybe thirty-five cops out front in the yard of No. 1 Legendre, a lot of them carrying video cameras. And there was the damn local news. Both channels.

She opened the front door and surveyed them slowly from left to right. She said, "Well, I'm so surprised you could just knock me over with a stun gun."

"Are you Miz Randolph Ralston?" Cop deadpan face.

"You know that."

"Are you the owner of a Land Rover Defender vehicle registration number 2536-double-o-7?" There the smirk slightly crept through.

She sighed exasperated. "I don't know the number, but I'm sure you do."

"Are you the only driver of the vehicle?"

"You're dam' right I am. And my vapid sister better not have . . ." Rannie paused, wondering suddenly if the question was loaded.

"I don't want to be alarmist or nothing but we gotta invite you for an interview. We could have just asked you to come in. But you're like in a perpetual state of pissed off. We figured you wouldn't return our phone calls. So we initiated the contact."

"I'm invited to a gab-fest by you all." She shook her head in wonder. "And the chief says there's not enough cops on the street. Budget's too tight."

"You're thinking there's a lot of buoyancy out here. Word got around was all. Some of the boys wanted to tag along. Membership in the corps de cops has its privileges."

"Yes, har-har. I'm the big fish on the grill. What am I accused of?"

"You seem to have locked Gaston Garnett in a death embrace with a decorative metal fence."

She flared. "That's the most off-the-wall, cock-and-bull … I mean this really takes the biscuit."

The cop looked up at the big house like he was calculating how privileged a life she led. "There's a percentage of folks everywhere who turn out to be killers. Pretty harrowing stuff not knowing where it'll come from next."

Rannie looked up in the oak leaves where gray squirrels chased each other and jays squawked. "What have you got on me?"

"It's not my job to analyze your prospects in the system. It's a maze I know. You'll hire some high-price boy to do the legal-eagle two-step. He'll kinda erode your personal assets the way them Robin Hood lawyers will do. But you don't want to think along those lines I guess."

Rannie's face cleared. "Which is to say you don't have jack. Well, I've got clients at nine, but I'm not a slave to routine. Let me get my briefcase."

He put out a restraining hand. "We can't allow you to go back into the house."

"Well, y'all seem friendly enough. Maybe you really do believe in innocent until proven the contrary."

"I can't argue with that. Lots of folks don't credit us for being on the side of decency. But to give you the full account, there's more."

"Since we're on such easy terms here, tell me the rest."

"Given that the said vehicle was abandoned and a pa-ticipant in a murder-one scene it kinda removed that need-a-warrant buffer. So we took the opportunity to search it and found a handgun in the glove box. And of course we couldn't resist running a ballistics on it."

She gazed out over the crowd for a full minute. "Okay, I'll bite. What did you find?"

"It's the weapon used to kill Claiborne Pusey."

Rannie gaped like she had gotten a good blow to the gut.

The cop shook his head. "Shame about that woman. My wife sure loved her novels. Well, kay-sirra-sirra. Is that how the song used to go? Say, you okay? You look like you got an abscess or something. Anyhow, amidst all this gloom, look at it from our perspective. As a bonus, we get to hook you up and take you in right smack in front of TV cameras."

He paused a beat.

"We can put a jacket over your head if you don't want to draw unwelcome attention, maybe got a fear of being stigmatized."

■ ■ ■

"Thank God you're alive!" barked Mary Canty Ralston, barging into the hospital room. "I thought I'd be confronted with rigor mortis!"

Gaston shrieked and would have rolled under the hospital bed had he not been bound by plaster and wires and tubes.

The turkey vulture with talons freshly sharpened. The battleaxe with balls. She had come to kill or torture him. Light matches between his toes sticking out of the thick plaster and pins and wires.

She pulled a chair up to his bedside. "You look awful. But then you usually do. Nothing but excess."

Gaston thought frantically. If he were nearly dead she might content herself with watching him breathe his last. He forced the weak seraphic smile. Serene. Slowly expiring. Inches from terminal.

"Morphine just hits the spot," he whispered. "Understand why gut-shot soldiers get addicted. My mind just meanders. Not the usual swift pace. No cavalry charge hitting on all four cylinders. A perpetual twilight. Moon glow on still waters. A country lane stroll in starlight."

"Good. Glad you're doing well. I'm not into bereavement. It's so morbid here I can't stay but a moment. Extremely busy day."

"Well thanks all to hell for the tea and sympathy," Gaston flared indignantly.

Her voice rose several decibels. "You? What about me? I slept terribly last night. All the fret and worry."

"You unceremoniously smashed me through the fence. And now you come in here oozing your charm at me."

"Well, I'm sure my behavior is not beyond reproach. But I do try to remember good manners."

"I was being sarcastic."

"That's uncharitable. After all I've done for you."

"I am mangled, wrecked, very nearly amputated. You did your best to kill me."

"Well, I'm sure the evidence is inconclusive. My daughter Rannie always says that."

He ground his teeth. Evil, obdurate harpy. "I *saw* you. I was, after all, first on the scene of the accident."

"You saw someone with a bandaged face. Could have been anyone. Sounds like a your-word-against-mine kind of thing. And you are an accused murderer in violation of your bond."

Gaston thrashed in the sheet, heaving against the wires and tubes that held him in place. "You're the dam of that vicious, vindictive daughter! You could be evil twins! There's no bounds to your savagery."

Mary Canty lit up a cigarette. "You always get over-excited about everything. You'd just be out drunk on a barstool somewhere. High as kite."

"I am riled up, het up and royally pissed off! This is like a trip down Memory Lane to Moira stabbing me through the thigh. The agony! The angst. The screams of anguish. And the food here is even worse than I remembered."

She blew smoke up towards the ceiling and looked around for an ashtray which of course wasn't to be found in a hospital room. "The food has to be bad. It's necessary for convalescence."

"I am a cripple for life! All I need is a goat cart and I can start begging like Porgy."

"Nonsense. They do wonders with physical therapy today."

Gaston grimaced. "Yes, I'll be jogging and playing tennis in no time."

Mary Canty stood up irritably. "Well, just lie there and revel in your grievance."

"Reprehensible cow!"

Mary Canty didn't seem to hear. She was gazing in the mirror. "I'm sick and tired of waiting on that plastic surgeon," she said under her breath.

She began to unwind the bandages.

Gaston stared in livid horror. What frightful monstrosity would emerge? A Lilith ghoul with teeth like a hacksaw?

Mary Canty fluffed her hair, looked at her image appraisingly. Then turned.

Gaston threw up his hands to block the Bride of Frankenstein image. He stopped suddenly. The vision of Mary Canty face-lifted . . . it was like she had taken a mega-dose of monkey glands.

It's a rare face-lift that doesn't have weeks of bruising. But Holy Moly she was pristine.

He opened his mouth and closed it again. His face stamped with incredulity. He was numb with awe. Felt like a cartwheel chandelier had dropped on him while he ate a t-bone and baked potato at the Western Sizzlin'. Which was oddly prophetic, but he of course had no way of knowing that.

She was glamorous. She was radiant. She was crowd stopping, hands-down beautiful.

He gazed earnestly at her. "I struggle towards the light," he mumbled.

"What does that mean?" she demanded sharply.

"You are spirituality refound in a materialistic and degenerate nation."

She looked at him suspiciously. "You just called me a cow."

"A mild sarcasm. You took me too literally." God she was arousing. He could feel his superlative spire rearing its head. Forcing up the sheet.

"You are a long draught of Pearl beer with a jigger of tequila on the side. You are a spread of Virginia ham and cold slaw after a week of muesli at a health farm. You should be lolling in the nude on a silk Chinese rug sipping a nice vintage Moët. I think it's time for hand-holding, endearments and nose-rubbing."

She flashed her strong teeth. Her voice nearly warbled. "Suddenly I feel all giddy. A debutante confronted by billing and cooing. With some doglike devotion thrown in."

Gaston smiled. And you are giving off active pheromones. "Dalliance time?" he asked. "With all forgiven?"

"I didn't just do it for fun. I had to make my point."

He could not take his eyes off her. "I'm sure I had it coming to me. We're doing much better now, aren't we?"

"After a rough start."

"Will you marry me?"

"Yes, of course, you bashful boy."

29

Rannie's night in jail had been sheer hell. No one read Dante these days, but it had to be in one of his inner circles. A junkie cut off from her heroin, her face a mask of pain, kept moaning "shiii-iiit" over and over. Then it was fuck this and fuck that and fuck the other. An alcoholic helpfully explained that if you stayed drunk you never had a hangover.

Then the biker dyke—busted for a van load of speed and ecstasy—came over and started stroking Rannie's thigh and said she'd like to work her into a lather, then eat her like a sushi platter. Rannie suggested she wait until she got sentenced to a stretch. She'd have plenty of time for activity then.

"In fact, it's almost a theme park for you."

"I got a strong take-off and a smooth landing," said the dyke.

Rannie told her to get back on her own bunk or she'd amputate her head.

All night clanging cell doors. Somebody into religion was wailing about false gods and transgressors and a needed plague of frogs.

Rannie lay on the hard thin mattress that reeked of urine. Somewhere out there was the wide sweep of the harbor and a cold wind that would whip the hair on her head. A V of pelicans would circle and drop into the trees on the edge of Jim Island.

She thought of the kitchen pantry at home with the shelves lined with mason jars of pickled okra, dilly beans and spiced peaches. She remembered the delicious odor as Mozelle the cook fried oyster sausages or baked bread pudding with whiskey sauce. Venison cooked in a deep, rich hunter sauce. Pulled pork with the slightest lashing of vinegar.

Morning came with a smell of cleanser and roach powder and clashing mop buckets. The sun was an orange smudge through the filthy wired window. Powdered eggs and French toast slid through the food slot on paper plates. For the first time in months Rannie had no appetite. But the others did. And they went for the watery coffee which was still strong enough to prompt a fight over the one commode with no seat on it.

The junkie shook the bars and screamed she had a sugar deficiency. The whore said she preferred to be called a 'sex worker' and gave Rannie a feminist lecture on male violators who took and never gave.

Just before nine, the cops came for them, hooked them up in lines in the corridor. Strings of five, all female troglodytes. A couple of them NFL-linebacker-sized. All of them compliant but sullen. Smelling of sweat and damp and peed in clothes.

In the grubby little hearing room, Rannie stared at the

back of her hands held in the steel bracelets, her carefully manicured and painted nails. Swallowed the bile in her throat. The magistrate set bail on one after the next, irritation evident in his voice. Rannnie was next up.

She did a double-take when her mother came in. At least she thought it was her mother. Mary Canty's face was radiant. It was out of a photo from when Rannie was two or three. Even the color in her eyes seemed deeper.

Judge Peaseley Chitwind took the magistrate's place. Only a circuit court judge could deal with murder matters. He dismissed the bond revocation on Gaston Garnett. Told Mary Canty her house was free and clear.

Thought a minute and said, "You wouldn't have been driving yo' darter's vehicle now would you, Miz Ralston?"

Mary Canty smiled at him. "That's impossible. I've been having elective surgery."

The judge nodded portentously. Rubbed his bristly chin. A patina of nicotine remained on his index finger from a ciggy habit he had kicked.

Rannie's name got called.

"You enjoying our hospitality?"

She grinned sourly. "It lived up to expectations."

"Says here you put Gaston Garnett through a piked iron fence."

"I was having lunch at the time. If you could call it lunch. A bunch of radishes and a hard-boiled egg."

"No point in trying your case in front of me. You know that. So save the shuck. Anyhow the real doozy is your gun being used in a murder."

"You're holding me while you investigate my gun?"

His mouth set in a hard line. He looked at the dingy slab walls and then back at her, thinking.

"All that blood on the car seats."

"You'll find it came from a wild pig and my sister who cut her finger."

That stymied him.

"Amazing but true," she added.

Little beads of light in his eyes. Knowing she had him. Nodding reflectively.

He set bond at $50,000.

Rannie was picturing the screaming headlines. Killer Criminal Lawyer Free on Lenient Bond!

Mary Canty said, "Well we're certainly not putting the house up as bond. I've had my fill of that."

Rannie's jaw dropped. "What?"

"Your life is like some crime thriller, and I'm simply exhausted with it. I try to see goodness and hope in the world."

Rannie's emotions were crackling with electricity like they had been short-circuited. "I'm standing here struggling to control my feelings."

Mary Canty threw up her hands. "Don't precipitate some crisis."

Rannie could hear herself breathing.

The judge's eyes actually flashed as he eyeballed her mother. "I tell you what, Miz Mary Canty. Allow me to say you are a damned good lookin' woman. I'd like to buy you a bourbon and coke with cherries and orange slices in it."

■ ■ ■

"Do you imagine I'm going to call him 'Daddy'?" Moira demanded. She was not taking her mother's engagement to Gaston Garnett well.

"You don't have to call him anything at all," Mary Canty replied in a serene voice. "Gaston thinks you need to return to Sweet Briar, and I agree. It will vastly improve the atmosphere around here."

"Never. That idea is just . . . just flat as a pancake."

"Let's not have a pointless quarrel."

"Writing is my new life. My new beginning. I'm twenty pages into *Passion Flower Bride*."

"Don't have the heebie-jeebies."

Gaston's hair was wet and brushed back. He seemed clean for once. The hospital had seen to that. He sat in his shiny wheel chair, his legs cased in plaster up to his hips.

Moira flung a hand in his direction. "After my upstanding daddy to marry this . . . this unholy dog's dinner of a poet."

"Ouch!" said Gaston, wriggling a bit as he feigned being cut to the quick. "The wildest rumors always circulate about me because I swim against the tide. My jut-jawed stances demoralize the envious. You can't believe all that truck about me."

"I can't bring back the past by remaining a spinster," said Mary Canty. "And what would be the point anyway?

Oh sure, little twinge of conscience here. But you can only blame yourself for throwing us together. You always were a matchmaker."

"Yes," Gaston chimed in. "Bringing me into the home and hearth. Fanning up our ardent flames." He beamed at Mary Canty.

"You told me you loved me!" said Moira. "Not that I care two pins."

"You stabbed me through the leg as you recall."

"Mother rammed you through a fence."

"She's such a spirited filly," he enthused.

Moira seethed. Seeing this self-pleased sugar lump in a wheel-chair putting on his charmer's voice just made her sick.

Mary Canty was calm, her agenda all laid out. "It won't change our lives particularly. I'm quite contented with my reading, my charity work. Perhaps Tabby could go to Sweet Briar as well. She would become a sister to you."

"Tabby is a murderess. And . . . and you're an ought-to-be-convicted murderer," she told Gaston.

"We didn't both do Claitie in."

"Well one of you sure as shootin' did."

He smiled wanly at Mary Canty. Recited:

"She's just a dad-blame young'un.
Needs a whippin' 'cross Pappy's knee"

"Well you're nothing but a mess of stains from deep fried cuisine," said Moira.

When Collier sauntered in, he was no more pleased

with the nuptials than his sister. Plus there was the add-on news that his mother was to tie the knot the same day as he and Dale. It would be a double wedding. Mother and son going down the aisle together.

The potential fall-out from that sank in. "Dale . . . Dale will never agree," Collier stammered.

"Well then don't marry Dale," his mother said flatly. "I had hoped you were going through a maturing process and had come to see how unsuitable she is."

"Of course I'm marrying Dale," Collier declared. "And I'm not holding my arms open to a stepfather. Gaston belongs with a wife who wears hair rollers in public."

"Well be that as it may," said Mary Canty, "I'm not going to be married in Irmo. The whole thing will have to be moved down here to St. Michael's."

"You know June is entirely booked," Moira argued. "People have been fighting over it."

"Well some bride will just have to change her precious little plans," said Mary Canty.

Moira looked like she was about to go into a swoon. "I'm trying to think of a bowl floating with camellias," she moaned.

"And we can't have all this Johnny-Reb claptrap," Mary Canty added. "St. Michaels would never tolerate that. Ghastly plan for a wedding anyhow."

"It was going to be a perfectly divine wedding," Moira insisted. "Or it was until this fly in the buttermilk came along."

Gaston smiled at her like the cat that ate the cream. Finished his verse:

"She needs a woodshed hidin'
Needs that fanny tanned
Whup that butt
Or switch them laigs
All the same in the end."

Collier was glaring furiously off into space.

"I'm through walking on eggshells on this," Moira said. "Does Rannie know about this? Where on earth is that girl?"

Mary Canty said, "I haven't the faintest. In jail or off with a pack of frightening looking people someplace."

Collier threw his hands up in the air. "I can't believe my sister. Talk about irresponsible."

30

Gaston sat back in his wheelchair, basking in the quiet of what had been Big Collier's study. Around him were floor-to-ceiling shelves of leather-bound volumes. Literature, law, history and philosophy. Black, tan, red. Some gilded. Some boxed. The highest shelves reachable only by a moving ladder.

Framed photos of Big Collier from the Citadel and the army. Grinning politicians shaking his hand. The dreadful sword that had skewered Gaston.

Two French windows that looked out on the quiet garden where the faint first sun of spring was beginning to show. Above the mantel a debutante portrait of Mary Canty at age 18, a remarkable simulacrum of her current face-lifted mien.

"Such large, sad eyes," Gaston murmured. Confident that he would banish her ache of loneliness. Give her a life full of meaning and significance in the service of a dick like a jack hammer.

Filled with breakfast sausages and contentment, he lingered over a final cup of *créole café au lait*. As Mary Canty's intended, he was at last experiencing some of the drugged charm of wealthy living. For tomorrow's breakfast he had ordered ham biscuits and pear chutney. And pan-fried quail with grits for the day after. He was one of nature's aristocrats, born to be ministered to and accepting it as his due. And now was a moment of perfect mellow decorum.

As the future head of household, he would do more than order up roast squab and brown oyster stew at feedbag time. He would lay down the law on certain matters. He was patient and reasonable, but it was time to put his foot down about all the children living under one roof.

Mary Canty was congenial in her shared concern over the constant assault on decorum by her offspring. Indeed, he sensed a growing awareness on her part that her children were the contents of some Pandora's box spilled out into the world.

And speaking of evil spilled out, Tabby Boone stepped into the dim room, shutting the tall double doors behind her. Eyes full of a lidless intensity.

O Momma, he had lusted for her when she was a coltish teenager. She had lounged by Claitie's pool in a blossom print green bikini and amber-tinted wraparounds. He'd picture her with her transmission in overdrive. Thigh muscles taut. Face glazed with perspiration. Juices sweet as scuppernong preserves.

She sat down on the floor cross-legged, staring at him. Saying nothing.

"What?" he asked.

She recited in a sing-song voice:

"When all resistance melts
I smooth your scented hair

And sing of nervous nipples
And taste the snake of paradise."

He smiled crookedly at her. "I've always thought of you as a Bloody Mary with a celery stick in it. Nourishment as well as entertainment."

"Anyone who wants to possess me must win my love daily."

"Is it purely an adoration on my side? I could be your galley-slave. Easily amused and anxious to please."

She shook her head in mild exasperation. "Marrying Mary Canty Ralston seems like a big fat *faux pas* in the wrong direction."

"It's all a put-up," he argued gamely. "I've got until June to weasel out. By then my legs will be back. A little rehab, I'll be good as new. Doing a buck and wing through life."

"You know, sitting in that chair you look about as unappetizing as a jar of big old pickled okra. Something a tourist would buy in a food shop in the market because it had a Charleston label on it. Then get it home and not want to eat it. Just heave it out with the trash."

"Is this some turn-coat routine? I'm invited to a testimonial dinner to get a cream pie thrown in my face?"

"The routine is that you are just a big old Capital-L for Loser." She planted an 'L' formed by thumb and forefinger in the middle of her forehead.

Gaston ground his molars. She was like all the others before. Struggling to express herself with a birdbrain vocabulary. He said, "You know the plan, my little blueberry muffin. Once we've got the lawsuit money it'll be loose the reins and let the horses run. Money galore. All our Cheerwine dreams come true."

"You are a passing phase," Tabby sighed. "I am eternal woman. I am grounded in nature and mystery. I am a very complex personality."

Gaston laughed out loud. "You're about as complicated as an empty egg carton."

"Well, you live in smoky bars thinking you're dangerous because you wear a hat indoors. Your body is fish-belly white. Love handles hanging over your belt."

Gaston blew out his breath. "I am the burly-chested Southern poet. You came into my life like jailbait. You touched my hand. Even years later I tremble at the memory."

"Don't make me up-chuck."

Gaston swallowed deep in his throat. His voice took on a tone of alarm. "All passion between the sexes is an adversarial position. It's best not to make rash decisions when we're roiling masses of emotions."

"I've thought about it all I need to."

"I'll give up the booze," he pleaded. "Eat roughage. Lose fifty pounds."

She put a finger to her lips, thinking. "You really swear you can stay away from the onion rings and hush puppies, all the nachos? Those giant tubs of buttered popcorn at the movies?"

He raised his right hand in the air. "Cross my heart and hope to die."

Tabby slowly rose from the floor. "Oh, I see. You're in the autumn of your life? Starting to feel the heavy mileage? All this is mellowing you."

He forced his most sincere smile. "I long for a late life baby."

Tabby scoffed. "That's a piece of light relief."

"What are you going to do?" he wailed.

She turned at the door to glare at him. "Something that you won't care for in the least."

■ ■ ■

The sky was a hard gray from one horizon to the next with just a slice of sunlight beginning to leak through. Rhett had the Ford pick-up window cracked letting in a draft and the smell of distant rain. His Labrador sat between him and Rannie on the long seat, tongue hanging out, happy to be out and doing things.

Rhett had seen her on the news and come up to the jail to post bail. Sir Galahad with a checkbook.

"So how was it?" he asked.

"I kept my face empty and my back to the wall," said Rannie. "At night I could hear the bamming of them unloading cargo containers over at the port on the Wando River. A real lullaby." She blew air, pushing the hair out of her eyes.

"They say it's right hard to get decent Crab-cakes Benedict in there."

The land narrowed to the neck that opened on the peninsula of Charleston. Rain dimpled the rivers on either side.

"It affects your confidence level," said Rannie.

"Doesn't sound real sociable."

"Oh everybody wants to talk. They've all got stories."

"They talk in that psychobabble the social workers teach them?"

"Yeah, they've got low self-esteem. Or they're victims of mental and physical abuse."

"But they feel with the right counseling they can learn to make wise choices."

"One of them told me her mission was to turn her life around."

"Yeah?"

"She had stabbed the owner of a North Charleston strip club. Six times."

"Did he deserve it?"

"He was drinking with the customers. Telling them which of the girls was the best lay. She was jacked up on black beauties. She said—her words—'I felt kind of bad I wasn't mentioned.'"

Rannie's eyes roved his face, body, the hands that held the wheel. Searching for that elusive something in the male animal that always eluded her.

She said, "You know I recall in law school that first tax course—estate tax—I thought if I could just force myself to focus on this. Then income and corporate tax, I could go on to tax school. Be in the élite group. Don't have to worry about your personality. Clients just hang on your every word. Because you are the keeper of the secret knowledge. How to screw the feds out of the money you earned."

"Tax law's pretty disgusting."

"I concluded that in the first course." Rannie stretched. "I'm feeling more confident now. Yeah, the further I get from that hole."

"Well, you made the news."

She snorted. "A buncha grinning cops. Everyone I ever beat in court. Showing up with video cameras to capture me doing the 'perp walk'."

"They were having a right good ol' time."

They were down in the old city now. Going slow down Legendre Street. Through one of the ornate iron gates, Rannie could see daffodils popping out. Some yellow, some white. Moira could identify the types. King Alfred. Thalia. Barrett Browning. They always marked the official end of winter.

The loons would go north to the lakes of Maine and New Hampshire. The swifts would begin swooping at dusk. They'd fly down the chimneys and roost. Red wing blackbirds in the marshes. Royal terns back from South America and the Dry Tortugas.

Then would come lawyers in seersucker suits and the onslaught of summer heat. Deviled egg and iced tea time.

Rhett told her he had gotten the smashed Land Rover back from the county garage after forensics cut big holes in the upholstery to get blood samples. Had to rip the fenders off it to get it to drive.

Rannie sighed. "Rough tough Land Rover. You'd think the thing would repel rhinos."

"The insurance company will probably refuse to pay up. Since it was intentionally crashed."

"I wasn't driving. Somebody stole it. So it's covered."

"From what I figure, your mother did it."

"Nobody knows that."

31

"Of course I'm buying insurance on your life," said Mary Canty. "We're getting married, aren't we?"

"Your plans are so rushed," Gaston argued feebly. "The recent death of my wife. I mean, is it strictly proper? What will people say?"

"When Big Collier died, the insurance was about all he left me. That man raised shiftless to an art form. And I'm not taking some tom-fool risk with you."

His morning was disintegrating. Little tattle-tale-tit Tabby had flounced out up to no good. A primitive feral quality about the girl. Cunning as a vixen. And now this. No more twinkling and sparkling at him. All business. Hard eyes and flinty heart.

Whenever Gaston felt trapped by women, he began to have a recurring nightmare. It was autumn on the Outer Banks of North Carolina. 'The blues are running,' someone would yell. And he would rush into the water with his casting rod and fall down. Bluefish in a feeding frenzy are berserk. They will eat anything. And he would be thrashing, fighting for breath. As they tore him apart.

Gaston reluctantly signed three different places on the policy. He was waiving the ten day look at the policy.

Once it was sent back, a half-million dollars of life insurance would be in force. Twice that if he died violently. It was like Mary Canty was relishing his impending death by lightning or falling meteorite. A slip in the shower. Choking on cheese straws.

A moment of foolish weakness and he was headed for the altar yet again. All Free Love had ever gotten him was married. Three times. And now the fourth coming at him like a freight train. It was never clear how it happened. He was a traveling banjo-picker just going haphazard in a search for truth. Following the road as far as it was cut. The Journey of Life. And suddenly he'd find himself trapped like a possum in a rabbit box. Girls so thoughtful at the outset would start making demands. And those would grow to obscene proportions.

Mary Canty was checking his signatures to make sure he hadn't deliberately misspelled his name.

O those long confabulations over brewskis and burgers with the sweet young things. Gaston the experienced seducer. Natchez Gambler hat pulled down level with his eyes. Man of the world in a commanding position. Ripe little tomatoes full of bright little thoughts. He could barely cope with their numbers as they competed hotly for his favors.

He had a duty to carry out. It was therapeutic for them really. And whatever small protestations they mounted, they had to come to it in the end. And be put in deep euphoria. As he stripped away that cover of virginal demeurity beneath which they raged to be sluts.

But they always wanted marriage.

And when married, they turned into grazing bovines. If he was a satyr, they had only themselves to blame.

Packing on the pounds. Claitey would sit down with a jar of Duke's mayo and a spoon. Make a meal of it.

And they always had their do-good reform projects in mind even before the marriage. They don't need a rationale for it. It's a natural female instinct. Claitey's tiresome lectures on his drinking.

Sober people are generally stupid, he would tell her.

Porcine wretch. Railing about his seraglios of coeds, his concubines.

Our interests happen to coincide, he would explain innocently. Mentoring the young people is part of my job description.

She forced him to sleep listening to a tape-recorded sermon urging monogamy.

Her sudden death had given him a pause for introspection. But now he felt he was being driven about in a hearse.

Mary Canty was putting the policy into a large envelope. Now licking and sealing it.

Moira Ralston stormed in and slammed a velour sack of Chop-slice knives down on a table.

"Where is that Tabby Boone? I am returning these unsuitable knives and demanding a full refund. If she doesn't like it then I'm getting Rannie to sue her for that products liability she's always going on about. The way that nasty thing just jumped up and cut my finger to the bone. I am asserting myself finally in this house. And Tabby can just paddle her own canoe straight out of here."

Gaston wondered why Moira never looked frail anymore? One more indestructible Southern woman. No wonder they survived Sherman and Reconstruction.

Moira focused on him. "And if you think for one minute you're going to come in here any old how you please and ruin all my plans for Collier's wedding, well you can just rethink the whole kit and kaboodle."

"Please, Moira. My injuries. I am bone-weary, weak and disoriented."

"At the bare minimum, I'm going to have Rannie draw up one of those pre-nuptial agreements that gives you not one darn red cent when you start cheating on my mother like you do with every flibbety-gibbet you get near."

Gaston stared unpleasantly at her. "Don't frivol with me, Moira. Your mother and I have a complete understanding."

"I think Moira has a point," Mary Canty agreed.

"Well while you've been sitting here listening to Gaston recite his limericks, I've been a busy little beaver. My brother is a highly respected state senator, and he's having a full investigation done of our Gaston Garnett's background. Our poet's got a well-deserved bad reputation, and we'll uncover every single shoddy bit of it."

"Is there something I should know about?" Mary Canty asked suspiciously.

"Mother, he's nothing but a primrose path to a dead end."

Gaston was in the grip of terror. Rapaciously invading his past. How well he knew the drill. Each college would welcome him with specious promises and hopeful slogans. After a year they would suddenly—surprise, surprise—discover he had less talent than they had believed. Calling his poetry bogus when he could make mincemeat of them intellectually.

The buccaneer poet—the troubadour, the bard—was

to vanish. The English major replaced by the utilitarian Corporate Communication. Versifying—as they called it—was an outworn concept.

Then they would drag out the accusations of some high-strung coed. Some innocent rhyme or playful action—if they could read an indecent meaning into it, they infallibly would. Some of the girls were clinically insane. The college campus is a classic playground for paranoiacs. And it's so hard to detect it straight off with hordes of leggy beauties parading past as his nose twitched with curiosity. The coed legions were cornucopias of free love, and there seemed no harm in extracting a percentage.

Is any one of us squeaky clean? he would ask.

Admin nazis would smile small frozen smiles. Jealous because he had nookie and they had nought.

And they would flail him on to other colleges where the I.Q. was even lower and the religion more primitive. Just how low was low? St. Enid's Normal School? Tonawanda Bible College?

Gaston's fears turned to fury.

Old Tartuffe, he silently raged. Falstaff. A bearded mendicant with a wooden leg. An inebriated dancing bear, my pelt full of mange. Trapped like some weakened, starved beast in the snow.

"You are the last and heaviest ball added to the chain of my damnation," he snarled at Moira.

"Well you're like somebody who never got over teenager-hood or something."

"I don't need your glib Freudianism. Don't think I ain't plumbed my darkest depths. Nor have I watched the she-male parade all these years without jotting down a few marginal notes. I am real boned up, for example, on the lurking force of woman's resentments. You want evidence? Just check out the lightning speed with which even the homeliest dog who catches a husband starts to take him for granted."

Always quick to resent anything in the nature of a slight, Mary Canty pointed a warning finger at him. Mother and daughter Ralston. A ruthless concentration of self-interest.

And he was full up to suffocation.

In a rapid and skilful maneuver Gaston whisked the Citadel sword off the wall. Slung off the scabbard. Felt the pointed tip of the blade that had once pierced him so neatly.

A sinister silence fell.

He looked at Moira murderously. These repellent Ralstons had stabbed him, and run over him and now they would drive him to Gehenna.

Pressing the guidance system of the wheelchair, he came at her, sword outstretched. "At daggers drawn are we? I'll show you daggers drawn!"

Moira frantically parried with the Chop-slice butcher knife.

"Vermin and disease!" Gaston bellowed. "Diarrhea and black vomit!"

Whack slap they hacked at each other.

She climbed onto the ladder, batting his sword away, creating a surreal tableau of Peter Pan and Captain Hook.

"Stop that this instant," Mary Canty commanded. "You're making a perfect exhibition of yourselves."

At which point Tabby walked in with a double-barreled shotgun and fired into the ceiling.

BA-DAM.

Shaking the huge chandelier.

■ ■ ■

Rannie Ralston, fresh sprung from jail, came crabwise into the room, squeezing between her mother and sister. She looked up at the ceiling. There was only one two-inch hole. Not the splattered devastation a load of shot would have done. She stared at it in surprise.

They were assembled under the gaze of Mary Canty's portrait. Tabby was in a great state of excited importance.

"Well I'm here to spill the beans," Tabby said brightly.

"Yes, yes," said Gaston. "We're all assembled here according to well-worn old literary formulas." He gave her a superior look. "The butler did it."

"Nooo. Little drum roll here. Ta-da. Gaston Garnett did it."

Guiding his wheelchair back into the middle of the room, Gaston scoffed. "You don't know shit from shinola. I've been exonerated. Rannie Ralston murdered your mother. The cops arrested her for it. It was on TV and everything."

"I'm ratting you out," declared Tabby. "It's not that I care a piddle about Rannie. I think she's hateful and sometimes I'd like to just slap her face. But it's a step I must take to assert my personality and put closure to my little *affaire du coeur* with you."

Mary Canty had lit a cigarette. She tipped some ashes

into an ashtray, eyed Gaston like he had been caught shaving dice.

He looked from her back to Tabby. "You're putting me in an awkward position."

"Quite the contrary. Life in prison is ordered and simple. You'll adapt easily." Tabby turned to the others. "Now, to understand this, you have to recognize that Gaston is stupid when he's drunk, and he's always drunk. Why I remember once Mummy dearest put in one of those electronic fences to keep the dog in the yard. Anyhow the dog got out of his collar and took off. Gaston was staggering around holding a drink in one hand and the dog's collar in the other yelling 'Here, Fido!'. When he got shocked he fell down and just lay there not knowing what to do. Zap zap zap. It sounded like one of those bug-zapper things. And he's squealing and writhing around. Isn't that a hoot?"

"Do you mind getting to the point?" said Rannie. "We are talking murder here, aren't we?"

"Premeditated?" said Tabby. "Well I should say so. He had to borrow your gun, I don't know, way back. When he wrecked a bar and you defended him. Put it back in the drawer when you weren't there."

Rannie said, "Well I'll be." Seeing where it was heading.

"He had to dig out the buckshot from a shell and replace it with a slug from Rannie's gun. That was after he had fired the pistol into the swimming pool to get the slug free and marked by the rifling in the barrel. That was why he really had the pool filled. Oh, he'd throw Mummy-dearest in it when he was in a wrath, but that was beside the point."

"Yes, yes," said Gaston in a lordly tone. "I roam abroad by night dressed in strange garb, committing lurid crimes. Turn Rannie loose on me. Twist me into a pretzel under cross-examination and then swing me at the end of a rope."

"You murdered your wife?" said Moira. "That's the most disgusting thing I've ever heard. You get out of this house this instant and go turn yourself in to the police."

"You have no evidence. And now my bride, after all this vitriol thrown by your family, we shall have a beautiful reconciliation." He reached out his arms for Mary Canty. Gave her the winning smile that never failed. His life was insured in her name after all. What more does a woman want?

She tipped some ashes again. Said, "You're a real worm." Indicating she did not return his ardor.

"Please pay attention," Tabby insisted. "It worked just like I said. Here, I'll show you again." And she let off the other barrel.

BA-DOOM!

Everyone jumped.

But this time a load of buckshot tore into where the chandelier base hung from the plaster.

Ripping the whole thing loose.

The ceiling being unnaturally high even for No. 1 Legendre, the chandelier came down with great momentum.

To crash squarely upon Gaston Bayard Garnett. Killing him instantly. His face was fat and squashed and full of disbelief.

"I won't be held responsible for this," said Mary Canty. "I've been after Rannie and after her about maintenance in this house."

"Who would have thought so much litter could come out of one ceiling?" said Moira.

32

"So you rushed out and got the insurance policy in the mail," Rhett mused.

"Yeah, the old acceptance of an offer's effective when put in the post," said Rannie. "First semester contracts in law school."

They stood apart from the garden of revelers behind No. 1 Legendre, Rhett in seersucker and a bow tie like almost every other man there. Both of them with gin-and-tonics, the glasses wrapped in napkins. A perfect June day without a cloud in the sky and, wondrous for summer in Charleston, temperature somewhere in the low 70s.

Collier and Dale's wedding had gone without a hitch. St. Michael's had miraculously had a cancellation when a bride caught her fiancé in the sack with an old girl friend giving him a warm send-off into the straitjacket of matrimony. Nasty rumor had it that Mary Canty tipped off the bride-to-be.

The rebel reenactors had been limited to a sword arch and single rifle volley although some of them were getting rowdy now at the reception. Their costumes were totally authentic, but most of the men were badly obese.

The bridesmaids were all supermodels and as meltingly

beautiful as Dale. Rannie overheard one of them saying she was "majoring in pre-med bo-tanny" when the Ford Agency discovered her. Rannie shook her head, thinking dumb? Did the girl know to come in out of the rain? Or did she just stand there with her mouth open like a chicken and drown?

Peckerwood state legislators swarmed around the girls jabbering a stream of yokel come-ons. There were no full stops in it, and their drool could have filled a wading pool.

"I teh' yew whut, honey-babe . . ."

"Lemme loose, sweet stuff, and I'll be on yew like a duck on a June bug."

"I'd kiss yore purty legs for a quarter even if you never did pay me."

Mary Canty downed a vodka tonic and lifted a second one off a waiter's tray. She had brought Judge Chitwind as her quote "date." Actually used the word. He told her she looked as good as quail on toast, and did the mother of the groom get into sexual heat at weddings like the bridesmaids?

She said, "You are a naughty man." But she didn't say it dismissively. There was a distinct gleam in her eye. And she wagged her finger roguishly.

Rannie looked up at Rhett and thought for the millionth time how loin-achingly good looking he was. She didn't know about the bridesmaids, but the groom's eldest sister was sure wet between the legs. Then she thought if he goes down to kiss the bride, I'll kill him. Grab that knife out of the hands of the man carving the roast beef.

Rhett gave a low whistle. "Accidental death. One million dollars. Sweet."

"Something's got to pay for the catering and open bar everyone's swilling from. The whole state senate and most of the House are here tucking in. Dale's parents actually wept with gratitude when I told them I was picking up the tab."

"But Gaston was dead."

"I'm convinced he was still breathing, had every prospect of living another full thirty years. So's everyone else. They're prepared to swear to it. He held mother's hand. Recited a poem called 'Hot-to-trot Hoedown'."

Rhett lifted his eyebrows. "Tabby's going along with this? What's in it for her?"

"Well, it wasn't exactly murder. But if we remembered it another way, she might face a manslaughter charge. And she seems to have a future in ad jingles. Plus she's racking out with a top honcho of a major ad agency in Atlanta. He likes her to dress like a Catholic school girl."

Rhett quoted Rannie's daddy verbatim. "The larger truth in the law that transcends petty facts that are all open to misinterpretation."

A look of something almost like admiration flickered across his face followed by a moment of bemused silence. "Yes, indeedy, the apple did not fall far from the tree. Well, if you've got colossal nerve, why not use it."

Arm-in-arm they strolled through the crowd, nodding at people they had known since childhood. Got fresh drinks at the bar, watched overweight men shag dancing to the band playing the old Embers song "I Feel Good All Over More Than Anywhere Else."

When Dale threw her bouquet, Tabby shoved Moira violently, but one of the bridesmaids, easily 6-four in her heels outreached the others and snatched it lightly from the air. She had a squat, bald man with a New York honk accent in tow. He managed a mutual fund with about a zillion dollars in it. She looked at him meaningfully, and he actually blushed.

Moira got up from the ground with grass stains and Bloody Mary spilled all over her. Rannie and Rhett strolled on, the torrent of Moira's tears and recriminations just part of the background noise.

Rhett said he guessed with the insurance money coming in, Rannie could take a breather. Tell the dirtbags to find other representation.

Rannie asked him what was on his agenda for the rest of the month meaning what are you doing tonight and how soon can I strip your clothes off?

"You know Bermuda is an interesting place. Tax and reinsurance haven. All kinds of tax litigation goes on there. Cases drag on for months with huge fees."

"Don't tell me you've been admitted to the English bar."

"Last year. It allows me to practice in anywhere they have English common law."

"You wear a wig?"

"I think I look quite distinguished in it. I have resisted faking a plummy accent. Sometimes you fall into it though. Just by accident."

"You probably look like someone from the cover of a Tabitha Boone novel. If you took your shirt off and wore the wig."

Rhett gazed mildly across the crowd. "You know I really ought to kiss the bride. Seems like the social thing to do."

Rannie stiffened.

Rhett turned back to her. "With that red hair, I guess you sun burn easily."

"There's such a thing as sun-block and umbrellas," she said a bit testily.

Rhett gave no immediate reply, but he looked her over from head to toe with what was, yes, it was a distinctly approving eye. "I've been accused of undue cockiness by perturbed women. Sometimes with vehemence. Get a real procession of negatives." He shrugged. "But they say your personality's fixed by age three. So I just roll with it. And I have got two plane tickets."

Rannie considered the implications of this for about a split-second. "They're right formal in Bermuda aren't they?"

"Yes, dress for dinner. All that."

"I can be packed in under a half-hour," she said.

About the Author

MARGOT SINCLAIR played front-row volleyball at Ashley Hall and studied ornithology at Cornell. She spends her winters in Barbour coats and Bean boots, owns her father's Purdey shotgun, and can pole a boat over a marsh at flood tide when the clapper rails can be seen among the Spartina grass.

Her grandparents were part of the Second Yankee Invasion of the South. Between roughly 1888 to 1940, Northern industrial wealth purchased vast tracts of worn-out cotton land, cut-over timberland, and abandoned rice fields. They restored old plantation houses or built new ones, and turned their estates into hunting preserves for duck, quail, turkey, and deer. The railroad brought resort towns to Pinehurst, Camden, Aiken, and Thomasville—golf, race-horses, polo, and quail.

Each winter, the Sinclairs migrated from Tuxedo Park, New York, to Run-a-Gate Hall on the banks of the Cooper River above Charleston. Margot's father was born there as she was much later. She is so much a part of the Low-country that she considers herself a valid "ben-ya."